CORPSE
IN
ARMOR

Martin McPhillips

Corpse in Armor

A THRILLER

ISBN-10: 1449541887
ISBN-13: 9781449541880

To Abbey

1

She was a still young actress, nearing thirty, very glamorous in that skin and bones way, blonde. I knew about her from the trade press and had also heard talk that she might be a major talent.

Chelsea Fall had cancelled two previous appointments, one already this week and one she had made for last week. Never a good sign. I had my legal assistant schedule today's appointment at 6:00 p.m. If Chelsea cancelled again I would call it an early day. But she showed up this third try, and I was prepared to politely let her waste my time.

"Mara Rains," I said as I took her hand and waved her into my office. I was looking up at her. She was an easy five inches taller than me.

She was working her first substantial film role, playing a lead in an indie production. The director, Ralph Keller, had made three films and for this one had a budget larger than those first three projects taken together. The word was that he had seen Chelsea in an Off-Broadway play and had to have her for the role of the broken call girl in the new film. For the indie weight class, she was being paid handsomely.

The usual creative honeymoon between Keller and Chelsea ensued, she explained after we sat down, until the first day of shooting. Keller then went the way of a lot of cinematic flesh and started in with abusive behavior on the set, of which Chelsea believed she was the principal target.

Someone who knew that I represented people in the entertainment business gave her my name.

The shoot, now in its eighth week, was expected to run just another month. The best thing to do, I told her, was to troop on and be a professional. Getting a lawyer involved right now would hurt her career. Keller's obnoxious behavior was nothing unusual in the industry. She was not the first actress to have this experience, and she would not be the last.

"You don't want the word 'difficult,' much less 'litigious,' attached to your name, at least until your name is big enough for it not to make a difference." I knew very well that no one got that big. Film producers had long memories and kept detailed accounts of their grudges.

I wasn't going to come right out and tell her that she was wasting my time, but she was. She had been in the business long enough to know what I was telling her, and I'm a lawyer, not a career counselor.

Then she said, "But all this gets very strange because I'm sleeping with Keller."

"Oh," I said, half deadpan, quizzing her with my eyes.

"And because," she paused to chew her lip, "he's going to kill me."

"Oh," I said again, with an entirely different meaning from the just previous "Oh," something more like "What the hell?" or "Did you just say what I think you said?"

She cried for a while. As she leveled off I asked her why she thought that Ralph Keller would kill her.

"It's a very distinct feeling," she said, staring off to the side, her hands fumbling together for calmness. "I can't explain it, but if you ever feel it, you'll know it as clearly as when a light is turned on in the dark. Ralph is going to kill me."

"Why? Does he have a motive?"

"It will give him pleasure, at first," she said, her voice taking the ironic turn of her thought, "and afterwards he'll be able to feel sorry for himself, that he felt compelled to do something so violent. He'll be angry at me because I was there asking to be killed."

At this point I had come around to the front of my desk and was leaning back on it, holding a box of tissues for her. I wanted to believe her, but was she just a good actress?

"Has he threatened you?"

"No. He's smarter than that."

I plucked out another tissue and handed it to her.

"Does he have a history of violence?"

"Not that I've heard about."

"Any known or rumored incidents of people getting dead around him?"

"I don't know of any, but that doesn't matter. He's going to kill me. I don't have anything solid enough to take to the police, and from there I'm so scared that I can't think straight."

I was taking her seriously, but I didn't know what to make of it. I recommended that she quit working with Keller, stay away from him, and find ways to protect herself.

She said yes, she had already thought of all that, but she was certain that he would still come after her. In the meantime, it would destroy her career to quit the film.

Now the picture became fuzzy again, because though she appeared genuinely terrorized, she was talking as if she was ready to surrender to being a victim. It was true that she had come to me urgently looking for help, but how did such urgency account for two cancelled appointments?

"Have you convinced yourself that no matter what you do Ralph Keller will murder you?"

"No. But the sensation I'm having, and I know it's not rational, is like being in a car that's gone off a cliff. It's like I'm just falling."

I leaned down and stuck my face in hers.

"I don't understand how you got there, but I believe that your fear is real and that for it to be real it is based on something real enough to you. But you do not have to be Keller's victim. Do you understand that?"

2

Chelsea agreed to stay for a few nights at a hotel under another name. She seemed happy to have me take charge, and told me not to be concerned about expenses, implying that she was sufficiently flush to cover them.

One of my assistants took her to the Sheraton at Times Square, and I called her agent. I explained that she would need two unscheduled days off from the film production. There were problems that I couldn't discuss. Chelsea would fulfill her professional obligations but she needed him to handle her brief absence for her. We agreed on the excuse of an unspecified medical problem that required attention. I asked the agent not to mention that Ms. Fall had communicated through an attorney, and by that request I was also testing the agent's trustworthiness. Sooner or later Keller would learn about me, but I preferred that he be playing catch up with what were going to be changes in his relationship with Chelsea.

Before she returned to work I wanted her set up with a security firm. Then there was the matter of breaking off her sexual relationship with Keller. That was going to be dangerous no matter what. The passions and dynamics of relationships are rarely subject to easy or rational resolution, and people in the film world often do believe that all the world is their stage and act out accordingly.

I put my private investigator Janice Greenberg to work on Keller. I wanted to know everything down to where he bought his groceries and back to grade school. Watching Chelsea, even more than listening to her, had unnerved me. I had a sick feeling about Ralph Keller that reminded me of the night a client, who had asked me to meet him for a drink, threatened me for refusing to lie to a judge for him. He had been menacing in a way I had not previously encountered, but that got taken care of when I told him point blank what I had never mentioned to any client before or since, that my semi-ex-husband was an NYPD lieutenant.

Chelsea's dilemma seemed much worse, but that one experience was enough for me to understand the kind of paralyzing fear she felt. It was also that experience that had marked my conversion from a typical Manhattanite who ritually abhorred guns, in spite of living with a cop, to learning to use one and keeping it with me all the time.

It was too soon to suggest to Chelsea that she consider that option, but I might recommend it once the immediate issue was stabilized. No woman should have to face that kind of fear without the means to defend herself. I knew that I didn't want my last thought to be 'I wish I had a gun.'

My semi-ex-husband Rob McAvoy works in the police commissioner's office. That is a 'homeland security' assignment too sensitive for me to know much about it. But all cops at all times attend to home front security, which means family security, even for a semi-ex-wife. Commonly understood to mean favors within the blue fraternity, such favors are nowadays limited. While having connections in the commissioner's office isn't what it used to be, it is still a good thing to have.

Calling Rob on his cell was reserved for emergencies, so I left a message with his office that it was 'very important,' our code for 'my hair isn't on fire but return the call right away.'

Rob got back to me within a half hour. After I laid out the story for him and asked him who could best handle Chelsea Fall's security, he gave me the number of Ryan Schell.

"He'll take care of you."

"So he's good?" I asked.

"Good doesn't capture it. Call him as soon as we get off and he'll move on it immediately. She'll be protected. And keep me in the loop on Keller as Janice fills you in."

"Now I'm worrying about overkill."

"Better overkill than her getting killed. I've heard people talk that sort of fear, and a lot of them had it right. Ryan will handle it."

"But I'm still skeptical about this woman's story. Maybe she's just a wild neurotic paranoid."

"Of course. But real or not you can get her to the other side of the situation and remain skeptical all the way there."

"You're so smart. You should have been a lawyer."

"No thanks."

We ended it there.

3

Ryan Schell was a no-nonsense professional. At the mention of Rob's name he took charge of the conversation and within a minute or two had me on hold so that he could dispatch someone to Chelsea's hotel. When he came back on he took the details I had on Keller. As we spoke he found a photograph of Keller on the internet and sent it to his man's Blackberry.

"You move fast."

"Situations like this can deteriorate rapidly," he said.

I asked him if my PI Janice would be in his way as he did background on Keller.

"No," was all he said.

He asked me to call Chelsea and tell her to expect his man within the hour and to ask her to cooperate with him. That was it. Ryan didn't waste a second. Rob's name was all it took. Nice to have that.

Chelsea seemed comforted when I told her that a bodyguard was on the way, and she agreed to work with him. There was an odd reticence to her voice, which I couldn't gauge. I was trying not to think too far beneath the surface.

I called Janice to tell her about Ryan Schell and that his people would be doing some backgrounding on Keller. She was fine with that and told me that so far Keller was coming up clean. He had no criminal record, no bankruptcies, his credit was good. He had graduated from Cornell in the top ten percent of his class. Went to UCLA film school. Janice needed more time to get the college background and pre-college years. Nothing about that was turning up in the standard biographies, so she was looking for some help to get her the Cornell admission records. She'd get back to me.

With all that lined up I felt like I'd had a pretty good day and decided to get out of the office. My most obvious choices were home, my claustrophobia-inducing health club, or Rembrandt's for a drink. The drink sounded like the better option. Maybe I'd even have dinner.

It was just past 6:30 p.m. when I swung my Prada bag onto Rembrandt's bar. Just three blocks from my office, it was a hangout for some Times people and all sorts of lawyers, many of whom I knew.

Jody, the head bartender, who bore an uncanny resemblance to a young Dennis Hopper, brought me a vodka martini without needing to ask.

"Are you going to want a table?"

"Maybe in a while."

"How are you?"

"Good," I said, "how are things with you?"

"Eh. Business is off. Once we get through the holidays, the New Year's resolutions kick in and everyone goes home or to the gym. Going out after work becomes the goblin."

"You were my first choice."

"You honor us. So I'll honor you." He reached under the bar and handed me the TV remote.

"You've made me an honorary man," I said. "Has any woman ever touched Rembrandt's remote? What happens if I put on the Food Network?"

"I take the remote back."

"So it is fleeting honor."

I switched the TV above the bar to CNBC and then ignored it. The market data that flashed continuously at the top and bottom of the screen warmed me even without paying attention to it. It was the world's economic heartbeat.

Chelsea Fall's face came again into my mind and again it bothered me. Was it a weak or a strong face beneath its glamour? Or was she just another humble artist through whom the Muses spoke? I rolled my eyes and reached for the martini.

4

Near the end of my second drink Jenn Marcus appeared at my elbow.

"Squirrels at their industry," she said, pointing up to the screen where a group of Congressmen were seen assembled in front of the Capitol.

"Still recovering from that round of dating with the Senate staffer?"

"Oh, dear, is that why I said that?"

Jenn was general counsel at a media conglomerate. A lawyer's lawyer, she was disarming and brutal. We were around the same age though our temperaments had matured in opposite directions. She cultivated fear where I cultivated trust. She liked me because I didn't fear her. Trust won.

A recent retiree from drinking, she had walked through the door carrying a Starbucks. When Jody came over she pushed it across the bar toward him.

"I'll have coffee," she said with her arch smile. He took the Starbucks and poured it into a mug for her.

"How do you sleep when you drink coffee this late, or is that decaf?"

"Mara, I can sleep anytime, but when I'm chatting with you I need to be fully awake."

"You're so sweet."

"So what have you been up to? Suing anyone I know?"

Jenn would have known if I was suing anyone she knew as soon as I did, so I moved on to the next question.

"Any interest in dinner?" I asked.

"I've been imagining eating dinner for three days, so the answer is yes."

My cell rang. It was Janice. I excused myself and stepped outside to take the call.

"I've gone back to your guy Keller in high school," she said.

"O.K."

"He appears in our world out of nowhere in the tenth grade."

"What are you telling me?"

"I'm telling you that unless something else turns up, Ralph Keller has no records before 1990, when he was fifteen years old. I can elaborate but that's the nut of it."

"So what are we looking at, Janice?"

"I don't want to speculate, but I know, for instance, that this is not the way a witness protection program cover turns up, so that's probably not it. I have some calls out that I'm waiting on."

My response surprised me, but it was instinctive.

"Would you go to this same depth on Chelsea Fall. Watch for a connection to Keller in the past."

"I think that's the smart move," she said.

"Later."

I wanted Ryan Schell to know about this turn of events. I got his voice mail and asked that he call me back. I thought about calling Rob, but decided that Ryan's guidance would be enough for now and there was, anyway, always the risk with Rob of running into legal conflicts. We both preferred the sidelines when it came to each other's business. But I did want to know more now about my de facto client, Ms. Fall.

The dead end that Janice had reached with Keller was giving me agita, though I preferred not to think about it, for the moment at least.

Jenn Marcus turned dinner into a surge of laughter. That girl can talk. The call from Janice had wiped out the effect of my two early martinis so I had a third, which barely took the edge off of my building anxiety about Keller.

While I sat amused and transfixed by Jenn's stories of corporate and political intrigue, I really wanted Ryan to get back to me, but it didn't happen. Maybe he ate dinner too, or had a family. But whatever was delaying his return of my call was starting to worry me, formally.

It wasn't until around 9:00, while I was on my way home in a cab, that my cell rang again. It was Rob.

"Should I be concerned," I asked instead of saying hello, "that Ryan hasn't gotten back to me for nearly two hours?"

"Mara," Rob said in a solemn tone, "Janice Greenberg is dead."

"Rob?"

"The detective who caught the case found my card in her wallet and called me. She committed suicide at home, in her apartment."

"It's not possible. I spoke to her a couple of hours ago. She's working on that matter we talked about. Rob, she was fine."

"I'm on my way to the scene," he said. "Meet me there."

I told the driver to turn around and head back uptown.

"How did she die?"

"Shot herself."

"Ridiculous. Never. She did not stop in the middle of being perfectly normal and shoot herself."

"We'll see for ourselves," he said.

5

The scene on the Upper East Side outside Janice's building was the standard spectacle of police and emergency vehicles, with the capstone a van from the medical examiner's office.

Rob was there, waiting. He had already been up to Janice's apartment.

"It's a mess," he said. "Can you take it?"

"I suppose so. I need to see this with my own eyes. But I'll tell you straight out that this is a murder. It is impossible that she killed herself."

He looked at me as we walked inside. "Do you know how many times I've heard that in twenty-three years as a cop?"

"Plenty," I'm sure. "But I knew Janice. Look at this crime scene very carefully when we go in there. It's not going to work as a suicide."

"What if it does work?"

"Then look deeper. When I tell you what she had just found out, you will listen to me."

"What was that?" he asked.

"That Ralph Keller's past disappears before 1990. He just shows up in high school."

Rob's expression changed, but he said nothing.

Janice had the perfect apartment. It had a big living room with a terrace and two bedrooms, one of which she had turned into an office. She was in there, at her desk, face down on it in pooled blood with the back of her head blown out.

I hung back as Rob spoke with the detective who had called him, looking the room over. Janice kept it neat and buttoned down. Her efficiency and clarity always impressed me, and her office reflected that same precise way. She was a runner too, among the fittest women I knew.

A delivery guy discovered her body. She had ordered food. The door was ajar when he arrived and he stepped inside when his knock wasn't answered. He said he often found customers who had left their doors open for him lost in headphones listening to music, so he looked around and saw the blood and Janice slumped on the desk.

The detective thought she probably had died minutes before the delivery guy got there. Rob looked back at me and then spoke to the detective too softly for me to hear his words. Cops like quiet talk in the huddle, especially with a civilian nearby. I sank into the background, to remove myself without actually walking away. I looked at Janice and remembered the first time she worked for me and how impressed I was by the quickness of her mind. She knew that looking beneath the surface of things carried risk, and so she always tried to step as lightly as she could.

She had hit some kind of tripwire today when she found the dead end in Ralph Keller's history. That was going to be my assumption, even if Rob and the detectives needed to be dragged to it. And if that was enough to get her murdered the very day she ran across it then I wasn't safe either.

My cell rang. It was Ryan Schell getting back. I left Janice's apartment and took the call out in the hallway. Composing myself I presented the facts to Ryan in my flattest manner. He was unflustered, though I could hear the change in readiness in his voice. This was someone whose heart rate, I thought, might actually slow down in combat. He said he needed to make adjustments and asked if he could call me right back. While I waited Rob came out.

"The lead detective won't make it a suicide until that is all that's left. I told him I'd cover him with his boss if there's pressure to close the case. He's going to look all the way through it, but I didn't give him your angle yet. He knows that it's coming. He's giving us time to work through what we have."

"Us?"

"You'll need my help, Mara. Looking at that scene, though, it's going to be hard to find anything other than suicide. These detectives are used to denial by friends and family, so that alone doesn't carry a lot of weight. They're going to need something out of the ordinary."

"How about," I said, "that women rarely use guns to kill themselves." It was a pointless comment and I knew it as soon as it was out of my mouth.

"But Janice carried a gun," Rob correctly noted. "She was a shooter. And that's almost certainly her nine millimeter."

"I know."

"What's obvious is often what's hardest to see."

"Spare me," I said.

I let Rob think about that while I answered my cell. It was Ryan. He had alerted his man watching Chelsea Fall, had sent a two-man team to my apartment, and there was another 'man,' this one a woman, on her way here, to protect me.

I asked him what he thought was happening. He didn't know yet but by midday tomorrow he wanted to see what was on the other side of Ralph Keller's dead end. He was pulsing his networks. His voice was less cool. He wasn't buying Janice as a suicide either. That was implicit to his series of moves. He assumed, as did I, that Janice was murdered because she had disturbed something while looking into Keller. If it turned out later to be a false assumption, that was fine. In the now, however, he assumed an enemy in motion. Ryan wasn't about getting beat.

"Could we be overmatched here, Ryan?"

"I'm not telling you everything," he said.

That could have had a dozen different meanings.

"Good," was all I said.

6

There were already so many crosswinds that I didn't tell Rob what Ryan was doing at his end.

"Can you take me back in there? I want to see Janice again and glance around her office."

I followed him back inside. Rob was one of the cops who other cops deferred to, so no one asked any questions when I stood next to the body and looked over the desk and surroundings. I knew how not to get in anyone's way and that I should keep my hands in my coat pockets.

"There's no note, right?" I asked the detective, who was keeping an eye on me.

"Not yet. Sometimes they show up later. An email to someone. We haven't gotten to her computer."

"Was that TV on when you got here?" I asked.

"No. Everything was quiet."

He was already annoyed, so I stopped asking questions. I wanted to do what I could for Janice. We had never been close friends, but we had a tight professional connection and her death had come mid-stride while she was working for me.

Rob put his hand on my shoulder.

"One of Ryan's people is here for you. In the hallway."

It was going to be the bodyguard. I stepped out of the apartment to meet her. She was dressed in a business suit and a wool coat. Trim, blonde, all-business, polite.

"Yael Martin," she said, extending her hand.

"Mara Rains."

"Ryan briefed me. Anything new?"

"That's my PI Janice Greenberg in there. Gunshot mouth to head. It's supposed to be a suicide."

"We start with the assumption that it's not," Yael said, "and that you are in danger. I understand that you carry a .32 caliber semi-automatic?"

I wondered how the hell she found that out but I just gave her a straight answer, "Yes, a little thing. Palm-sized."

"I will loan you a nine millimeter. I have it in the car."

"I'll take it. I need to finish up inside."

"I'm right here."

I went back in and found Rob. He was in the kitchen talking on his cell. He got off.

"I know her. She's good."

"Yael?"

He nodded.

"This is no suicide. I want to say that again," I told him.

"They're going to keep an open mind."

"I know just how open minded cops are, Rob. You see what happened here, right? The killer surprised her, got her gun, made her eat it."

"Let the detectives work it," Rob said. "They'll canvass the building and the neighborhood. Look at the tapes from the surveillance cameras. Test for powder residue on her hands. They will put it together. I've motivated them."

Now I broke down and leaned into him.

"I know," he said. "Janice was one of us."

"What did I get her into?"

"It's too soon to know. I'd rather not guess. It's not the moment to take chances, not even a chance on a guess."

"I know what Janice knew about Ralph Keller. Will they come after me next?"

"We don't know that this is about Keller. But Yael will protect you and Ryan doesn't cut corners.

"You've talked to him?"

"I don't have to talk to him. Where he's been this is light duty."

"Iraq?"

"Iraq, Afghanistan, and worse."

"And Yael?"

"Different gigs but just as serious."

After one more stop at the door to Janice's office, where the people from the medical examiner were preparing to move her body, I met Yael back in the hallway. It was time to go.

She had retrieved a black vest from her car and was holding it at her side.

"Would you mind?" she asked.

"Kevlar?"

"A little extra something, in case," she said.

7

The plan was to get me back to my apartment, pack a bag, and then move to an 'undisclosed location' for the night. Yael didn't actually use that term, but it immediately came to mind.

"You're a shooter?" she asked, double-checking my bona fides.

"I've spent a few quiet evenings at the pistol range."

She took a nine millimeter in a soft holster from a locked compartment between the seats and passed it to me.

"Just in case I go down you won't be left empty-handed."

"I do have the .32, in my bag."

"That's good for muggers. The nine is for slightly bigger game. You a good shot?"

"Very good, for a girl." I was in fact a crack shot.

Yael laughed. "Yup."

When we got back to my apartment, Ryan's two-man team was already inside waiting for us. The one who did the talking, Jimmy, said there was no sign anyone had been there, but wanted me to look around for anything that might not be how I remembered leaving it. They had already gone through the tapes from the lobby, elevator, and hallway surveillance cameras.

"How did you get access to those?"

"That was no problem," was all Jimmy said. "There are no listening devices and your phone is clear."

"So I have nothing to worry about."

"There's plenty to worry about, ma'am."

"I was just joking."

"I know," he said, smiling.

Before I packed a bag or did another thing I wanted to check in with Chelsea Fall. It was closing on midnight as I called her.

She was wide awake. I had to remember that she knew nothing about what had happened the past several hours. She said she felt safe and had a very tough looking man guarding her.

"Are you O.K. with some questions?"

She was. I asked her what she knew about Ralph Keller outside his career as a director. Did he talk about his life or his family? Had she ever met any of his family or friends?

No. They shared nothing outside the world of the film production. That's all they knew together or spoke about.

"And thinking about it," she said, "being able to think for the moment without fear, Ralph is not some creative genius with a bad bruise. He's human wreckage with some skills left intact. Outside of film he doesn't seem to know anything. He's infantile, but even that might be giving him too much credit."

I resisted saying "welcome to the club," but it was comic relief just thinking it. We chatted for a minute or two, to stay comfortable with one another. I didn't hint that things had gone wrong. I told her we would talk in the morning and ended the call.

Jimmy and the silent one, Eli, were playing stud poker on the coffee table with a laptop to the side that showed four views: hallway, elevator, lobby, front entrance. They had placed their own wireless cameras.

"Won't someone notice them?"

"They're very small," Jimmy said, "but no one really pays attention to cameras anymore."

"What about the stairwells and back alley entrance?"

He touched the laptop and those views appeared.

"Just checking," I said.

He smiled again. Jimmy had a fantastic smile.

"Help yourself to whatever you need. I see you figured out how to work the coffee maker."

"Hope you don't mind, ma'am," he said, lifting a mug.

Yael was in the kitchen talking on her cell, so I got to packing a bag. When I was ready to go, dressed in jeans, a big black wool sweater, and my hiking boots, Yael helped me back into the Kevlar vest. Jimmy and Eli led the way. Yael was right beside me. No one said anything.

The men took the lead in their car and we followed. We zigged and zagged for about fifteen minutes before pulling up in front of a townhouse about twenty blocks from my building. I thought we would be heading to one of the outer boroughs, or perhaps, gasp, to the suburbs.

We parked in two spaces that were marked off with traffic cones as a construction zone. In Manhattan that constitutes real power.

Inside, the townhouse felt as tight as a vault and was as clean as a furniture showroom. In its current incarnation it had not been lived in. Someone had tried hard to make it look like a real place but had fallen way short.

We settled spontaneously into the leather chairs and couches in the main room and acknowledged one another. It was a breather. We were taking a moment to remind ourselves that we were the good guys.

"So," I said to my three protectors but looking at Jimmy, "does this all scare the crap out of you the way it does me?"

"Scared, ma'am?" he said. "Our job is to keep you safe. Scared is something people like us left back down the road."

"That must be liberating, to have conquered fear," I said.

"There's that," Jimmy said.

Yael just looked at me and smiled, the way my sister would. It was comforting, and I could tell she meant it to be.

We sat there for a while, the four of us, not saying anything, and then I grabbed the bag I had packed and headed off to my bedroom on the second floor, where the miracle of sleep actually happened. It was as though the transcendent calm of my security team had rubbed off on me and put me right out.

8

I knew that something was wrong before it began to happen. A clock on the night table said 4:07. My mind had come fully awake. I heard nothing, but I instinctively reached for the nine millimeter. And then I was out of bed, pulling my jeans on, getting dressed without putting the gun down.

Then came an explosion. It was muffled, not heavy, but the townhouse trembled. Then flurries of gunshot, sounding almost like popcorn in a microwave. Then single shots exchanged, popping in desperation. I stretched out on the floor alongside the bed and trained the nine millimeter upward at the door. I guessed that whoever came through that door would be guessing about where I was, but in this position I was not immediately exposed and the light from the hallway wouldn't hit me. I would have a chance to get off a few shots.

The shooting stopped. When none of my guards came to check on me I assumed that they were hit and down or dead. I would have expected my mind to be racing, but it was calm, almost cold. I could feel parts of my brain focusing and measuring. I was getting ready to kill or be killed. But no one came through the door. I waited four, five minutes and I moved.

I had my cell phone ready, to call Rob, but I didn't feel safe doing even that until I looked outside the room. Yael was lying back on the top stairs. Her eyes were open and she was applying pressure to a neck wound. She didn't speak and her eyes were glazing. Another wound above her knee was pulsing blood. I quickly tied that off with my belt.

"Are there any more gunners?" I asked her.

She gave an infinitesimal shrug to indicate she didn't know. I stayed there with her, training my gun on the bottom of the stairs and called Rob.

"Everything's gone bad here. Yael's shot and needs help."

"Hold tight," he said.

It's an amazing thing how fast emergency response is in New York. In five minutes NYPD was there followed seconds later by an EMT truck and paramedics. They saved Yael. But my two other guards were dead, as was the four-man hit team that had come to kill me, the last one shot through the forehead by Yael as he turned to come up the stairs. The explosion had been them blowing the door to the townhouse. Everything had happened in a span of about ten minutes from the moment I woke up to when I came down into the main room as the emergency teams arrived.

My guys had been hit repeatedly but clearly kept returning fire and killing the first three gunmen with Yael getting that last one.

A uniformed NYPD lieutenant arrived and was speechless at what he saw. There were no questions. Rob arrived a minute later and took me into the kitchen.

"This makes no sense," he said. "That sort of tactical competence doesn't just happen, not for the bad guys. How would they even be able to find this location, let alone get inside? They had to beat the surveillance system."

Rob was rarely confused by anything.

"If they know we know about Ralph Keller," he said, "then they know it can't be contained, so why go this far? Why come so heavy after you when it has so clearly gone beyond you?"

"Maybe that's not the job," I said. "Not to contain something that's already out, but to keep something else from getting out. Ralph Keller isn't the item."

"Ralph Keller is dead." The voice was Ryan Schell's. I recognized it. He stood in the entryway to the kitchen.

"Are you O.K.?" he asked me.

"Two of your men died for me. I'm sorry."

He nodded grimly. Tall and muscular, with short, almost black, hair, Ryan had a Special Forces look that I recognized from cops who had come out of the serious end of the military.

"What happened to Keller?" Rob asked.

"We were watching him, listening to his communications. I didn't figure him for a target. He wasn't doing anything that seemed out of the ordinary. Didn't appear to have a clue that the actress had come out on him or that the dead end in his background had been turned up, or that we were watching him. When I got Rob's call about this I sent my team into his apartment. They found him with his throat slit."

"What about Chelsea?" I blurted.

"She's O.K.," Ryan said. "The team on Keller went to her hotel. We have something by the tail, and it doesn't want us to see its face. But this was a win for us tonight. You're alive, Mara. They blew in here big time and didn't get what they wanted."

Rob said that this level of capability felt like it had to be attached to a foreign government.

"A few years ago I say yes to that," Ryan said, "but it's no longer a safe bet. And it's not just about the raw capability, but the stones behind making it happen. But whoever did this is now the hunted; whatever else they know they know that."

"I'm feeling hunted," I said.

"Make yourself the hunter," Ryan said. "That's the survivor's M.O."

"He's right," Rob said.

"O.K., then," I said, "where do we go from here? What about those dead guys in there. Can we trace them back somewhere?"

"We'll try," Rob said.

"Have we found their vehicle?" Ryan asked.

Rob left to check on that and to see where NYPD was on developing the crime scene.

"Did you see Yael?" I asked Ryan.

"In the ambulance. She's stable. She'll be fine."

"Did someone give up this location?" I asked him. "I don't know anything about your operation, but are you worried that someone inside betrayed you?"

"No. My people would die first. They couldn't be tortured into turning on the team. This is an outsider with a fix on my outfit. We have our business interface. These people most likely got under that and had a look around."

"Can you deal with that?"

"Done. We have a survival mode that can't be backgrounded."

"Where should I go?"

"Stay here. We have a protected NYPD crime scene in front of us. Besides, this is all out in the open now, between us and our opponent. You stay safe. We find our opponent and kill him."

"What if he is too big to kill?" I asked.

"Good question. I'm betting that once we see his face, he's not going to look too big to kill."

"Then?"

"Then we kill him. That's the only option here. This isn't a criminal matter. This isn't even a matter of warfare. This is just plain kill or be killed survival."

9

Early morning light began to seep into the townhouse as I made coffee. My adrenaline was now turned off, and my body felt weak and rubbery. My mind was cloudy. Given what happened the last time I drifted off I wasn't sure when sleep would come again. I was oddly longing for an hour of comfort with my hairdresser, my eyes closed, leaning back for a shampoo, and then I remembered that I had the nine millimeter loaner from Yael tucked in my jeans.

Ryan had gone to Chelsea Fall's hotel. He hadn't decided how to handle her, and wanted to evaluate both her and the hotel. He would not tell her that Keller was dead. I didn't think that was fair, but Ryan said that it didn't have anything to do with fair. He would tell her when he knew more about both Keller and her.

She had been getting protection from Keller, but even with Keller dead Ryan didn't know whether she was still in danger. He would assume that everyone connected to this affair was in danger, but nothing was certain. Chelsea didn't know what Janice or I knew about Keller, but her safety came down to what our opponents might suspect her of knowing and the doctrine of better safe than sorry.

Rob had also left, to meet with the commissioner, get this sorted out downtown, and establish some sort of ad hoc protocol. He was worrying about the federal agencies. If their curiosity was aroused the usual eighty-car pile-up of conflicting jurisdictions and bureaucracies would result. No one understood the potential of that disaster better than the commissioner, who didn't resent federal interference so much as he feared it. He saw their bull-in-china-shop ways as a danger to New York City. Everything he had done to strengthen NYPD's antiterrorism capability was done with an eye on keeping the Feds at a safe distance. He intended to leave that as part of his legacy.

The term Rob used to summarize the style of his boss was "no bullshit." It would take fifty years, Rob said, before the story could be told of what the commissioner had done to protect the city from the next attack after 9/11. The insights, the strategies, and the tactical angles he developed were astonishing. He thought five or ten moves ahead, and always challenged assumptions and conventional thinking.

The first objective was to find out who Ralph Keller was. That would unlock the big door. If we knew who Keller was the bet was we would know why this had happened and who was behind it. That Keller himself had been murdered said that he had not been the larger issue.

Chelsea Fall's dread that Keller intended to kill her had led, in the course of one afternoon and night, to the death of Janice, two of my guards, and Keller himself, and I might be among them if Yael had not finished the last man of the hit team.

My imagination, replaying it like a viral video on the internet, ran through that next ten seconds that didn't happen, where the last gunman came through the door of my bedroom and I finished him. I chose to believe that I had been ready to win that one because the next time I might have to.

The loss of Janice, coupled with the mortal threat to my life, made me feel an angry love for my ordinary everyday routine. Something as simple as standing on line to get coffee seemed an immeasurable pleasure because it was free and relaxed and so perfectly kicked into the rhythm of this big wave of a city. I thought about all of the good manners that people show, quickly, subtly, in the rush of things, making room on sidewalks, holding doors, nodding acknowledgment in momentary encounters. I realized how acutely joyful it really was, all that freedom, and how dynamic it was, how it propelled me and made me want to do what I do better.

It was my angry yearning love for that simple freedom that straightened out my thoughts about what this all came down to besides simple survival.

Ryan called me from the lobby of the hotel.

"Is she safe there?" I asked him.

"They won't come after her here. She's on an upper floor in a room now heavily protected. It would be more of a suicide mission than last night."

"So it's safe?" I asked again.

"I'll put off moving her for the moment."

"O.K., it sounds like the right call. What about Keller?"

"Nothing yet. The high school can't find his transfer or admission records. He was an only child. His parents, if they were his parents, are dead, and their backgrounds are sketchy as well."

"Is this some sort of terrorist sleeper cell?"

"Consider the year that Keller shows up, Mara."

"Ninety?"

"Yes."

"The Communist regimes in Eastern Europe have collapsed. The Soviet Union is about to go down. You think Keller's arrival could be connected to that?" I asked.

"I see it as a door ajar. Could the energies from all that political power just dissipate in the historical rubble of its collapse?"

"Don't get too far ahead of the facts, Ryan." I realized that I had no need to say that to him. "Sorry, I'm being a lawyer."

"I know," he said ambiguously. "I'm having Keller's DNA analyzed. That can tell us where his family, at least, originates from."

"But he might not be from there."

"That's right."

"Small steps," I said.

"Small steps," he echoed.

We ended the call and I realized that I had been holed up in the kitchen of the townhouse for hours and had nearly finished the pot of coffee. I braced myself and turned into the short hallway that ran side-to-side between the kitchen and the main room, so that I turned left into the hallway and then turned right at the other end to enter the main room.

The dead had been removed and the crime scene people were still at work, carefully collecting samples and bagging evidence. The mess of carnage now had a legal, official stamp on it, like a document accumulating footnotes.

Four uniformed cops controlled the blown-out front entrance and beyond that I could see the still-flashing lights of emergency vehicles. I wondered how this would be played in the media, but NYPD knew how to downplay an event like this and make it seem ordinary enough.

That no detective had even approached me to ask about the events told me what I needed to know about the special handling that was in place. When I needed to know more Rob would fill me in.

Despite my status as target, Rob wouldn't make this about me with the commissioner, and it wasn't about me. Whatever the intent of the kill operation, the purpose behind the killings, it had run into the wrong end of NYPD, one of the most serious counterterrorism operations on earth. Rob was a key player in that, and that's why he wouldn't make this about me, even though everyone from the commissioner on down would know I had been a target.

What mattered now was that a terror-capable outfit had dared to strike in the city. That was what it would be about downtown.

10

Rob returned to the townhouse just before 11:00 a.m. The commissioner had been predictably steely-eyed and unemotional about the attack, but still very concerned about me. He made the Keller case the highest priority. It turned out that everyone who counted downtown knew Ryan, so Rob was cleared to work with him, and Rob was in charge of the case on the direct authority of the commissioner, reporting directly and only to the commissioner.

As for all the potential conflicts involved the commissioner was blunt. He didn't care about that, just get these guys. Rob was to use the Feds' resources as needed, but not let them inside the core operation where they could make a mess. It was the frequently spoken unspoken commandment at NYPD to keep the Feds back.

The commissioner had special skill at cutting right through or circumventing bureaucracy in NYPD and city government, but the federal agencies were like the Amazon rainforest of bureaucracy, and the major tropical disease was getting stabbed in the back over some turf war you hadn't even known existed. Similar conflicts happened inside NYPD, but when the commissioner wanted something all parties to those squabbles stood down and accommodated him. With the Feds no one had that capability, not even the President, who was seen in the heart of the bureaucratic heart as always a vaguely transitory figure who was unlikely to ever reach too far beneath the surface.

At NYPD the commissioner took names, rewarded success, and punished failure, especially the failure of procedural obstruction. NYPD is a big organization but the commissioner regards every member as an individual with character and a personality, and he could find his way to you very quickly if he needed to. That was a very different attitude from a head guy who actively doesn't want to know what's going on below him.

That see-no-evil tendency was not uncommon or confined to large organizations. I had seen it often in my law career, at big firms and small. Some of the blokes I had dealt with seemed to believe it was evidence of their manliness that they were oblivious to what was going on around and below them, as if paying attention was only for neurotics. Yes, I had witnessed the obsessive types get lost in details, but that was not the same thing as paying attention and taking responsibility.

Rob wasn't wearing his usual dark suit and white dress shirt, the unofficial uniform of the commissioner's office. He wore a tweed jacket over a blue oxford cloth shirt, which was what he most often wore in cold weather during his days as a homicide detective.

He was keeping a hard eye on his watch, waiting, with the sort of patience that was pretty damn impatient, for someone to tell him who Ralph Keller was. NYPD intelligence was pulsing the global network as we sat there in the kitchen of the townhouse.

"Did you get any sleep?" he asked me.

"You're kidding."

"You look pretty fresh."

"You're still kidding."

"This is the fort for at least the next few days," he said, "so you might as well make yourself at home."

"Yes, home sweet home, with blood all over the place and the smell of death hanging in the air."

"It could be worse. We could still have the girls at home and in the middle of this." He meant our two daughters, both in graduate school now, one at Duke, the other at Georgetown.

"They're safe aren't they?"

"I'm not assuming anything."

"You've got people on them?"

"First thing I did this morning when I got downtown."

"Did you tell them?"

"The girls? Not yet. That, I didn't have the strength for."

I chuckled. "They'll be furious."

"About having people on them or not being told immediately?"

"Both," I said.

"Well, that's O.K. That's the way they're made. Stubborn and independent."

"They both scare the hell out of me," I said. "What have we unleashed on the world?"

Rob smiled and then laughed. He exhaled the tensions of battle. I saw him reach, unconsciously, to the inside pocket of his jacket for the cigarettes that were long gone from there.

He saw that I had caught it and gave his head a little shake.

"How is this playing in the media?" I asked.

"As a gas explosion."

"So, let me guess, there's a Con Ed truck parked out front?" I hadn't so much as looked outside yet.

"There is indeed."

"Block closed to traffic?"

"Of course."

"So, we're officially safe in here," I said.

"You mean from the media?"

"I mean from whatever did this invading and killing here last night."

"If we're not safe right now, in here, then no one is safe. Those bastards got their bite on the apple. They're not getting another."

I believed Rob, or wanted to believe, but that's what I had thought the night before as I went to bed and fell off to sleep. My instincts had been updated on that score. There was confidence, which I had. There was overconfidence, which I feared. I wasn't able to draw the line between them where Rob was drawing it. I let him know that with my eyes and the wary tilt of my head.

"We're on offense now," he said.

"But we still don't know who the opponent is."

He eyed his watch.

"Soon enough, we'll know soon enough," he said. "Do you have any idea what Ryan is capable of?"

"My imagination tells me that the sky is the limit."

"He was on the ground in Afghanistan ten days after 9/11. Then he did five years in Iraq. Five years, from the beginning through the worst days and into the Surge."

I didn't argue with that. The moment was right for me to get cleaned up, so I waded out through the now dried blood and crime-scene footnotes and went upstairs past Yael's blood and into the bedroom where I had been prepared to make a last stand just hours ago.

The bathroom and its shower felt like places that had not been used since they were remodeled. They had the smell of construction beneath the smell of clean. I left the exhaust fan off and let the bathroom cloud up with steam and spread towels on the bare floors, and when I was done, wrapped in towels, I threw myself down on the bed and closed my eyes, not intending to sleep, just to rest, and I was gone.

11

The knock at the door was too formal for it to be Rob.

"Yes?"

It was Ryan. There were developments and I should come downstairs. The light from outside was fading. The clock on the night table said 4:30. I had been out a few hours. My head was sour. Normally I would be in my office now tying up a day's loose ends, and I had the sudden panic of falling behind on my work and neglecting my clients. I shook it off, dressed quickly, and forced my hair to behave with a brush and clips.

As I headed downstairs I realized that I hadn't yet put together a stoical attitude toward the mess in the main room so I pulled myself tight and held my breath until I was back in the kitchen.

Rob and Ryan were both leaning back against countertops holding coffee mugs.

"Let me get some of that," I said as I reached to the cabinet where the mugs were kept. They waited while I poured my coffee.

"We know who Keller was," Rob said.

"That's impressive," I said. "Who was he?"

"His real name was Rolf Schantz," Ryan said. "He was born in Germany, more specifically in the former East Germany and his father was one Gerhard Schantz, who was a high officer in the Stasi."

"The former secret police of the former East Germany," I said. "Your hunch was on mark, Ryan."

"It was the year that he showed up here that gave it away," he said.

"So Keller, or Schantz, was sent here," I said, "with a fresh identity so that he could live a normal life and avoid the risk of getting caught up in whatever the old man had done with the Stasi."

"That's what we're thinking," Rob said.

"And when Janice looked at Keller it set off an alarm somewhere and then they sent someone to kill her," I said. "So who are they and what were they worried about? It obviously wasn't Keller they were trying to protect."

"We think that there is a Stasi remnant out there," Rob said.

"Out where?"

"That's the question," Ryan said.

Ryan had people talking to Keller's high school classmates and though Keller spoke perfect unaccented English, one of them remembered once catching Keller speaking German on the phone. In a turn of luck, Keller looked just like his father, which some old hand in German intelligence who was familiar with the former Stasi hierarchy caught at a glance.

The Stasi were brutal murderous bastards who were like a fusion of the Nazi Gestapo and the Soviet KGB. They had made the lives of East Germans hell. When the Berlin Wall came down the fear of retribution had the worst of them looking for an exit strategy. Ralph Keller, a/k/a Rolf Schantz, innocent of his father's crimes, was probably first among Gerhard Schantz's concerns and was given a new life and identity in the United States.

"And what became of the elder Schantz?' I asked.

"He didn't want to be too far from his son," Ryan explained, "and took up a new life of his own one town over from Rolf, far enough away for purposes of safety and close enough to see him on occasion, I assume. He died five years ago."

"Natural causes?" I asked.

"Heart attack."

"Natural causes?" I asked again.

Ryan laughed. "We don't have time to exhume his body, Mara."

"I'm just saying."

"There's more," Rob said. "We have a match between one of the members of last night's kill team and an airport surveillance tape from a month ago. He came in on a flight from Buenos Aires. Obviously not for last night's job, but it's him."

"Who was he?"

"The passport he carried for the flight used the name Luis Adolph. We've gotten nowhere with it. It's a fake and very professionally so, as it would need to be."

"Is he former Stasi"

"Too young for that," Rob said.

"Whoever he was," I said, "if it's an old Stasi remnant employing him then we're dealing with one of the most dangerous and paranoid outfits ever, and good enough to keep themselves hidden for two decades. And the quickness and deadliness with which they acted yesterday and last night doesn't feel like something one does from retirement. These boys are still in business. No?"

Ryan looked at Rob as if to say, 'You weren't kidding about her.'

"That's what we're thinking, of course," he said. "They're not just protecting themselves. They're protecting their business, whatever that might consist of. That no one knew they were still operating, at least no one on our side, was their big advantage."

So I had unwittingly poked a stick into this Stasi hornet's nest. My mind froze on that point. There was no exit out of the situation, at least none that was apparent. Rob and Ryan knew it, and we were grimly and silently acknowledging that this would go on to the finish, if we only knew what that meant. Then I remembered that Ryan had been through Iraq and Rob had been in NYPD when the city was called ungovernable with two thousand murders a year. These guys had already seen their way out of no-way-out situations. The Stasi murderers might not be so daunting after all, maybe.

"What do we do with these people when we find them?" I asked.

Rob excused himself from the kitchen and left me alone with Ryan, so I knew what was coming.

"Like I said before, we kill them," Ryan said.

"You make that sound easy."

"It's easier than the alternative."

"You mean like bringing them to justice?" I asked.

"That is justice."

"Frontier justice."

"Yes," he said.

My mind raced through all of the calculations, moral and practical, and it wasn't hard to see that Ryan had been through them already, and not for the first time.

"We're getting ahead of ourselves," I said. "We still don't know for sure who these people are or where they are or how many mutations they've gone through. Yes, it's probably a Stasi faction, but how big, working for themselves, like a mafia outfit, or for others or both?"

Ryan was the calmest human being I had ever met.

"They're still in there," he said, "in the mist, but we know they are in there, and as we look closer we'll see their outline first and then we'll see them."

"They'll be looking back at us too, Ryan."

"Yes," he said, "but over their shoulders."

12

It had been only twenty-four hours since Chelsea Fall walked into my office and spilled out her fear of Ralph Keller to me. As bizarre as that had been, it seemed relatively normal now. It was as though I had since stepped into another dimension. I realized that everyone in the former East Germany once lived with these very same monsters in control of their lives. What sickened me was that these Stasi leftovers thought they could get away with murdering Americans and, worse, that they would have had they not run up against the wrong people.

Which was the real face of humanity, I wondered. Was it the vicious murderers, the secret police of tyrants? Or was it the everyday citizens trying to go about their business? It struck me that at least in part each existed because of the other. Civil society existed as a united effort to fend off the plunderers while the plunderers could only exist if there was something that could be plundered. I had to believe that the true face of humanity was the face that was animated by a conscience. That a person ceased to be a person without a conscience, or could not even become a person without one. I chose to believe that. If simple vanity could be destructive of character, an absence of conscience was fatal. The full-blown narcissism of a human without conscience was like a reflection in a mirror without anyone standing in front of it.

I chose to believe that the words 'true' and 'person' could not be used together where there was no active conscience. But was that rotten state of being – having no conscience – a place that one simply slid down towards, requiring nothing more than an unwillingness to resist the slide, or did one have to strive to be that awful? Or did someone have to be born that way?

Rob and Ryan had each dealt with more than enough men without conscience. Ryan had even yanked their power, and often their lives, away from them in the very place they controlled. I flashed on Yael, ready to die, making a last stand on the staircase to save me, and my two other guards, Eli who never said a word and Jimmy who did all the talking, fighting on with mortal wounds, and I understood Ryan's life and death clarity and how he and his kind could give attention to the fine details of the task at hand until their hearts literally stopped beating.

This old corruption, this artifact of a dead tyranny that uncoiled its dumb horror on the accident of Janice finding no bottom to the life of Ralph Keller was the reason why Ryan had to exist. Many people would know the meaning of this corruption without knowing what to do about it, but Ryan would know what to do about it.

What a gaping hole would be left if Ryan went down. I knew that this Stasi outfit was dangerous in its own terms, but the possibility existed that it was plugged into and drawing power from a government or a faction within a government. I put it in exactly those terms to Ryan.

"Then you unplug them," he answered.

"Easier said than done," I said.

"That's true of everything worth doing, Mara." He smiled big.

The plan, subject to improvisation, was to locate the Stasi cell, grab one of its members, and get the details of the Stasi network from him. The steps in this process were nearly automatic for Ryan, who had done it many times in Iraq. He also had his own network, a shadowy team that existed by implication, but which he had yet to explain to me. I had very limited understanding, so far, of Ryan's operation.

We were waiting for the next pieces of intelligence. Ryan had people pouring through the background of Ralph Keller's – Rolf Schantz's – father, Gerhard Schantz, during his years in the United States.

"That was a sloppy man," Ryan said. "With power in East Germany he enjoyed a certain immunity from his lack of care with details, which might explain why his son's new identity was not properly covered from birth. Gerhard was used to getting away with things. He was lazy. That laziness was his son's death sentence."

I looked at Rob as Ryan said that and my eyes said "the girls."

"Don't worry," Rob said, "that coverage has gone from enough to a lot."

Ryan understood and nodded that it had been seen to.

"Two questions," I said, "how long can we stay in this place?"

"Indefinitely," Rob said. "The gas explosion was very serious and the NYPD presence is available as long as it's needed."

"And when can I get out of here?"

"Can you wait another day?"

"I can but do I have to?"

"You should wait," Rob said.

That was good enough. I had been prepared to hear it would be longer.

Ryan believed that the Stasi cell knew that it had blundered and was now calculating the risk to its whole operation. Their habit of substituting brutality for being smart had backfired. Now they were thinking more clearly, he believed, but if they get frustrated at being so far behind the curve they would look for another angle from which to try brutality.

"How are they behind the curve?" Rob wanted to know.

"No matter how fast they might have updated their capability, their technology, even their methods, they cannot update their past. Their secrecy wasn't just an operational advantage; it was also a shield against that past. Now that we know who they are, even without names and places, it's just a matter of time before that past betrays them."

I was digesting that insight when I excused myself for a bathroom break and left the kitchen intending to go upstairs. I entered the hallway that ran side-to-side between the kitchen and the main room. As I set foot into the main room I noticed a uniformed cop standing just inside the blown-out front entrance, which was now covered with a thick blanket of translucent plastic.

It only took one look at him to know that something was not right. He was glassy-eyed and the uniform looked wrong on him. He was out of place. He saw me and smiled thinly, and I immediately backed into the hallway intending to return to the kitchen to get Rob.

Rob and Ryan saw my face and began to move before I said a word.

The force of the explosion blowing me across the kitchen was what I remembered when I woke up minutes later. Rob was kneeling next to me calling my name. He had a cut on his face but was otherwise all right.

The heavy, old-fashioned construction of the townhouse had resisted the blast and the kitchen had been protected by the thick walls of the hallway that ran side-to-side between it and the main room.

"What the hell was that?" were my first words. "I saw a cop in the front and he looked wrong. Then this."

Ryan had just stepped back into the kitchen. He had fury in his eyes.

"You saw a cop out there, Mara?"

"Yeah," I said, realizing that my head ached.

"It was a suicide bomber," Ryan said. "They put a suicide bomber in an NYPD uniform and he just walked through the door. The balls on these people."

"Just another gas explosion," I said. "This is New York."

They both managed a smile. I was showing grit.

"Anything left of the bomber?" Rob asked.

"DNA is probably all that's left of any value to us. His face is gone. What did he look like, Mara?"

"He seemed glassy-eyed and too skinny inside the uniform."

"Did he say anything to you?" Rob asked.

"Not a word."

Two paramedics arrived in the kitchen and one of them said that I likely had a concussion.

Rob left to take charge of the scene and find out where the bomber had come from and how the hell he got through the police presence outside.

Ryan was worried about a follow-on attack and was looking at the paramedics like suspects.

I let them check my vital signs and clean up my cuts, but had no intention of going to the hospital and was ready to resist any attempts to take me there.

"How bad is it?" I asked the paramedic taking my blood pressure.

"It's normal," he said with a surprised little laugh. "Do you take medication for it?"

"No."

"You're very unexcitable."

"That's not really true."

"Blood pressure doesn't lie," he said. "We need to take you to the hospital though. You're going to need some x-rays of your head."

"Sorry, I don't photograph well," I said.

"I haven't heard that one in a while."

"How long?" I asked.

"A year, maybe."

"Did he, she go with you?"

"No, she didn't, if my memory is correct."

"And nothing bad happened to her?"

"Not that I heard about."

"Then we have a precedent. I'm staying."

I was getting used to being under attack and, always a quick study, how to shake it off. It was the next best thing to being young again.

"You're being dumb," the paramedic said.

"But it feels so right," I said.

13

"The cops on the watch were suckered," Rob said as he approached us outside on the sidewalk. He wasn't angry. Just telling us the facts. At the end of the block the bomber, with sergeant's stripes on his uniform, came out of nowhere, mentioned Rob by name, and got waved by. He was more aggressive with the cops right outside, using Rob's name again with a degree of urgency.

"I spotted him as a fake right off," I said, "but maybe I've been around cops longer than the cops out here."

"Or maybe what you picked up on was a man who knew he was about to be blown to pieces," Rob said, always a defender of NYPD no matter what.

"It's done now and we're alive, he isn't," I said, "but that was certainly a bold move. And they know you're the NYPD point man, Rob. They've gotten inside the department."

Ryan watched the street like an x-ray machine. He didn't like the number of emergency vehicles that were arriving at the scene.

"We have to move," he said.

Rob's car was just down the block. He looked at me and nodded his head toward the townhouse.

"Need anything from in there?"

"Yes, but the staircase is blown out. When they get to the second floor, maybe someone could find my bag. My wallet and cell phone are in it, and my .32."

Any man who can overcome his natural contempt for a woman's purse and show it all due respect is absolutely the manliest of men. Rob went to one of the cops who had screwed up and charged him with recovering it for me. I felt much better as the three of us drove off.

"They went to considerable trouble to get that zombie in there but the explosive charge was a third of what was needed to bring the building down," Ryan said. "Why?"

"Mistake?" Rob asked.

"Professional courtesy?" I wisecracked.

"No. They're thinking about media impact. That's got to be it," Ryan said. "They saw how we played the first attack as a gas explosion. So they're thinking 'we like that, let's not turn it into world news.'"

"It's a theory," I said.

Rob nodded. The little smile that brought his face back to life when I said 'professional courtesy' was still sitting there. I knew his moods and it didn't take much to adjust a bad one upward. He had been mortified that the cops fell for the bomber's ruse.

We were heading downtown. Our destination was a building on the Lower East Side. Ryan had rented it that morning. It was a fresh location and our opponent wouldn't know about it, yet. An old bank building that had later been an artist's studio, it was big, cold, empty, and built like a fortress. But there would be no NYPD presence to maintain a perimeter. This was a hidden in plain sight deal.

As soon as we were inside I said, "I'm not comfortable with this."

"Comfort almost got you killed twice," Ryan said.

"So," I answered, "if constant fear is comfort, then total unrelenting immediate fear is what?"

"We call that total calm," Ryan said.

"I get that. It's not that far removed from being in front of a judge who is furious at you, with the small difference that the judge won't try to have you killed later that day."

"There you go."

I remembered what Jimmy, my dead bodyguard, had said to me last night, "Scared is something people like us left back down the road." Jimmy would be too busy doing his job to be scared even when he was being shot to death. That was indeed total calm, and I was beginning to feel it.

Time had always meant anxiety to me. It couldn't be stopped, but this was as close to having it stop that I had ever known. I was beginning to grasp how some soldiers found everyday life unsatisfying after long exposure to combat. It wasn't a love for violence, but the stopping of time and the relief from the slow death of everyday anxiety. It was the calm. I was feeling exactly that when the paramedic had examined me and my blood pressure was normal. For a change, I wasn't even clenching my teeth.

"There's no coffee maker," I said.

"Tomorrow morning try the hardware store down the block," Ryan said. "I noticed it driving up. For now there's got to be a place where you can pick some up to go."

"You're saying it's safe for me to go out?"

I looked at Rob who looked at Ryan.

"If they are already on top of this place we'd be dead. Enjoy it while you can," Ryan said.

Rob shrugged; I got some cash from him, and went out for coffee. The bodega down the block had it all. Cans of coffee, milk, sugar, coffee filters. I laid all that on the counter and then asked the guy behind it for three large coffees to go. He looked at my supplies.

"For the morning," I said nodding down at the groceries, and he went off and prepared the three big ones for me. When I turned outside with the two shopping bags, I felt like a free and normal New Yorker. The street was busy with cars and pedestrians. It was already 7:30 and I remembered that it was a Friday night. I could see the relief in people's faces, to be done for the week.

No one would pay much attention to the dust from the explosion that covered my jeans and sweater. I might be working at a construction site. Maybe they would wonder about the fresh cuts on my face, but New Yorkers were adepts at ignoring things. Most of the time most things out of the ordinary might draw a glance but would be forgotten in the next thought. It took a big effort to give prolonged attention to more than a few of the thousands of busy people you saw every day.

It was like a holiday to get even a block's worth of the city after a long night and day holed up. Back at the new temporary location Rob and Ryan were seated on folding chairs at the end of a long cafeteria table and while they were not angry at one another, they were at odds about something. It had to do with me.

"Spit it out," I said to them as I unbagged the coffees.

"I want you out of this, Mara," Rob said.

"Out to where?"

"That's what Ryan is saying, that you're safer with us. After today I don't see that."

"Well, for instance, what do I do? Go hide in a convent in Peru? Just the feeling of helplessness in that sort of retreat would make me insane. But tell me I'm in the way and I'll go to the convent."

"No, you're on the team," Rob said. "But you're safety trumps that."

"If you two are the rest of the team and your safety doesn't trump the team, why should mine?"

Rob had no answer. Ryan didn't say a word. The controversy passed and what had become the regular order among us was restored.

"There's something else," Rob said as he looked at Ryan.

"We've located the Stasi cell," Ryan said. "We followed the lead of the shooter who had come in from Buenos Aires and he was indeed a contractor they used. They're based in an Argentine suburb. We have a plan to grab one of their members and bring him to a facility we use in Pensacola."

"When will that happen?" I asked.

"The plan is to have him there early tomorrow morning," Ryan answered. "His cohorts will know he's gone missing, probably within a few hours, and we can't be sure how they will react. My people on the ground think they'll run. Rob thinks they'll try more violence. I think they are unpredictable. We need to have a very fast, very successful interrogation."

"What's the biggest worry?" I asked.

"Everything that we don't know. We've been running on conjecture. We have their outline. We've found them. But we don't know what we really have."

"Why waste time flying this guy into Pensacola?" I wanted to know.

"We have people and resources there that will save time and get us a more reliable product."

"You mean an interrogation product?" I said, smiling at such a term.

Ryan nodded.

"What is it?" I asked, sensing that Ryan had more.

"Perceptions always evolve. Sometimes you see enough. Most of the time you don't. Occasionally you can even see and know too much. But our model of the Stasi remnant in business for itself, something is wrong with it."

"Be more specific," I said.

"I can't," he said.

"Because it's gut instinct?"

"Yes."

14

I didn't get to ask where the beds were hiding in the old bank building and wouldn't have the opportunity to buy a coffee maker the next morning. We were soon on a private jet to Pensacola. We caught it out of Teterboro and I slept the entire flight. When we landed in Florida we were met by a van and driven to a warehouse district. The air outside was warm and thick, and it was the middle of the night.

Someone watching on a surveillance camera buzzed us into a windowless cinderblock and aluminum building. From inside a badly lit vestibule we were buzzed through another heavy door. The interior was not open warehouse space, which I was expecting, but was finished like a generic office with carpeting and white walls. We followed a hallway around to a conference room. A young guy who looked like military but was wearing only a crisp grey jump suit told us to help ourselves to coffee and donuts laid out on a table at the back of the room.

We did help ourselves and sat waiting, mostly in silence, for about an hour. Then a man of about sixty, very handsome, dressed in a business suit, came into the conference room. I could tell that Ryan was relieved that he was there.

"Rob," the man said, "good to see you."

"General," Rob said.

"Ryan."

"General."

"Who is this?" he said with a displeased tone, pointing at me as he walked to the other side of the conference table.

"She's part of our team," was all Ryan said.

"I've never seen her before," he said. Rob cautioned me with his eyes to keep quiet.

"We've taken some casualties," Ryan said, perhaps to explain my unfamiliar face.

"Yes, I know. That's unacceptable."

I didn't know what he meant by unacceptable, whether he was being critical of Ryan for letting it happen or saying that no one would get away with that. The 'General' so far seemed like someone who lived on the other side of the looking glass.

"Get this right," he said as he finished circling the table, and then he left the room.

Rob just shook his head slightly at me. He was telling me I didn't need to know who the General was, what all that was about, and that I shouldn't ask. Not usually willing to let such an oddity pass, I did grasp the perfect simplicity of saying nothing. And for a change I did exactly that.

More time passed and I dozed off again, with my head resting in my palm. The young guy who had graciously directed us to the coffee and donuts came into the room and said, "We're ready."

We followed him down the hallway and he ushered us into a room that was like a theater with seats facing a large screen television monitor. On the screen was a room lined with bookshelves and two men seated across a table from one another. We all sat down and Rob and Ryan put on the headphones attached to their seats and I did the same.

No one explained anything to me but it became clear that the man on the left of the screen with a pad in front of him, tapping his pen on the table, was the interrogator. The man on the right was the ex-Stasi officer who had been grabbed out of the Buenos Aires suburb. He appeared to be in his mid-fifties, was very fit, and had the stone-faced affect of an executioner about to be executed.

The interrogator began to speak but what I heard on the headphones was a simultaneous translation in English. I assumed that the interrogation was proceeding in German, but I didn't know that for absolute fact because I heard only the translator. They could have been speaking Albanian for all I knew.

The Stasi guy did not know who had him, why, or where he was, and didn't seem to care. He did seem to know that the game was up, and there seemed to be an implicit assumption between the two men that this was the 'easy way' and that the 'hard way' was immediately available.

A few times the interrogator stressed how important exact details were. He was not, he told the Stasi officer, interested in vague or subjective answers. Names, places, and addresses flowed. This fellow was not taking one for the team, and it was pretty clear, from the context, that he knew it was pointless to attempt to bargain. My sense was that he believed he was working toward an outcome that didn't involve torture, a painless death perhaps. He was not going to resist.

I attributed these efficient results to the acting skills of the interrogator, whose flat affect and piercing questions played the uncertainty and the unknowability of the situation to perfection.

It was an hour and a half before he began to ask about the events in New York, as if they were side details in which he had some mild interest because he was vaguely amused by those silly Americans. At that point I was certain that the Stasi officer hadn't a clue that it was Americans he was talking to. He was responding as if, on the question of the Americans, he and the interrogator were on the same side. It was something like, 'even though I don't know who you are and I expect you to kill me, surely we are both better than the Americans.'

Then the interrogator asked the Stasi officer, "Did your group assassinate the private investigator whose name was Janice Greenberg?"

"Yes," he said.

"Why?"

The Stasi officer became visibly uncomfortable and hesitant. He looked away from the interrogator.

"I will ask again. Why did you assassinate the private investigator in New York?"

"Isn't an admission that we did it enough?"

"No. You must tell me why, and you must tell me the truth, please."

The Stasi officer continued to hesitate and look away. It made no sense to me that this could be a bigger deal than everything else he had given up.

"Answer the question, please," the interrogator demanded.

"No, I cannot," the Stasi officer insisted. "You want only the truth and here I cannot tell you the truth."

"Why is that?" the interrogator asked in a more relaxed tone.

"Who are you, who do you work for?" the Stasi officer asked defiantly of the interrogator.

"That's nothing you need to know or that would do you any good," the interrogator answered.

"My answer to you is the same."

"But our positions are not equal, you know that. Once again, why did you assassinate the private investigator in New York?"

The Stasi officer's eyes darted around the room. He looked as though his head was going to explode.

"For our friends," he blurted out.

"Your friends? Who are your friends?"

This made no sense to me. They killed Janice because she was on to Ralph Keller's real identity and Ralph Keller led back to them.

"What do you mean when you say 'our friends,'" the interrogator asked again.

The Stasi officer looked the interrogator in the eye, his mouth now swollen with anxiety.

"KGB," he said.

Ryan, without a word to either of us, got up from his seat and left the room. Seconds later we saw him on the television monitor. He went right to the Stasi officer, grabbed him by his collar, and shoved the barrel of his nine millimeter into his face. What he said to him was not relayed over the headphones nor were the Stasi officer's responses, but the Stasi officer was answering Ryan's questions without hesitation.

That exchange went on for fifteen minutes. It was like watching a silent movie without the occasional subtitles or music. Other than the placement of his gun in the Stasi officer's face, Ryan's usual composure remained intact.

Ryan spoke briefly to the interrogator before leaving the room. He didn't return immediately to the room we were in and the interrogation did not resume. The Stasi officer composed himself while the interrogator wrote on the pad in front of him. Rob looked over at me but said nothing. He knew I had questions but was telling me not to ask them.

"Stop trying to get ahead of the facts," I told myself as my thoughts raced.

We waited another twenty minutes before Ryan returned.

"This is really a cauldron of shit now," were his first words as he came back in. Strangely, he looked younger, with fire in his eyes.

"KGB?" Rob said.

"Can you believe it?" Ryan turned to me, "Your PI wasn't killed because she found a false bottom in Ralph Keller's life. She was killed because she was going to find out the same thing about Chelsea Fall. She's the daughter of a former KGB official who set her up in the U.S. with a new life and identity. They put the arm on their Stasi friends who put the arm on Keller to give Chelsea the part in his film. See, it really is all about who you know."

"What do we do with Chelsea?"

"I've already told the team watching her to get her out of the hotel."

"To where?"

"I left that up to them."

"So let's back up a second," I said. "What's the KGB daughter doing bringing her neurotic beef with Keller to me in the first place? Keller wouldn't dare cross her. Or doesn't she know who she is?"

"Why did she choose you, Mara?" Rob asked.

"She heard I represented entertainers."

"No references?" he said.

"I didn't ask her for any."

"I'm going to assume that this is about Rob," Ryan said, "until the facts show that it's not."

"If it's about me, then it's about the commissioner," Rob said.

"And the commissioner runs the tightest anti-terrorism operation anywhere. New York is target one," Ryan said.

"And KGB, which no longer exists, by the way, wants to accomplish what and for whom?" I asked.

Rob left the room. I assumed it was to call New York and alert the commissioner. The stakes were getting higher and the pace was picking up.

"Where does this leave us, Ryan?"

"In a hall of mirrors," he said.

15

Randall Wolfe was the name that came up at the top of the list when Ryan searched around for an expert on the KGB. Wolfe was a scholar who went to Moscow right after the Soviet Union collapsed. For a few years there had been somewhat open access to Soviet archives, access that has since been shut down.

Ryan arranged for Wolfe to be contacted so that we could meet with him later that day. We were returning to New York.

The plan had been for Ryan to oversee the roll-up of the Stasi faction in Buenos Aires, but someone else would have to manage that now. That was old news. We didn't have enough time now even to listen to more of the interrogation of the Stasi officer. Details from that would be passed to Ryan on the fly.

During the flight back I listened to their sides of phone conversations as Ryan and Rob built a more complex model of the situation we faced. They were asking the dreaded Feds for more help, while still holding them back, outside of the core.

Ryan was so anxious to talk to Randall Wolfe that he was having him meet us at Teterboro. We would use an office in one of the hangars.

I gave some pro forma consideration to whether I still had any responsibility as an attorney to Chelsea Fall and I quickly decided that I did not. Her approach to me had been made in bad faith, a ruse to somehow get close to Rob and through Rob to the commissioner, though none of the purpose for her doing that was yet clear.

I caught Ryan's attention between phone calls and asked where Chelsea had been taken. Her handlers had her at a house in a suburb north of New York, in Rockland County.

"Is she safe?" I asked.

"From everyone but us," he said. He had lost two men and nearly lost Yael and was fresh out of sympathy for Chelsea. I hadn't quite gotten that far, yet.

When we landed we went directly to the office where Randall Wolfe was waiting for us. He was a very large, tall man with dark hair and a beard and wore old-fashioned thick black-rimmed glasses. He seemed pleased to have the opportunity to talk about his work, but didn't ask us who we were. He had probably been told enough already. Ryan got immediately to it.

"Can you tell me anything, Professor," he asked, "about rogue KGB factions surviving the Soviet collapse?"

"I can tell you two things," Wolfe said. "First, the KGB was for a long time in business for itself, before the collapse. Second, the KGB knew for twenty years that the collapse was coming and had long prepared for the transition to, what should I call it, the private sector."

"Where do they operate out of?" Ryan asked.

"Everywhere," Wolfe said. "They were everywhere and they stayed everywhere. Finding work is easy for them. When they can't find work; they make work. The cells are now autonomous, but they of course know each other. It's a brotherhood, a network. Dying out in some places, getting stronger in others, especially in the homeland."

"Russia?" Ryan asked.

"Yes, indeed. Look who's in charge there."

"Is the network controlled from Moscow?"

"'Control' is too strong a word. It's certainly nothing like the old days. These men are self-interested capitalists now, in a manner of speaking. They might long for the power of the old Soviet Union, but they are, most of them, uninterested in the ideology."

"Do you consult with CIA about this?" Ryan asked.

"I can't answer that question," Wolfe said.

"I know you can't," Ryan said. "In your opinion, as a scholar, how does CIA approach the KGB now?"

"Strictly as an historical matter," Wolfe answered.

"The KGB no longer exists," Ryan said.

"That about sums it up," Wolfe said.

"We could go wild from there, couldn't we?"

"There are some who think that of CIA's many blind spots that this one is the most consequential." Wolfe was pointing into the intellectual woods.

"Have you pressed your case or published anything about this?" Ryan asked.

"If I did that," Wolfe said, "I would be pigeonholed as a Cold War obsessive."

"But it's your area of expertise," Ryan said.

"Ironies abound," Wolfe said. "I am the expert until I offer my conclusions. Then I'm still fighting the Cold War."

I could tell that Ryan took to Randall Wolfe. Straight answers were something he could always use and Wolfe had them.

"Would these people use a suicide bomber?" Ryan asked him.

"It's not one of their usual methods, not one they would use directly, is what I mean to say, but why not. They reinvented terrorism through their stooges in the Middle East before the collapse. It's not as if they are above it, and since they no longer answer to any authority there's nothing to restrain them. Remember, they no longer exist."

Ryan got quiet, trying to calculate all the angles in this mess. It was an almost impossible task. He thanked Wolfe and asked if he could call on him again. Wolfe said he was available anytime. He had found someone who would listen to him talk about the KGB.

"I hardly need to warn you about these people," he said, "but you must always be very careful."

Ryan thanked him again and we left the small office and retrieved Rob's car. We were headed for Rockland County. Ryan wanted to talk to Chelsea. I wasn't sure I wanted to be in the room for that. I brought it up.

"It's not going to be like that," Ryan said, rejecting my implication that it would get rough. "She doesn't know that we know. I want to question her as her ally and protector and see what I can sift out of her cover story. I want to get the name of her contact. I need to light up the network around New York. You will be a big help with her."

"What's my role going to be, then?" I asked.

"Be her friend and help her believe that she can play this all the way through and walk out the other side."

The house where Chelsea was being kept by Ryan's team was a nondescript older place on an equally nondescript wooded block. We pulled into the driveway. A van was visible inside the garage, which was attached to the house. We went around the side of the garage to the back door and were greeted by one of the men.

I played my role with Chelsea, greeting her warmly and inquiring about her mood while the men huddled elsewhere. She hadn't been told anything. She didn't know that Ralph Keller was dead. For her it had been two nights in a luxury hotel and a trip to the suburbs. She had questions for me, but I told her that Ryan would explain everything.

"I'm getting a little crazy," she said, referring to her confinement.

"I know," I said, "this has been terribly hard on you." I was so reassuring that I almost made myself laugh.

Ryan joined us and asked Chelsea to sit down. I took a chair as well.

"You are safe, Chelsea, and everything is going to be O.K."

Her relief seemed genuine and Ryan continued.

"I don't want you to return immediately to your regular routine, but there is no reason for you to stay cooped up here."

"So I am safe from Ralph now?" she asked.

"Well, yes, for all practical purposes that situation has been straightened out. But I would like you to stay a day or two with a friend or relative, someone you'll be safe with."

"But you just told me I am safe," she said.

"You are, as best as we can tell. There is no immediate threat to you, but I would prefer that you not jump back into your routine."

"Why?" she demanded to know.

"Ralph Keller has been murdered."

She was stunned and turned pale.

"What happened to Ralph? Who killed him?"

"It's under investigation," Ryan said. "It was very brutal. There are no suspects yet. That's why, just as a precaution, I prefer that you not go back to your apartment and your routine. Just to be reassured that this involves no threat to you. You don't know of any possible connection to you? I should ask that."

"No," she answered, "it couldn't have any connection to me. My personal relationship with Ralph was only between the two of us. No one else was really even aware of it."

"But you see why I want to keep you buffered from even the possibility that this could affect you. Who would you feel safe staying with?"

He had convinced her. She now wanted to do what he wanted her to do, which was to go where she knew she would be safe. Watching her face it seemed that she was worried that Keller's murder was about her or at least about "it." And that was the direction Ryan wanted her moving in.

"I have a cousin in Brooklyn," she said. "I can stay with him."

"What's his name?" Ryan asked, taking out a pen and a small notepad, as if just attending to details.

"Les Rogoff," she said.

Ryan got his address and telephone number. He recommended to Chelsea that she relax for a few more hours and he would give her the go ahead to make arrangements with her cousin. At this point she was anxious but compliant. Ryan had put her in a state of mind where she would, for the time being, do what he wanted her to do.

Chelsea and I said goodbye. I assured her that everything would be fine. And then Ryan, Rob and I left. The moment we pulled away from the house Ryan was on his cell. The hounds were unleashed on Les Rogoff.

"Do you think he's her contact?" Rob asked Ryan.

"He's something. She said he was her cousin. I think Rogoff has got to be in the network."

16

The three of us were in need of sleep, showers, and food. There wouldn't be any time to sleep, but the other two were available. I requested a stop at a mall along the highway and then set a new record for buying anything, grabbing some pre-washed jeans, a few pullovers, and socks and underwear. Then we found a motel with a restaurant and took three rooms.

By the time we were assembled at the restaurant Ryan already had the life story of Les Rogoff, including every bank account, credit card, phone record, and medical procedure.

Ryan's plan was efficiently illegal, comprising about a dozen felonies, but no one was counting those anymore. He would tell Chelsea to go ahead and contact Rogoff, then see who Rogoff called or went to see about it. Rogoff would be under a surveillance blanket.

He would set off all sorts of alarms, Ryan believed, and the communications surveillance team would follow that daisy chain. Every call in that chain would be matched to Rogoff's recent known calls and a pattern would emerge. Then Rogoff would be grabbed and interrogated. A specialist was already on the way from the Pensacola facility to handle that. My head spun.

"Back to motive," I said. "At bottom we think this whole move is about getting to the commissioner."

"We're not forgetting that," Ryan said. "We're trying to outrun and pre-empt it."

"How do we know we're staying ahead of that?"

"We're still alive," he said. "That's always a good rule of thumb in a situation like this."

I asked what would happen to Chelsea, and got the quick prospectus. After she calls Rogoff and sets off the chain reaction, she is taken to his place. But he isn't there, because we will have him. Then she makes her next move, we watch that, and Ryan decides whether or not to pick her up again. He was leaving it open when and how that might be played, depending on her relative value to us at that point.

"What is the immediate objective?" I asked.

"To map the network of this KGB faction," he answered.

"And?"

"To break the mirrors."

"The mirrors?"

"Remember when I said that we had stepped into a hall of mirrors?"

"Yes."

"In that dilemma you smash all the mirrors. Destroy their capacity to bring confusion and misdirection."

"And then?"

"Then they are stark buck naked and very ordinary."

"That can happen to those people?" I asked.

"Especially to them. What are they besides their deception?"

"Violent," I said.

"Violence is the easy part," Ryan said.

I could tell from the look on Rob's face that he was skeptical about all of the pieces of the plan falling together.

"What are you thinking?" I asked, turning to him.

"These people," Rob said, "they are not so easy to understand. Their roots run deep."

"Be more specific," I said.

"Look at the implications of what Randall Wolfe said about the reception his work gets – the attitudes, the denial – in the academic world and at CIA. Two arenas where you would think there would be plenty of interest in what actually became of the KGB apparatus, but where instead you get treated like you're chasing sea monsters if you raise the question, or at least raise it outside of a very narrow context. To whose benefit is that?"

"To the remnants of the KGB," I said.

"Well, there you go," Rob said, "like the devil, the KGB's first post-Cold War win was to convince everyone that it no longer existed. Or simply that it no longer mattered. Is that just the power of deception, as Ryan seems to suggest, or is that real power to somehow make these institutions adopt certain attitudes and behaviors?"

"You're a counterterrorism insider," Ryan said to Rob. "Has the old KGB network ever been discussed in your circles?"

"I've never heard anything about it. I don't think it's even on anyone's mind. That's my point. It's not just a fade into the woodwork. There's a cultivated denial. And you've dealt with CIA, Ryan, in particular. You know how that place runs."

"All the resources and talent in the world," Ryan said, "saddled with the fear of making the wrong move. There's a not so fine line between prudent caution and paralyzing fear. At CIA all those resources and people get folded down into the batter of process and bureaucracy."

Rob made his point again. That somewhere along the line CIA, the academic world, what he called the 'knowledge establishment' had been disciplined and trained not to consider the leftover KGB apparatus, even when, he emphasized, someone from that apparatus had assumed power in Russia. It just amazed him. How deep did KGB's roots have to be in that knowledge establishment itself to turn the mere consideration of KGB into a taboo?

"If everyone has conveniently forgotten to remember that KGB exists," Ryan said, "then no one will miss them when they're gone."

"Except the rest of the KGB network, Ryan," I said. "What do you think the reaction of that network will be to the crisis you inflict on the New York node?"

"Adverse," Ryan said, "I expect it to be an adverse reaction."

Rob was even blunter with Ryan. "Those people found your safe facility in a matter of hours, had the Stasi remnant send a kill team, and when that didn't work had a suicide bomber walk through an NYPD cordon, using my name, and attack the same facility hours later."

"Are you trying to discourage me, Rob?" Ryan said, with a smile.

"I'm just saying that we are picking an awfully big fight."

"We didn't pick the fight, Rob. I'm here because you called in a small favor, which was to help Mara protect a woman from a potentially homicidal boyfriend. I missed the memo that he was the son of a Stasi general and that she was a KGB love child, or whatever."

They were both right. It was too big a fight, but we hadn't asked for it.

"I don't think there's any walk-away option here," I said.

"Of course not," Rob said. "The commissioner isn't flustered by a plot to get at him. It's not the first. And unless they succeed, whatever their objective, it won't be the last. But the commissioner always sees his duty as that of a civil official operating within the rule of law. Where I am right now is anyone's guess. And Ryan, you're launching a plan that will leave dead bodies all over the jurisdiction. What I'm saying here is that holding all of that aside, how are we going to deal with the blowback from the rest of the KGB network?"

The question hung there. Ryan nodded and leaned back and drank his coffee. There was a lot I didn't know about Ryan and his operation and I knew better than to ask. I wondered how much Rob really knew. But Ryan had said that the opponent had backgrounded his outfit, which was how they found and attacked the townhouse. He had to switch his operation to what he called 'survival mode,' which I took to be a fully ad hoc situation, where everything moved through new channels on the fly. Everyone scrambled to new locations and essentially disappeared.

Without any formalities, I was now a part of the operation, safer than I would have been if left on the sidelines, but safe only in the sense that I was at the center of maximum danger, which was also a moving target in 'survival mode.' I could fantasize about being back at Rembrandt's after work, sipping a martini in anticipation of some laughs over dinner, but that was another world now. That was the world that Ryan made possible, but not the world he would ever be comfortable in. I began to doubt I would ever find my way back there either.

But here I was running with a pack whose leader had survived five years in Baghdad encircled by the most vicious murderers on earth. On that basis I believed we could get this mission done, even though 'this mission' was as ambiguous as, say, the mission in Iraq had been.

Rob had challenged Ryan to think, not challenged him to stop. And he had been thinking.

"You're right, Rob," he said. "We don't want to be killing old KGB soldiers."

"O.K.," Rob said.

"We want them killing each other," Ryan finished.

Rob smiled and shook his head. He didn't know what to say to that. Ryan got up from the table and stepped outside the restaurant. He was on his cell phone, and I imagined him on a cell phone on a street in Fallujah with bullets flying back and forth between people who were supposed to be on the same side. I didn't know how Ryan would make that happen in New York, but I didn't doubt that he could.

Rob seemed bemused. He had long been telling me that the world we knew had been turned upside down and that I just couldn't see it yet. Now I was seeing it. I understood where the new lines in Rob's face came from. I had watched the commissioner, always a taut, chiseled figure, become an even harder man. I knew many of the facts but never grasped their implications. Now they were spontaneously assembling in context.

Of course the commissioner was used to threats and plots, against the city and himself. It was his way of life now. Just as it was Rob's way of life. I was grasping the unending war it really was, now from the point of view of a combatant. I can't say I liked it, but it didn't have anything to do with liking or not liking.

We paid for the food and joined Ryan outside.

"Next move?" Rob asked.

"Manhattan. We'll go back to the old bank building."

"Is that safe?" I asked.

"Define safe," Ryan said.

"Our opponents don't know about it yet."

"It's safe," he said.

It felt like theoretical safety to me, but I was beginning to see all safety as theoretical. In this case, the theory could be readily falsified by another exploding bomb or flurry of bullets.

The rest of the trip back into the city was uneventful. Rob drove fast. Ryan made calls. I was along for the ride and tired. When we got back to the Lower East Side, Rob left us and went to see the commissioner. I found a couch in what had been an office and fell right into it. Ryan was continuously on his cell.

I didn't know how long I was out, but the light was fading on another day when I was awakened by a conversation out in the big space that had been the bank's lobby and then an artist's studio. I didn't listen to what was being said, but I was uncomfortable being half asleep and I could smell coffee brewing. Ryan had picked up a coffee maker. O, the little things!

When I pulled myself together and rubbed the sleep out of my face, I walked out there and found Ryan talking with the handsome man from Pensacola who Rob and Ryan both called 'General.' The man who I thought lived on the other side of the looking glass.

He immediately turned his head in my direction and, just as he had before, pointed at me and asked, "Who is that?"

"She's on the team," Ryan said, "she was with us at the facility."

The General grunted and indicated to Ryan that he wished to be elsewhere. Ryan led him off to another former office, politely excusing himself and pointing out the fresh coffee. "It's very strong," he said.

I liked the General and was reassured by his presence. He wasn't trying to charm me, that was certain, but he exuded confidence. I took his arrival on the scene as a positive sign, even though I had no idea who he was or what he could do for us.

17

Ryan and the General spoke alone for more than an hour. That gave me time to drink coffee, do some stretching, and get more awake. I was oddly reassured by the length of their conversation. Surely they were detailing a plan to which the General would bring another dimension of resources. I would be content with knowing only so much as I needed to know.

When they came out they both helped themselves to coffee from the fresh pot I had made and sat down at the table with me.

"You're on the team," the General said.

"Is that a question or a statement of fact?" I said.

"They are only men," he said.

"Excuse me?"

"These Russians, the KGB, they're men, but they have dug themselves in very deep, like termites."

"I see the analogy. I like it," I said.

"They lost their world, but they keep going. It's a discouraging comment on the human heart, don't you think? They produced nothing but ruin and misery, but they keep going."

"Or," I said, "it's an encouraging comment on human tenacity, that such a strong will to continue survives after the original cause is dead."

"But," the General asked me, "is that human tenacity or, again, the mere biological tenacity of the termite?"

"No matter how broken, their souls are human," I said. "No matter how corrupted, so are their minds. That makes them much more dangerous than termites."

"And they are just still men," he said.

"We have to remember that," I said, smiling.

The General laughed. It was a good uproarious laugh.

"She's on the team," he said, looking at me but speaking to Ryan, and then asking me, "Do you understand that there is no team?"

"But that is the team's great advantage," I said, "that it doesn't exist."

"Exactly," he said.

Then the three of us sat and drank our coffee in silence. It was again the serenity of maximum danger. After a while the General got up to leave. We remained seated.

"They are not stupid," he said to me before turning toward the door. "It's quite the opposite. But they do not know what we know." Then he left.

I stared at the door for several moments, and then looked at Ryan.

"Who is he?" I asked.

"You'll have to ask him that."

"Well, then, while we're on the subject, who are you, Ryan?"

He laughed. "Me? I just do what you see me doing and, to be honest, what you don't see me doing. I discovered my vocation in Iraq: give the bad guys nightmares."

"Is that it?"

"No. I think that the real bad guys don't have nightmares. They have animal fear."

"And where are we right now?" I asked.

"Fear is rippling through our opponents. While you were napping I sent word to let Chelsea Fall get in touch with her supposed cousin, Les Rogoff. And when she did that the switchboard of the local KGB affiliate lit right up. She's on her way to see cousin Les right now, but we already have him, grabbed him right after he exhausted his panic button. He's talking to one of our interrogators right now."

"You're not there. We're not there."

"Division of labor, Mara. We don't need to see the warm-up. We have a decision to make on Chelsea, whether to let her roam free or grab her back and get her talking. I still don't know how valuable she is. I'm talking about her value to whoever her benefactor is on their side. No little trouble was taken to give her an acting career, but when push comes to shove she might be expendable. If we leave her out there they might kill her."

"Then you must bring her back in," I said.

"You think we owe her that much?"

"We owe her her humanity, Ryan. Isn't that what the General meant when he said that 'they don't know what we know'?"

"That was part of what he meant, yes. But we're also about to disregard the humanity of a lot of these people."

Ryan pulled out his cell phone and got up and walked away. He had made a decision about Chelsea. He wasn't going to let her loose. The order of her life would be upside down now. She had gone from asset to liability for their side and as paranoia grew in the ranks she would likely be at the front of the line for a bullet.

When Ryan came back he nodded that it was done.

"What happens to her, ultimately?"

"Ultimately?"

"I mean in this life. What will you do with her?"

"After we're done with her, she'll get a new identity. We'll set her up someplace, and she'll live a very mundane life in constant fear of them catching up with her. She is Russian, so in the end she knows how to get along with being unhappy.

"I found her to be very American," I said.

"Maybe on the outside. Her real life was attached to the dictates of a ruthless outfit."

"You think so? All the way?" I asked.

"When she first came to your office, if she had been ordered to kill you she probably wouldn't have hesitated. And if she had resisted the order, they would have threatened her in a way that made her comply."

I asked Ryan if it was possible that she might be incapable of violence. He said that I needed to factor in the element of terror. The Soviet system had survived on terror. The KGB wielded that weapon, just as the Stasi had wielded it in East Germany. They knew how to terrorize ordinary people. He doubted, from what he had seen of Chelsea, that she had enough inside her to resist that sort of control.

But I insisted that it was possible that she did.

"Anything is possible, but the probability is low," he said.

"What about us?" I asked.

"You mean us, you and me?"

"No, I mean us Americans. Would we be so easily terrorized like that? Or is everyone everywhere just equally susceptible?"

"I always thought that the point of being an American was to not ever be used like that, by anyone" he said.

"Me too," I said.

"But everyone has a breaking point."

"I can't say I know where my breaking point is, but I'm guessing that it would be considerably harder to reach than it was a few days ago."

"You think so?" Ryan asked, challenging me.

"Yeah, I do."

"You should hope you never have that tested."

"Where's your breaking point, Ryan? You say everyone has one."

"That's easy."

"So what is it?"

"Death," he said. "My breaking point is death."

"That's the breaking point of the unbreakable."

"Exactly."

It was, despite the grimness, a cheery point, precisely because there was no hesitation or regret or apology to it. It was measured and cut. I knew that I couldn't say it and believe it. But I could look at Ryan and believe he meant it absolutely. He knew exactly how much pain and fear there was in his body and he would endure it all if he had to. And I sensed that it gave him the ability to know the breaking point of others. I wasn't ready right now to have his estimate of mine. I was on the team, but I was a rookie. I understood that.

18

Les Rogoff, the KGB contact who Chelsea Fall had said was her cousin, was not an easy subject to interrogate. A van had come to the bank and taken Ryan and me to an empty commercial building in Brooklyn where Rogoff was being questioned. We were in the basement. With less carpeting than we had enjoyed in the Pensacola facility, the interrogation set-up was roughly the same. Rogoff was in a room that looked like a library, sitting across from the interrogator. We watched on a large-screen television monitor from another room.

The interrogation was in English, so we weren't listening through the barrier of simultaneous translation as we had in Pensacola. Where the Stasi officer, realizing that it was over for him, gave it all up, hoping to win some small favor, or an easy death, Rogoff was slippery, evasive, and defiant. Those were also the qualities of Rogoff's demeanor, a face he had built over a lifetime. It was a thin and sloppy face, a face not meant for looking at unless you had to. It was a face you might look at only if you needed something from it or owed something to it, and that was the way Rogoff wanted it.

"He's not helping," I said to Ryan.

"That will change," he answered, looking at his watch. "I've seen this type before. Never the Russian version, but the type is predictable. He doesn't know where he is right now or who, exactly, has him, so he doesn't know the stakes yet. He doesn't know yet whether he can walk back out of here and resume his life as a KGB hack."

I asked Ryan how he knew Rogoff was no more than a hack, and he said that Rogoff was too much of a slob to be more than that.

"So he's not going to have much for us, in that case," I said.

"He'll have plenty for us. This guy is like a sponge who soaks up his surroundings so that he'll know how to react or not react to the people who use him and pay him. He probably started out as an informant and worked his way up to fixer. When he's squeezed, all that detail will come right out. The interrogator is preparing him."

"Preparing him for what?"

"For me."

"Are you going to stick a gun in his face like you did to the Stasi officer?"

"The first thing I'm going to do with Mr. Rogoff is let him see me, because he'll know in an instant that the tactical side of things is anxious to hear what he has. This interrogator is helping him get comfortable. When I go in the room, and I won't have to say anything, he'll know that sense of comfort is an illusion. That sudden contrast will get him straightened out."

"You think he's that smart?" I asked.

"No. I think he's that feral. Let's test the theory. It's time."

Ryan left the room and seconds later, on the screen, Rogoff's attention was drawn sharply past the interrogator. Ryan had entered.

He appeared on the screen, approaching the interrogator from behind. He laid a single sheet in front of the interrogator, who looked only at the paper as Ryan looked into Rogoff's eyes and held them for just three beats. As Ryan turned and left the room Rogoff straightened himself up and swallowed. He had just gotten a burst of information about his situation that he hadn't expected.

"Did you see that?" Ryan asked as he sat back down next to me.

"Yes. Rogoff is a new man in there. He's ready to join the team."

"Not quite that ready."

"What was written on the paper you put down in front of the interrogator?"

"It said 'would you like some coffee?'"

"What does that mean?"

"It means 'would you like some coffee?'"

Seeing Ryan got Rogoff started on his life's new journey. Ryan's hardened Special Forces presence announced to Rogoff that the page had been turned. He began to talk and he had been a careful observer over his years as a hack, and he was revealing things that had probably once been too dangerous to even have as thoughts.

The KGB operated around New York as an international political mafia. Its greatest asset was that it didn't exist, so the effects it created could never be traced back to it as the cause. The United Nations was like an outdoor market where the KGB got a percentage on every booth, though it was far more subtle than that. As the financial and media capital as well, New York was an unparalleled business opportunity. The connection with the KGB-controlled government in Russia was like that of an autonomous franchise to a corporate headquarters. There were arrangements and fees and a sense of vague duty, but it was not like the old days when Moscow called all the shots.

Then the interrogator asked Rogoff about the commissioner and what the KGB's interest was.

"That commissioner has too much face for someone," Rogoff said.

"Too much face?" the interrogator asked.

"Too zealous, too much a boy scout," Rogoff insisted.

"Who is 'someone?'"

"I don't know."

"Not someone in the New York network?"

"No," Rogoff said, "this is a customer. I don't know who. Not my department. But I know something like that is very expensive. Very very expensive, to kill an important public figure."

Then Rogoff described what had happened the past few days as a false start. Chelsea Fall was an asset who was going to use me to get close to Rob, who was inside the commissioner's office. But there had been an 'unfortunate' miscalculation.

"Who knew these private detectives would be so efficient," Rogoff said, referring to Janice. "The whole thing became a mess and my friends got carried away. They see themselves as having many prerogatives and other people as not so smart. You understand me? They are expert at killing. They have done a lot of it."

After the arranged suicide of Janice, they were annoyed that a quasi-military outfit, which is how they viewed Ryan's team, was protecting me, so they called in another favor from the Stasi faction in Buenos Aires and tried to kill us all in the townhouse and create confusion while they plotted another angle on the commissioner. Rogoff was out of the loop on that new plan and was relegated to waiting on the return of Chelsea and was then to dispose of her on the assumption that she had been or would be turned on KGB. She was from an important family, but nobody was that important.

"This piece of shit is lying about something," Ryan said leaning forward in his chair as he focused on the screen.

Then, as if Ryan's declaration had invoked him, the General appeared in the interrogation room and tapped the interrogator on his shoulder. The interrogator left and the General took his seat.

"He caught it too," Ryan said.

"Where did he come from?" I asked.

"He's been here."

The General flipped through the interrogator's notes for a minute and then looked up at Rogoff.

"Mr. Rogoff," he asked, "do you believe in an afterlife?"

"I have no use for fairy tales," Rogoff replied.

"So this life is all that you have?"

"Yes, and before you ask, yes, I would like to keep it. That is why I help you."

"By lying to us?"

Rogoff offered no denial. His face was full of calculation.

"All right. You already knew, I'm sure. The actress is KGB officer, next generation. Master of manipulation."

The General got up and left the room and Ryan got up and left our room. I assumed they were meeting somewhere in between.

Chelsea had effectively fooled us twice. She was good enough not to lead us to suspect her as being that deep into the game. The irony, though I was sure she wouldn't appreciate it, was that our decision to be merciful by not letting her loose and leaving her to her fate meant that we still had her. And according to Rogoff, unless he was again lying, she was much further inside the New York KGB outfit than he was.

Ryan rejoined me as the interrogator sat down again across from Rogoff.

"What did the General think?" I asked, perhaps impertinently.

"That he would like to let a sushi chef loose on Chelsea."

"But instead of that?"

"He wants you to take a crack at her."

"Me?"

"That's right. Don't worry. You'll do fine."

Well, I was a lawyer. I had taken many depositions and despite the fact that the truth was required for those, there was always a lot of lying.

"How did you know that Rogoff was lying?" I asked.

"He slipped into a groove. He became too smooth. The truth is hard. It has bumps and sharp edges."

"Is that how I'll know if Chelsea is telling me the truth?"

"She's not going to tell you the truth. But we want you to turn over a few cards in front of her and we'll watch how she lies about them. Remember, she had you all staked out and was going to use you. Now you'll have an opportunity to return the favor."

That grabbed me and my teeth clenched automatically. I understood the General's urge to unleash the sushi chef. I saw Janice face down on her desk and the sick glazed eyes of the suicide bomber in the NYPD uniform. I shook my head to make those pictures go away, and when they did Chelsea's glamorous face replaced them. I had to gag back the urge to throw up.

19

When I walked into the interrogation room Chelsea was waiting for me, but she believed she was meeting with me as her attorney. She had not been told about her new status.

"Why wasn't I allowed to go to my cousin?" she asked as I sat down.

"There's a problem," I said.

"And that is?"

I told her that she and Rogoff were now suspects in a plot to kill the NYPD commissioner.

"That's ridiculous," she said, "I want you to get me out of here right now. Those people holding me are not the police. Who are they?"

"Who are they?" I repeated her question. "They aren't anyone or anything."

"What?" she said, flashing anger.

"You're not familiar with that sort of arrangement?"

"What are you talking about? Do your job and get me the hell out of here."

"Chelsea, your 'cousin' has given you up. It's over."

"You are insane," she said while projecting violent anger at me with her eyes. Ryan had warned me about that modality. It was a way to find out if I was bluffing, without anything to back me up. In any case, the glamorous actress mask was now hanging to the side. It was the real, and far more accomplished, inner actress who I was seeing.

"Who are you, Chelsea, and what is your real business with Les Rogoff?"

"My god, lady, would you please shut up and get me another lawyer. I'm going to make sure you never practice law again. You're a lunatic."

"O.K.," I said, "here's the easiest way for you. These people who have you, they will take whatever they have to from you to get to the truth. Your beauty, your teeth, whatever it takes. They told me to tell you that. As best as I can tell, they mean it. So the best thing you can do is just tell me what they need to know, and I assume you know what that is."

She straightened out her demeanor as she digested my words. It was pretty clear that her Plan B was about to make its appearance.

"I am a minor functionary," she said.

"For whom, a minor functionary for whom?"

"For the Russian people."

"What does that mean?"

"It means exactly what I said. I am a minor functionary for Russian people. I do things for major functionaries of the Russian people, and I don't ask questions about it."

I laughed. "You have a good sense of humor, Chelsea."

"I am telling you the truth."

"And the truth is whatever you want it to be, right?"

"Shut the hell up," she said rather quietly.

"How exactly were you going to use me to get close to the commissioner?"

"I don't know anything about a 'commissioner.' My assignment was to get close to you, to make a big bill as your client, pay you a lot of money, and get inside your life. That was it. No one told me any more than that."

"So that whole story about Ralph Keller wanting to kill you?"

"Was acting. Ralph Keller was a ball-less wimp. He couldn't have killed a cockroach."

"So you are a minor functionary who was told to get close to me and that's it. You were acting – lying is the more accurate term – about Keller. Beyond that you know nothing."

"That's correct and you can't get more than that from me because there isn't any more. No one tells me anything more than what role to play."

"Define 'no one,'" I said.

"By that I mean the people who tell me what to do."

"The major functionaries?"

"Yes," she said.

"Tell me about them. Who are they?"

"All of my contact is through my cousin. That's the extent of what I know. I am a very minor person and a waste of your time."

"But that's not what your cousin has told us. He says you are big time."

"He's lying to you."

"So," I said, "you are saying you know nothing that would help us and are of no further value. Where do you think that leaves you?"

I could sense Ryan leaning forward in the other room and smiling when I got there. Chelsea was left flipping through her extensive mental catalog of ruses. She had raised her closed hand to her mouth and was resting the knuckles of her forefinger on her upper lip, softening her eyes, looking straight at me, thinking hard.

She took a deep breath and slowly closed her eyes and opened them again.

"Why would serious people send in an amateur like you to talk to me?" she asked.

"To exhaust your lies," I said bluntly.

She laughed. "Lies are inexhaustible."

"You're welcome to make that bet with my friends," I said, as I got up from my chair. "It's been good chatting with you, in a manner of speaking."

As I left the interrogation room the General was waiting for me. He didn't say a word. He only shook his finger at me as if to say 'that was good' and he walked away.

I rejoined Ryan in the observation room and he nodded approvingly and pointed to the screen. The regular interrogator entered the room and sat down across from Chelsea.

There was a silent assumption apparent in his approach that the jig was up and that Chelsea understood the business at hand. He proceeded methodically, not asking her about her real KGB status, just taking the facts that she was privy to, with questions clearly based on and weighed against what had been gotten from Rogoff.

I was watching both the screen and Ryan. At first he seemed satisfied as he listened to her recitation of names and front organizations and methods of operations. But I could see his mood gradually change.

"This is too easy," he finally said.

"How so?" I asked.

"That woman is rotten down to the depths of her soul. She told you that lies are inexhaustible and she meant it."

"But what she has said so far tracks with Rogoff."

"Yes, but it tracks too closely. Her perspective should diverge more from his. She's the insider. Rogoff's the hack."

I got that. Rogoff had called Chelsea the 'new generation' and a 'master manipulator.' I recalled now how he said that with a mixture of fear and admiration. He was an old school guy talking about the latest model of operator. Ryan was absolutely right; her account of things did track bizarrely close with Rogoff's, as if she had anticipated everything that he might have spilled.

Ryan concluded that she was continuing to play us. He left the room in a hurry and moments later the interrogator got up from his chair and left that room. Ryan must have been at the door. Then roughly a half hour went by. I sat and watched Chelsea fidget as a welcome blankness washed over my mind.

Ryan came back in with me just as the interrogator sat down again across from Chelsea.

"Did you watch her?" Ryan asked me.

"Yes, nothing."

"Nothing is right. She's ten degrees below absolute zero. This is not a human being as we understand the term."

I honestly hadn't seen that far and that much. She had seemed just the same calculating bitch waiting calmly for the interrogator to return.

"Put the headset on," Ryan said, "he's going to continue in Russian."

I reached for the headset next to my seat and listened to the simultaneous translation.

"We need to know," the interrogator said, "who was contracting for the operation against the commissioner."

"That," Chelsea answered, "I cannot tell you. It is above the level of information that I need to know and I would certainly never ask."

"It's above your pay grade?"

"You could put it that way."

"I don't believe you," the interrogator told her.

"Whether you believe or not, it is the truth. It does not help me to know who a customer is, and it would be very unprofessional for me to try to find out."

"You're lying."

"Why would I lie to you?"

"Why?" the interrogator asked, "because lying is all you know and what you do. But now there will be consequences if you continue."

"Like what?" she said. "You'll kill me? I'm already dead. You just can't smell me yet. Now you know the truth."

Ryan looked over at me. "She's right about that."

A thousand different things ran through my mind but they all were heading in the same direction, toward the awful void that had appeared in this world in the form of Chelsea Fall.

20

Throughout my life and career I had believed that the force of everyday evil was best demonstrated in the lives of stubborn and dull men whose great desire was to have unfettered access to the sound of their own voices. They were like heavy equipment stalled out, broken down, rusting on a highway, blocking passage of those who wanted to get somewhere. They didn't even want others to listen to them. They just wanted to listen to themselves and then demand admiration for having enjoyed their listening experience. I had run into this so many times and had my own honest path blocked by it so often that I had come to view it as the pure destructive evil of vanity.

I don't believe that it is more evil, or as evil, as hardened criminality. Just that it is more pervasive and subtle and a chief cause of anxiety and frustration for people of good will.

But my experience watching the unmasking of Chelsea Fall now made those old bonfires of vanity seem as harmless as someone wearing too much perfume in an elevator. Unpleasant, but nothing to let get in your way.

I could not think of Chelsea as a mere criminal or even as an exceptional psychopath, a low probability occurrence of human nature. She had been cultivated, or manufactured, by other human minds, to do what she did. And what she did was calculated by her makers to destroy in others the humanity that had been already destroyed in her. It only added to her perfection in this that she was so perfect an actress. I never imagined in my life seeing anything like it, but I finally did understand that she had been built from the leftover parts of a machine that had once sought to control the world, had in fact controlled more than half of it, and engaged in industrialized murder for the better part of a century.

How could anyone have believed that the Soviet evil simply evaporated into thin air one day? That was like believing that the magician on stage really did make the rabbit disappear again. It was the will to believe.

Now I had just seen in Chelsea the fruit of that undead evil. As the slippery eel Rogoff had announced, she was the next generation, more efficient, glamorous, perfected in her charms.

I asked Ryan if he thought she would kill herself if she had the chance. His answer was no, because she wasn't kidding us when she said that she was already dead and that we just couldn't smell her yet. From her point of view, Ryan said, there was nothing to kill.

I suppose that we could have stopped everything right there and spent the rest of our lives just studying this woman. But we weren't scholars and this was far from being an academic matter. Chelsea was a part that had fallen off the machine, and we were going to have to deal with that machine before it could turn and deal with us.

We left the basement interrogation facility in Brooklyn in the early morning hours and headed back to the old bank in lower Manhattan. Chelsea would be transported to the Pensacola facility where she would be dredged for every bit of information she had about the KGB, its modes of operation, her training, and anything else she had, including the horrible shape and consequences of her own psychology.

Rob met us at the bank and reported that someone working in the commissioner's office, a civilian employee, had been taken into custody for selling information about the operation of the office. How much damage had been done was unclear, but the assumption was that the security of the commissioner had been seriously compromised. The civilian mole gave up his contact and that person was also in custody. Their operation had been in progress for almost three months and the information sold had mostly to do with NYPD antiterrorism protocols and the commissioner's personal security routines.

The contact was himself a reporter for a news agency who passed his information along electronically in exchange for bank deposits. All that was being chased down, but Rob believed it could all end up in fog and misdirection.

Rob looked ghastly from lack of sleep. I'm sure I looked awful too. Even Ryan appeared to be a little tired.

What we had in front of us though was the structure, the names, and the addresses and institutions of the KGB network in New York. Rogoff and Chelsea had laid it out. This was our target and Ryan had been continuously mapping its destruction.

He believed that the greatest efficiency would come from causing elements within the network to turn on each other. Without the strong force of ideology to bind it together this outfit survived on discipline and brutality but not on loyalty. Just from listening to Rogoff and Chelsea, Ryan understood that the total suspicion in the network was greater than the sum of its parts. He planned to sow panic while creating a sense of cross-betrayal. That, he believed, would result in a fratricidal kill-off, much like a mafia war, but far more brutal and immediate. Not tit-for-tat vengeance, but an urgent kill or be killed war of survival.

"Rogoff's closest ally in the network," Ryan explained, "has already been tipped off that Rogoff, who he now cannot get in touch with, is plotting his murder with his most zealous rival."

"What is supposed to have set the rival off?" Rob asked.

"The dangers to the network that resulted from Rogoff's ally having ordered attacks on us," Ryan said. "Meanwhile, we are feeding the suspicions of other elements within the network so that when they talk to one another they don't believe each other and the suspicion is compounded."

"Suppose that's not enough to inspire the circular firing squad?" I asked.

"We're not taking any chances on that," Ryan said.

"What do you mean?"

"I mean that some of these people will be found dead by the exact methods they use themselves. The rest will fear it is coming their way, and with our help they'll look to strike first inside the network. Their instincts for self-preservation will be matched with their ready capacity and skill for murder."

"It sounds dangerously theoretical, Ryan," I said.

"With these sorts of people," he said, "it's totally predictable. The truth is, Mara, we have done this before."

"In Iraq?"

"Yes."

"But these are Russians in New York," I said.

"It doesn't depend on the geographical map, but on the mental map. These men don't live in Brooklyn or Manhattan; they live in the precincts of suspicion, paranoia, treachery, and violence. Yes, they think with rigorous objectivity, which is why we've acted so quickly on what we've learned. We are creating what they will believe to be an objective landscape of threat within their own organization. There is nothing original here. In fact, it is a very concentrated variant of what KGB practiced in target countries throughout the Cold War, turning faction against faction and factions against governments. Here they will get their own medicine in a lethal dose before they know it."

I could see in Ryan's eyes the watery fatigue of someone who didn't want to face this in our country, but had forced himself to see it exactly as it was. From his point of view, I was certain, it was just his job as a soldier. He must use what he had learned, applying it tactically to the situation at hand. To me, though, it seemed like genius.

Rob, I knew, saw it with the eyes of a cop dedicated to the rule of law, and he no doubt saw it as a catastrophe that could run wild. He would never say a word about it, because for him it was all outside even the margin of civil society. It was the raw state of nature to him and because of who he was it, like Ryan's team, could not exist. I also had no doubt that he understood that Ryan's plan would work.

I was not yet convinced, and would not be convinced until I saw it happen. This was just my way of not falling prey to too much hope. I was also thinking ahead to what the reaction would be throughout the global network of autonomous KGB remnants. If Ryan succeeded with his plan, what would happen with the unintended consequences among those old monsters around the world? There were always unintended consequences. I asked him, delicately, about that.

"We haven't thought about that," he said, "but let's get through this day alive."

21

Despite Ryan's plan to inspire self-destruction within the remnant KGB network in New York, there remained the question of who had contracted with it to kill the commissioner, and why. For that line of inquiry Ryan needed someone close to the arrangement. Les Rogoff fingered Yuri Stellikov, a sixty-seven year old KGB officer who fronted himself as a prosperous restauranteur, as the man most likely to betray everyone with the least amount of pressure. When asked about Stellikov, Chelsea responded with a bitter laugh and condemned him as weak and greedy. She confirmed that he would know who had contracted for the assassinations.

Concluding that Stellikov was unpopular enough to be an early target when the network began to consume itself, Ryan had him grabbed that morning and taken directly to the Pensacola facility where the General would oversee his interrogation. At the same time his hasty disappearance would be used to further stoke fear within the network, arousing greater suspicion and recrimination.

"Any guess about who Stellikov will name as hiring them to kill the commissioner?" I asked Ryan.

"Stellikov will be able to tell us who the middleman is, most likely. We can deal with whoever that is, but it is still going to be a step away from the real customer."

"The world of vipers is a complicated world," I said.

"Just consider how this KGB network has operated in the mist all these years," Ryan said. "They could get away with that because within Western intelligence organizations there was a will to believe that they were done with KGB. I had never given a moment of thought to them or the Stasi as living outfits until a few days ago. We stumbled over each other in the dark."

"But you have to wonder," I said.

"Yes, you do have to wonder how much more than the simple will to believe it took. Not that the will to believe is anything to sniffle at."

The KGB had been everywhere, and then suddenly nowhere when the Soviet Union fell. After decades of infiltrating Western countries and governments, much less the Third World, they were supposed to have vanished into the dust, with no ideology or government left to feed off of. No one wanted to consider how resourceful and dangerous they might continue to be. It was never the KGB's intent to die off, not when it produced a next generation in the mold of Chelsea Fall.

"It might be true, Ryan, that KGB is better off without the Soviet Union. They could make a fortune from their transnational network without the burden of paying tribute to a dying empire. Then there is the special advantage of not existing. What could be better than that?"

"It might be better to have something, don't you think?" he said. "A reason to exist in your non-existence, something greater than your own suspicion-filled, paranoid survival. The Soviet Union was a crock of murderous bullshit, but it at least owned a pretense of standing for something, even if it was a lie. What does this leftover KGB network stand for?"

"Its own criminality," I said.

"Exactly. Maybe, though, and this seems absurd to me, they continue to believe they carry the secret banner of communism.

We didn't explore that with either Rogoff or Chelsea. We need to go back to them with that question. Maybe they'll surprise us with their secret dedication."

"Randall Wolfe would be interested in that," I said.

"Remember what he said? As long as he stayed within the bounds of scholarly restraint and pressed none of his conclusions he was just a scholar, but if he made the meaning of his research clear, he was a Cold War obsessed crank."

"What do you make of that?"

"I make of it," Ryan said, "that at least within the field of history that some history, past and unfolding, is regarded with hostility."

"Wolfe encountered the same attitude at CIA," I said.

"Those people," Ryan said, clenching his jaw.

"Those people?"

"You know how Rob and the commissioner regard the federal agencies. For my money, CIA is the worst of them, and the competition for that title is fierce. They are capable of good work, but inside the bureaucracy it's one treacherous bastard after another. It is mostly a lot of people, smart people certainly, but people with too much time in at the universities and no experience other than CIA. In fact, experience from outside of CIA is viewed with suspicion."

"They use a lot of people from outside of the organization," I said.

"Of course," Ryan said, "but the bureaucracy is an insider's culture. It doesn't have a head or a face; it's just all insider culture and process, with everyone watching his back because backstabbing is the routine."

Rob, who had left us for a while to attend to things downtown, came through the door. He was carrying my Prada bag.

"This is yours?" he asked.

"Thank you so much," I said taking it. I looked inside and saw my wallet and my .32. The .32 reminded me that I now carried the nine millimeter as second nature, and didn't foresee a time when I would not carry it, ready right there in my waistband as the last line of defense. I was so far from my old typical Manhattanite disdain for guns that I saw the .32 as merely cosmetic protection. As Yael had said, that was for muggers.

"My cell phone isn't in here," I said.

"That's right," Rob said. "As a precaution, that's gone elsewhere. You'll need to get along without it."

I shocked myself by not whining. In my world, you didn't mess with someone's cell phone, but I wasn't in my world anymore.

"I'll live," I said.

"That's the idea," he said.

Rob relayed to us that the commissioner was grateful for the work dismantling the plan to assassinate him. It wouldn't be the last plan, at least until he retired, but he was very thankful.

"Does he know about the KGB role?" I asked.

"Yes," Rob said.

"Did that strike him as, well, outside the box?"

"The commissioner lives outside the box," Rob said. "I could have told him that it was a gang of leprechauns and he would have said the same thing: 'let's get it taken care of.' He makes Ryan seem like an emotional basket case."

Ryan enjoyed the comparison.

"The commissioner's emotional excesses are legendary," he said, wryly.

"What's the word from Pensacola?" Rob asked.

"Nothing, yet," Ryan said. "They're probably just gearing up with Stellikov. I expect that we'll have a name for who contracted with the KGB in an hour or two."

"Meanwhile," Rob said, "the media has been making inquiries about the second explosion at the townhouse."

"They're not buying that it was a second gas explosion?" Ryan asked.

"That's what they're reporting, but the neighbors on the block aren't buying and they've been talking to the reporters, so..."

"We can't afford a media outbreak," Ryan said. "They're behind the curve right now. If they break out of the original misdirection they've got to be left still chasing their tails. How's your office handling the repercussions from the civilian mole?"

"We're adjusting," Rob said, indicating it wasn't a topic he wanted to discuss.

"Good," Ryan said, and dropped it.

I had spent my career dodging and dancing around the treachery of law firm politics and the politics of the law. That was the main reason I was out on my own and not a partner at a big firm. But now I saw all that treachery as a norm and then just how high the stakes could go. The whole world was not corrupt, but corruption was a constant and it could show up when and where you might least expect it. A week ago I would not have believed that a civilian employee in the commissioner's office would have the balls to sell classified information. But there it was. Was the world falling through the cracks or was it already down in the cracks.

Ryan had taken a call on his cell and walked away. When he was done he turned back to us.

"Let's go," he said, "this place isn't secure."

We just turned and walked out of the old bank, like that, leaving nothing behind but the coffee maker. Rob went to his car and a van pulled up for Ryan and me, and we were gone. I didn't ask Ryan how the bank building had been compromised. This was a fact of life now, not anything to be surprised about. Just another crack opening and something else falling through it.

Then I saw that sometimes things and even people come back up out of the cracks. It was Yael driving the van.

22

"Thank you for saving my life," I said.

Yael looked quickly back at me. "Thank you for saving mine. If you hadn't tied my leg off I would have bled to death."

"How did you get out of the hospital?"

"Walked out," she said.

Nothing was said about where we were heading or a new location, but Yael was driving to the west side of lower Manhattan.

Ryan was on a laptop and he turned it so that I could see the screen. He had received the video of the interrogation of Yuri Stellikov at the Pensacola facility. Stellikov was resisting the interrogator's demand that he reveal who was paying for the assassination of the commissioner. He wanted to know that his family was safe. The interrogator told him that they were not safe, and could not be safe until Stellikov revealed who had contracted for the murder.

It was all that Stellikov had left now, that bit of information, and he was determined to bargain on it. This went back and forth until the General came into the interrogation room, showed Stellikov a photograph that wasn't visible on the video, and then walked back out. Stellikov's demeanor straightened out and he told the interrogator that the money for the hit came from the North Koreans.

"Of all the things I could hope he wouldn't say, that would have to be at the top of the list," Ryan said.

"Why?" I asked.

Yael answered for him. "Because that place is locked down. It's closed off."

"A dead end?"

"No," Ryan said, "but as close to it as you'll find these days. It's a terror state where the terror is directed inward. The last Stalinist paradise. It is ruled by the rigid discipline of absolute fear."

"No cracks in that armor?" I asked.

"Some."

"How do we get through them?"

"My bet is that the General is contacting the Russians," Ryan said.

"The Russians? Aren't we already in a death match here with the Russians?"

"I mean the Moscow Russians, who don't control and probably don't see more than nominal tribute from the New York KGB Russians. The sentimental ties are about as strong as Russian sentimentalism, which is strong only in the sentimental sense."

"Are you sure?" I asked. "How do you know they're not together in this?"

"Randall Wolfe told us that the nodes of the global KGB network are autonomous. Everybody's in business for himself. All arrangements are matters of self-interest."

"But suppose," I said, "it's the Moscow Russians themselves who are using the North Koreans as the middleman to pay the New York KGB to kill the commissioner."

"That would be too inbred. The Moscow Russians wouldn't want any of their stink on a job like that in the U.S."

"But no one," I said, "even knows that the KGB is still active."

"But look how fast we found out," Ryan said. "Besides, Russians don't trust Russians. And that is the North Korean blind spot. They don't trust anyone but Russians."

"So you think the General is contacting the Moscow Russians to find out who used the North Koreans?" I asked.

"Correct."

"How long will that take?"

"It better not take too long because we need to stay ahead of all this. You know the old Irish toast?" he asked me.

"'May you be in heaven a half hour before the devil knows you're dead'? That one?"

"Yeah, that one. We need to find the instigator of this plot and do unto it about a half hour before it knows we're coming. It's move fast or die, Mara."

This was the race that Ryan had learned to run in Baghdad, where he had to be faster than murderers without conscience on their own turf, hunting them down at a pace they couldn't stay ahead of because they couldn't conceive of it.

Yael pulled the van into a nondescript warehouse south of the Holland Tunnel. It was large, dark and empty with a glassed-in office that would become our next temporary operations center.

When she got out of the van I could see that Yael was dragging the leg that had taken the bullet, and I recalled the blood that had been pulsing out of it. Her neck wound had been less severe but the bandage on that was thick nonetheless and she had it covered with a turtleneck. She was wiry and hard, and thoroughly unimpressed with her own toughness. Her focus was singularly on the task at hand.

For a moment I thought that Yael must be a marathon runner, but she had no time for anything like that. She was no recreationalist. She was a warrior, plain and simple. I thought about the bunch of them I had seen so far, Yael, Ryan, the General, dead Eli and Jimmy, the nameless interrogators, the faceless translators. Who the hell were they and where had they come from? It was obvious that they were out of the military, and within that the Special Forces, but surely this wasn't just the usual next stop on the career path after that.

As the General said, the team did not exist. How long, in that case, had it not existed? As Yael and Ryan got older, assuming they would live long enough to get there, would they take on the executive functions of the General? Would this continue on that long? And I had been declared 'on the team' and had been assumed into it and was inside the operation. I had seen it in action breaking innumerable laws. It was pretty clear to me that without even thinking about it I was enlisted for the duration. Enlisted by events and by the very mortal threat to my life.

Ryan had taken a call and walked out of the glass booth. When he returned he said that the kill-off among the New York KGB faction had spread rapidly. The circular firing squad that Ryan had engineered was doing its job. These KGB people were not the kind who waited months or years to satisfy their killing urges. Their lessons had been passed down from Stalin and Beria, and the essence of those lessons was that if you suspected someone then they were guilty and, since they were guilty, needed to be executed immediately.

Though there was no longer the altar of a people's revolution at which to offer such sacrifices, there was the kill or be killed motivational standard. As Ryan had said, in a world where the highest values are suspicion and paranoia, triggering that standard is easier than one might suppose.

Yuri Stellikov, Les Rogoff, and Chelsea Fall would turn out to be the lucky winners from the New York network. They would get to live and there would be very few of their old comrades left to point fingers at them, although their cousins in other cities and around the globe would certainly not be welcoming them in from the cold.

Then there were the unintended consequences that would result from this, which could show up immediately down the block. By now I knew enough about Ryan to know that he was not only thinking about them, but how to shape and use them.

"How will the North Koreans react when they get wind of this?" I asked him.

"I'm thinking that they will be more receptive to the Moscow Russians and more ready to give explanations in order to get explanations."

"So are you going to pass that along to the General?"

"I already have," he said.

"What did he say?"

"He was already on it."

"Results?"

"Are forthcoming," Ryan said.

"In exchange for what?" I asked.

"You mean what do the Moscow Russians want from us?"

"Yes."

"The General will have something they want."

"And we'll know who used the North Koreans to order the hit on the commissioner?"

"We're about halfway there."

"And then what do we do?"

"That's going to depend on who it is."

"Do you think it's going to be an Islamic terrorist outfit? That's where this is headed, isn't it?"

"Don't assume that, Mara. The jihadists are not, as you've seen, the only bad guys in the world."

"How will we even know if the Moscow Russians tell us the truth or if the North Koreans tell them the truth?"

Ryan paused for a moment. "We'll know," he said.

23

Over the next few hours bad news broke from two directions. The General did get the Moscow Russians to sucker the North Koreans into talking about the assassination of the commissioner. They admitted to paying the New York KGB Russians to carry it out but also explained to the Moscow Russians that they did not know who was using them as middlemen.

"Is that possible, for them not to know?" I asked Ryan.

"Why not?" he said. "That regime is desperate for hard currency. Put enough on the table and it makes perfect sense that they will ask fewer questions."

The other bad news was that two of Ryan's men who had gone to feed the flames of the New York KGB war by killing an important member of the organization had run into trouble. One of the men had called in from an apartment in Brooklyn where he was hiding from a Russian search team. His partner had earlier taken fire and had just died. Ryan and Yael were going in to get them both. I wanted to go along. Ryan said no. That wasn't going to happen.

"What if you don't come back?"

"We're coming back," he assured me.

The plan was almost ridiculous in its simplicity. Yael's mobility was too limited for her to enter the building, but she would drive the van and provide cover. Ryan and the trapped team member had the KGB search team surrounded, in Ryan's conception. His man had the front. Ryan had the rear. Together they would destroy the Russians, who numbered four or five. The only serious challenge was bringing the body of the dead partner back to the van, but that was an absolute requirement. They would sooner die than leave anyone from their team behind.

"Hold the fort," were Ryan's parting words to me, and I was left alone to worry. I had no cell phone. There was a laptop in the glass booth and so I monitored local New York news stations on the chance that the team screwed the proverbial pooch and produced a media storm. If that happened I supposed I would be on my own. To occupy myself I kept scanning radio and TV for close to three hours, an eternity, before the door to the warehouse went up and the van came inside, Yael at the wheel.

The team member just rescued had gone on his mission dressed as a postal worker. Yael introduced him to me. His name was Paul. The body of his dead partner was in the back of the van. His name was Andy, and the atmosphere among the three survivors was grim over his loss. I did not presume to look at the body, but Andy was not, I learned, one of the team's younger members. He was in his mid-40s, and had been with Ryan in both Afghanistan and Iraq. This was a tough loss for Ryan, and when another van arrived to retrieve Andy's body Ryan quietly oversaw the transfer.

I asked Yael how they dealt with a loss like this.

"Our team stays together, even in death. A year, two years from now, we'll be looking at a situation and someone will say 'Andy would do it this way' or 'Andy would say,' that kind of memory. They're not here but their acts are alive. They are still on the team. We never leave anyone behind."

I felt weak. A lot of what Ryan and Yael were had rubbed off on me. I had a mental attitude that I could not have conceived of having a week earlier, back when I actually thought of myself as being tough, a tough lawyer, a tough woman, with street smarts and a handgun in her handbag next to her lipstick. I had no idea what tough was.

The hours spent on the recovery operation had put us behind, Ryan said. We were faced now with the dead end of not knowing who the ultimate buyer had been on the plan to assassinate the commissioner.

It was easy to understand why the contractors wouldn't want the North Koreans to know their identities. They didn't want to risk being betrayed by them. On the other hand, the assassination hadn't happened.

"Will the purchaser demand his money back?" I asked Ryan.

"More likely the demand would be for fulfillment," he answered.

"Then they absolutely want the job done, but the North Koreans have failed to deliver. Won't that get the North Koreans, what, a bad reputation in the business?"

"The North Koreans already have a rock bottom reputation," Ryan explained.

"So who goes to them for a job like this in the first place?" I asked.

"That's what we're trying to decipher, Mara."

"No, I mean who would have enough money but be naive enough to go through the North Koreans? They want to lay the work off to a brutal regime to which they attach an unjustified belief in its competence."

"Well," Ryan said, "the North Koreans were competent enough to hire an old and invisible KGB outfit. They didn't attempt to do it on their own."

"Still," I said, "some entity paid a luxury retail price and wound up not getting their money's worth. The commissioner must really represent something of an immediate and insurmountable obstacle."

"Again," Ryan said, "he has been the key to protecting New York against terrorist attacks."

"But in the process also made it a very difficult place to carry on regular criminality. So it doesn't have to be terrorists who want to soften the target by removing this commissioner," I said. "The drug people, for instance, might see him killing their biggest market."

"This trail has a very expensive coldness to it," Ryan said. "Whoever made the contract was trying to make it impossible to follow."

The conversations had circled the dilemma one more time, and what we needed was more information. And we had no time to wait for it. Falling behind the situation meant that the other side had time to catch up. Ryan was worried about multiple fronts, most pointedly other KGB nodes outside New York coming in to pick apart the New York crisis. He believed that could happen very quickly, and he reminded us that his own operation had been compromised right off the bat, when the Buenos Aires Stasi outfit located the townhouse and attacked it. That was part of Ryan's visible operation, which he had used to work legitimately with NYPD and other agencies, but sooner or later, if there was still pressure in the pipeline to eliminate the commissioner, the team's core would inevitably be exposed to the enemy, despite its ability to disappear into the mist.

Everything always depended on staying ahead of the situation, outrunning it, until the situation itself was taken apart. All of that depended, according to Ryan, on getting back to the original maker of the assassination contract and dealing with it, if that was in fact possible. Ryan had not ruled out that it was impossible, which in his terms meant that it would be, at the least, a serious military matter and something beyond the scope of his operation.

"We are stuck. We need to catch a break, and we need it soon," he said.

Ryan left the glass booth and got on his cell. He paced the warehouse as he talked.

"Who?" I asked Yael nodding in Ryan's direction.

"Probably the General, in a situation like this," she said.

"Who is the General?"

"You'll have to ask the General that," she said.

Ryan finished the call but didn't come back into the office booth. He sat down against the far wall of the warehouse and stared straight ahead. He remained fixed in concentration like that for about an hour, the longest I had seen him in one position in one place in the days I had spent with him.

That came to an abrupt end. He jumped up as the warehouse door opened. A black limousine with tinted windows pulled in. A uniformed driver got out and opened the rear passenger door and it was Randall Wolfe who got out. I wondered what we needed an expert on the KGB for now. We had already walked the cat back beyond the KGB's involvement. Maybe Ryan was looking for help to forestall other KGB elements from taking up the New York outfit's portfolio.

Ryan brought Wolfe into the booth and invited him to sit.

"We need you to tell us," Ryan said, "who you believe would be comfortable using North Korea to orchestrate political violence for them." Ryan made no mention of the plan to kill the commissioner. "It can be a government, a terrorist organization, a political faction, but we need to get a list and to hear what you think the attraction would stem from."

Wolfe looked more than perplexed. He realized that the air around us had gotten a bit thicker since our first meeting with him.

24

"The first thing any entity," Wolfe began, "whether terrorists or a government or a faction, would need to feel comfortable with the North Koreans would be to have nothing to fear from them. That means there would have to be a certain fundamental compatibility. The Cubans are compatible with the North Koreans. They share a last-of-the-Stalinists viewpoint, though the Cubans offer a much more diluted variant than the North Koreans."

"Who else?" Ryan asked.

"The Iranians would be unashamed dealing with the North. If they were the last two nations left on earth, each would need to destroy the other. But they see themselves as fighting the same enemies even though there is no ideological compatibility."

"Continue," Ryan urged.

"Well, any of the terrorist organizations would appreciate the North and would have their appreciation reciprocated. The North has an upside down view of the world in which the terrorist is presumed to be on the side of the revolution, even where the individual terrorist group does not profess revolution. So, terroristic violence is sufficient in its own right to the North. It sees it as implicitly revolutionary."

"So killing innocent people," I said, "is a gateway to the North Korean heart?"

"To the heart of the regime," Wolfe said, "which is all-powerful in the North, totalitarian in every sense of the word. To it there is no such thing as 'innocent people.' Violence is what is innocent. People never are, unless they perhaps die in a war with the United States. From the North's view even the most murderous terrorist is an innocent victim when killed by the Americans."

"And the way you just described the North's way of thinking," Yael started to say.

"My way of describing the North would in turn," Wolfe picked up Yael's thought, "be described by the North as counterrevolutionary and right-wing ideology."

"And if we protest that we are right," Yael continued, "and they are wrong."

"They laugh," Wolfe said, "and smile knowingly among themselves. We can't understand the revolution, you see, because we are afflicted with false consciousness and are fundamentally out of touch with the progress of history and our place in it. Hence, no one of us is innocent."

"The North then," Ryan said, "is pure and only those as pure as it is would have the comfort level required."

"That's only a rule of thumb," Wolfe said, "but I think it represents the core reality of the North and those who would approach it on its level."

"So," Ryan asked, "North Korea could work hand-in-glove with al Qaeda and vice versa and each has no fear of, or moral qualms about, the other."

"Not at this stage of history. No fear. No qualms," Wolfe said. "But North Korea, while it doesn't fear al Qaeda does have practical fears about being caught in bed with it."

"Which means that al Qaeda," Ryan interrupted, "or any other terrorist group or any nation like Cuba might conceal itself from the North Koreans even as it was trying to work through them. They are drawn to the North's compatible nature but remain aware of the practical limits."

"Right," Wolfe said, "the chief practical limit being getting caught by the Americans."

"So it's not that many who would ever approach the North, and none that would want to get caught at it," Ryan said. "What are we missing here, Dr. Wolfe?"

"Well," Wolfe said, "the North does have rather considerable influence with a global network – and this has been one of the benefits to the North from the internet – of small, very marginal, but astonishingly well organized political parties, all of them staunchly Marxist in the old Stalinist sense and for whom North Korea remains the most significant, perhaps the last, surviving outpost of the real revolution. Cuba, for instance, is for Hollywood stars. North Korea is for true surviving Marxist-Leninists, who think their thoughts in Marxist terms.

"But that's just out on the fringes," I said. "They are of no real consequence."

"They can't be dismissed like that," Wolfe said, shaking his head.

"Why not?" Ryan wanted to know.

"What nearly derailed the mission in Iraq?" Wolfe asked Ryan.

"Broken confidence back here," he said.

"That's right," Wolfe said. "A relentless drumming that success was not just far off but impossible. Now, I was against the mission in Iraq from the beginning and for many reasons. But it never occurred to me that success there was impossible."

"What has that got to do with the North Koreans?" Ryan asked.

"It was one of those small fringe Marxist political parties devoted to the North that orchestrated the so-called peace movement from day one. Staged the first rallies, sponsored the big marches, and most important of all set the mimetic stage, so to speak. That is to say, it threw out into the public square the slogans and concepts that would be imitated and repeated over and over again by virtually everyone who became antiwar."

I had been against the Iraq war, in fact, and I took exception to Wolfe's implication that I was therefore a follower of North Korea and fringe Marxist political parties.

"You're making too much of this Dr. Wolfe," I insisted. He seemed to know exactly why I was objecting.

"I'm not suggesting," he said, "that those opposed to the war were without sincerity or didn't have perfectly good reasons for their position. My reasons were good and I could argue them right now. But the mass psychology that more or less took over the peace movement was riddled with typical Marxist rhetoric and falsehoods, and I can document with precision how that was orchestrated by a specific fringe political party, with intimate ties to the North Korean Stalinists. That fringe party used pre-existing front groups to step right into the forefront of antiwar activity, and many of its frankly lunatic attitudes worked their way into the mainstream and became everyday antiwar bromides."

"Such as?" I asked.

"Such as 'Iraq was better off under Saddam,' which is like saying that Russia was better off under Stalin or Germany better off under Hitler and then marshaling all the positive evidence of the wonders worked by both Stalin and Hitler."

Everyone was silent for a moment while Wolfe's point sank in.

"Your point then," Ryan said, "is that we have a small, fringe homegrown faction in the U.S. that is very well organized and therefore, I assume, well funded, that has perfect compatibility with the Stalinist regime in North Korea."

"That is my point precisely," Wolfe agreed.

"And their money comes from where?" I asked. "North Korea?"

"That is not so clear. The ideology is hard Marxism of a Stalinist bent. North Korea is seen as the last great practitioner thereof, hence the pilgrimages to North Korea."

"Pilgrimages?" Ryan said.

"Yes, the U.S. Stalinists actually go on pilgrimages to North Korea," Wolfe said, "but as I was about to say, the North isn't exactly a cash-rich regime and it's not clear that they contributed anything to their American devotees other than the purification and sanctification of their ideology."

"So the money," Ryan proposed, "might flow the other way, from the American faction to the North."

"That had actually never occurred to me," Wolfe said, "but you're on to something there."

"And where would the U.S. faction get the money?" I asked.

"That's the question," Wolfe said.

"Maybe," I suggested, "before the war it came from Saddam himself. He could certainly have believed that an effective peace movement would be worth the investment."

"There's nothing off base about that," Wolfe said. "It makes perfect sense on its face. Remember that Saddam was trained by the KGB. He was a Soviet client. He not only knew how to crush dissent in Iraq, he knew how to work on public opinion abroad. But having clear evidence that he funded the Stalinist faction that orchestrated the peace movement in the U.S. might take decades to uncover. In terms of who stood to benefit most immediately from the peace movement, well, that would have been Saddam, even though that's not how it worked out."

I held my hand up as if to stop the stream of the discussion.

"I know we are in a hurry here," I said, "but could we slow this down just a bit. Dr. Wolfe, would you please explain how these associations of the principal organizers of the American antiwar movement with North Korea were not reported in the media?"

"They were reported," he answered, "here and there."

"So that means I, all of us, should know about it. Why don't we?"

"Because it was not repeated again and again and again. It never became *the* story, in other words."

"Why not? Isn't it an important thing to know that the lunatic fringe is organizing a mass movement inside the U.S.?"

"The American media treats this sort of thing the same way the academic world does. One can offer information about these fringe Marxist parties but to press the case of their Marxism is treated as unsavory. Remember how I told you that it's all right for me to focus my scholarship on the KGB, but the moment I press my conclusions about the KGB legacy today I'm labeled a Cold War obsessive. If I take another step after that, I'm engaging in McCarthyism. So I stay with being a scholar, and leave it to others to press the conclusions. But that has yet to happen, either with the fringe party origin of the peace movement or my work on the KGB, through the American media."

"There was never a day in Iraq," Ryan said, "when we didn't understand it was a two-front war. One front in Iraq, the other in the American media. Forgetting of course that things were even worse in the European media. Even as we were clearly winning in Iraq, we were just as clearly losing in the media."

"And what the hell is that all about?" I wanted to know.

"That's what I call the Soviet ghost," Wolfe said, "and it haunts the world. I can tell you first hand that it roams the halls of American universities. But it dare not be mentioned."

25

The session with Randall Wolfe ended abruptly when Ryan took a call, stepped away for a moment, and then came back into the booth.

"Let's go, we have to move, right now."

Ryan didn't give us a why. We packed Wolfe back into the limousine, thanking him for his help, and by the time the warehouse door was open, Ryan, Yael and I were in the van following the limousine out. It turned right and we turned left, heading uptown. Yael was driving.

"That call was from Rob," Ryan said. "They hit the commissioner."

"Dead?" Yael asked.

"Not yet. He might survive. But he's out of the picture."

"What happened?" I asked.

"It wasn't too subtle," Ryan said. "His SUV was rammed by a tractor-trailer. The commissioner and his security detail were crushed inside. He was on his way to meet with the mayor."

"Did they get the driver of the rig?" Yael asked.

"No. He fled the scene on foot. So far there is no description. The rig was carrying a full load so the force behind it was tremendous. It was probably stolen not long before the attack. A very clever, simple plan."

The mood among us was not desperate but we knew without saying so that we had been outrun despite all our efforts. We were heading to a new location. It wasn't clear whether the warehouse had been compromised or we were just making a precautionary move. Either way, it amounted to about the same thing. Since the second attack on the townhouse, the suicide bombing, any location would get old fast for me.

Ryan was back on his cell as we made our way uptown on the west side of Manhattan. He didn't finish his conversation until Yael pulled up to the gate of a chain link fence around the lot of a closed down car dealership. She had a key to the lock on the gate and opened it.

We drove onto the lot and then into a garage bay toward the rear of the building. Inside there was yet another glass booth office. Just like home.

"We think," Ryan said without explaining who 'we' meant, "that the taking out of the commissioner means that there was more than one prong to the plot. This might have been the backup or one of the backups. We don't think that this one came through the New York KGB, which has been decimated. We caught that prong of the plot. We missed this one that just succeeded, missed it completely."

Ryan believed that the take-out of the commissioner was the decapitation of the New York counterterrorism effort. He said that very few people understand how important the commissioner was to that effort, but that it was clear the enemy knew it. The commissioner had pumped vitality into safeguarding New York against attack. He was a visionary, Ryan said.

"We think this is a prelude to an attack. The enemy will launch an attack on New York believing there is confusion in the command structure, and there is," Ryan said.

"Who is the enemy?" I asked.

"We don't know," he said. "The enemy has concealed himself. We don't know who hired the North Koreans, nor do we know if whoever hired them acted on their own behalf, and is the main enemy, or acted on behalf of the main enemy. But we don't believe the takeout of the commissioner was any end in itself. That's all we feel certain about. We see an attack on New York as imminent, and we see that attack as an attempt to level a major blow against the United States."

"So I'm guessing that the federal agencies are all lit up over this," I said.

"Yeah," Ryan said, "they're rushing to the scene with their crayons and fire hoses. Congressional hearings to follow. The commissioner had eyes in the back of his head. These people don't walk out the door in the morning without their blinders in place."

"Where does that leave us?" I asked.

"Out in the cold, basically," Ryan said. "Rob is with us, but his capability drew on the commissioner's authority. All of this is going to fall on the mayor now and our estimate of him is that he's in over his head, way over his head."

"Do you want my thoughts on this?" I asked both presumptuously and boldly.

"Go for it," Ryan said.

"We've got a huge horizon we're looking at now, and we're stopped in our tracks unless we find the real target on that horizon," I said.

"Keep going," Ryan said.

"Let's think about what Randall Wolfe was telling us about the fringe domestic faction that is comfortable with the North Koreans."

"Let's think what about them?" Ryan challenged.

"What I'm saying is that we choose them as the point on the horizon and pursue it, immediately and exhaustively, right now."

"You mean," Ryan said, "we follow it like a hunch, and the hunch is that it was the fringies who threw the deal to the North Koreans out of trust and affection and faith that the North would pull it off?"

"That's more or less what I'm saying."

Ryan thought about it.

"We have nothing to base it on other than a suggestion from a scholar. On the other hand, we are at another dead end. So, we'll pursue Wolfe's lead until something better comes along."

Ryan said he had to speak to the General. He left the glass office and paced around the garage as he spoke on his cell.

Randall Wolfe had pointed to a new direction. Ryan needed to get angles on it but there might not be any time. My gut tightened at the thought that we were left helpless.

The team never grabbed anyone it didn't know to a reasonable certainty was deeply involved in serious business. And it was from individuals like Rogoff and Chelsea Fall that you got the kind of information that broke things open.

Yael explained to me that the team always tried to work with facts and that once we knew a particular group or person was involved and factually guilty, then we would grab someone and get the goods from him. Here, in this situation, we were flying blind.

"Ryan never stops," Yael said, as if reading my mood.

"I know," I said.

Ryan came back into the office, his call with the General finished.

"Where are we?" Yael asked him.

"The General says we have to break the rules. He thinks the circumstances warrant that we grab someone from the fringe party. It's a risk."

"A risk of what kind?" I asked.

"A risk that we get nothing and then have to let a relatively innocent person go. Our rule is to grab people who we know are guilty up to their eyeballs and who are happily sent off to live a new life somewhere after they betray their comrades. When we don't have that in advance, we don't grab people. Break that rule and we risk having to let someone go. We might break laws, but we aren't criminals."

"Where are we doing this?" Yael asked.

"Here. The General is coming in. He's finished with Stellikov."

"This is a long shot," Yael said.

Ryan half-laughed, half-grunted.

"Once they got the commissioner it all became a long shot," he said. "Funny how things so often come down to one man, good or bad. We'll follow Wolfe's lead until we get something better, and if we come up with nothing we'll start over, and if time runs out, then we'll get a new clock."

When Ryan said 'clock' it threw me back to the night in the townhouse when I woke up just before the attack and looked at the clock. I remembered the time was 4:07. My instincts woke me up and told me something was about to happen. Now my instincts were telling me that Randall Wolfe had pointed us in the right direction, toward the laughable little fringe political party that, while hidden in plain sight, more or less worshiped at the shrine of North Korean Stalinism. Ryan was willing to follow my hunch only because there was nothing else at the moment. Ryan's own hunch was that New York was going to be hit with a terrorist attack within days if not hours. So we would take a chance that I was right. It would cost us nothing but time, but by Ryan's calculation we were about fresh out of that.

26

Rob drove into the lot and joined us in the office inside the garage. He had just left a meeting with the mayor.

"The mayor is panicky and inaccessible," Rob told us. "He's afraid that they'll come after him next and he's looking for someone to blame in advance. He's falling back on his political advisors."

"How about the city," Yael asked, "any concern for its safety?"

"We're at highest alert, but headless without the commissioner. The mayor, I think, senses that, but can't really face it. There's a lot of fear in the air, but it's undefined and that leaves it feeding on itself."

"You can't tell the mayor what he needs to hear, Rob?" I asked.

"I tried, and more than once, but the mayor sees me as just one of the commissioner's aides. He doesn't listen carefully to someone else's helpers. I'll put it that way."

"What about Ryan?" I said. "Maybe if Ryan briefed the mayor."

"I don't know about that," Rob said. "I'm not sure the mayor would be able to handle it. Ryan?"

"Where we are right now," Ryan said, "I'll do whatever you think is best, Rob. There's always a chance that a politician will turn and run from harsh facts. But what would I tell him and how much could I tell him? If all I did was sit down with him and say I believe a terror attack is hours away, what makes me more than another security specialist with another opinion. If I show him a tape, for instance, of the Stellikov interrogation, then he could see himself implicated in a crime and turn on me. How much did the commissioner really tell the mayor and how much, in fact, did the mayor really want to know?"

Rob said that the commissioner kept his conversations with the mayor private. He had described the mayor to Rob as a good but limited man. Rob's own view of the mayor stressed the limited side of the equation. The best thing about the mayor in Rob's view was that he had trusted the commissioner.

"But did the commissioner trust the mayor?" I asked.

"He trusted the mayor to be who he is," Rob answered.

"Where are the federal agencies around all this?" Ryan asked.

Rob laughed. "Strutting, posturing, vowing total cooperation, and getting ready to stab each other in the back and shift blame for anything that happens. The usual. The predictable. But their resources are at our disposal."

"What's their interpretation of the hit on the commissioner?" Ryan wanted to know.

"That it's too early to know the reason or if it's related to terrorism."

Ryan expected exactly that, but he was still taken back by it. He excused himself from the office and got on his cell. I assumed he was calling the General, but I had learned not to assume anything.

What I understood now about Ryan and Yael was that, while they were willing to die doing what they did, they were not willing to let others die. Their entire objective was to stop the murderers before they could murder. Every move they made had that as its end, and they were ready to die in service of that goal.

That wasn't me, not yet, and they understood that. I was among the protected still, not one of the protectors. Yet I was 'on the team.' It was a curious in-between state. From being someone whose life they were determined to guard – and Yael had nearly given her life doing just that and Eli and Jimmy had died saving me – I had almost become one of them, even though they were still protecting me. They did not expect me to give my life, give the last full measure, but I think I gave them a sense of what they would die for, a sense that the flesh and blood people of the civilian world were worth their commitment. Yet I wasn't symbolic and I wasn't a mascot, I was real and on the team. I felt some of the life and death commitment of that rubbing off on me.

Ryan finished his call and came back into the office. He focused on Rob, but he was telling us all what the play would be.

"This is what we assume," he began. "The weapons that will be used to attack the city are here already or are directly on their way. We don't know what they are or who has them. We don't know how they will be deployed, but we assume that they exist and that they will be used very soon."

He ran through a series of probable scenarios, any one of which would result in mass destruction. They were nothing new, but Ryan was refocusing on them to shake the dust off of the familiar. He went down the list, everything from nuclear weapons to busloads of tourists unknowingly infected with diseases to a combination attack. It was everything about potential terrorism that people in the everyday world tried to put out of their minds in order to stay sane. It was the reality that the commissioner had faced every day. It was very simple, Ryan explained. We assume the attack is about to happen. That it is in motion. That the methods used to bring it are more clever than we have so far imagined, and that we had better be lucky because we are already good and they just beat us by taking out the commissioner. That, in fact, might have been their one mistake, their obsession with the commissioner, because that tipped their hand. That could be, paradoxically, our one bit of luck.

The message Ryan asked Rob to take back to the mayor and the Feds was that they needed to look at this situation as an attack already underway. To back that up the tape of the Stellikov interrogation was coming from Pensacola as soon as it could be sanitized. Rob was getting it from an 'anonymous source.'

"Did Stellikov say anything about an attack?" Rob asked.

"No," Ryan said, "but he made clear how much the North Koreans paid to take the commissioner out. It indicates how high up the terror chain this is."

"Hold on," Rob said, raising his hand in a stop gesture. "If you let the agencies have the Stellikov interrogation they will just go off on the North Korean angle. They'll chase that and won't get the rest of the message."

"You've got to tell them the rest of the story, that the North Koreans only acted as the middleman," Ryan said.

"I don't think they will buy it. They are going to demand my source, and if I give them the team, Ryan, they will start after you, or they will think I've become a lunatic and shove me aside. I'm telling you. This is what the commissioner had to deal with, all the time. Even if we focus them on the attack and successfully stop it, the next move will be to come after you, because you are outside the process. They will think that you have gone rogue."

Ryan was determined not to care about any of that. The General, he said, had contingencies for blowback against the team. The main objective was to stop the attack, and the tape of the Stellikov interrogation was the best evidence available right now of the seriousness of the matter. It was a card that had to be played. Rob would have to do his best to steer the agencies away from their predictable behaviors.

While Rob tried to get them turned around, Ryan said, we would play our hunch on the fringe Stalinist party. Ryan looked at me when he said that, and I thought again of waking up just before the attack on the townhouse knowing that something was about to happen. The team was placing a bet on my instincts. That included the General.

As Rob prepared to leave there was no sense that any of this would work but there was satisfaction that there was at least a plan.

"What's the commissioner's condition?" Ryan finally asked, not as an afterthought, but as something that the urgency of things had crowded out.

"He's not expected to make it. It's something of a miracle that he's still alive, but there's no hope." Rob's eyes filled with tears.

"The commissioner inspired us all," Ryan said.

"He had his ways," Rob said. "We would meet and go over and over and over the same vital questions, every day. It could be maddening. He insisted that we go back and look at the basics and take new angles. He was never content. He never stopped thinking about the basics, the angles, the things we needed to look at. And we would be sitting somewhere, his office, in a meeting, at a restaurant, and he would stand up, excuse himself, and leave. He'd be gone five, ten minutes and would come back with a whole new set of insights that would just amaze everyone.

We never had a clue how he did that. It was his genius. That was the commissioner."

27

After Rob left we said goodbye to the garage of the closed down car dealership. That decision was made after a phone conversation between Ryan and the General. No reason was given. Ryan only said, "We're out of here."

The target chosen from the fringe party for interrogation was a man by the name of Steven Flaum, a member of the party's top leadership. Flaum had not been to North Korea for six years but his communications with the regime were frequent and at a high level. We knew that much. There was no evidence that he was involved in contracting with the regime for the assassination of the commissioner. We were targeting him because I had argued my hunch.

"When will we grab him?" I asked Ryan.

"That's done," he said.

I should not have been surprised, but the mysterious capabilities of the team, dispersed, often faceless, above all unhesitating and efficient, still did surprise me.

Yael drove us downtown again, but we didn't stay in Manhattan. We took the Williamsburg Bridge into Brooklyn and were soon back at the commercial building with the interrogation facility, where Les Rogoff and Chelsea Fall had been questioned.

When we took our seats in the room with the television monitor, it was the General himself who was in the book-lined interrogation room with the man I assumed was Flaum.

Flaum was in his early forties, fit, with a fixed smirk on his face. As the General questioned him it became apparent that Flaum believed he had been grabbed by his own side, and that he was suspected of betraying the cause, his own fringe party, and the grand global revolution of which it was a part.

The General had transformed himself into a severe, disciplined, Marxist ideologue. Flaum did not know him but he knew Flaum, and he spoke to Flaum in a tone of imperious condescension, and as I watched and listened I understood why the General was handling him this way.

The smirk etched on Flaum's face and his tone indicated that he worked from precisely the attitude that the General was taking with him. To keep Flaum open, the General had gotten him to believe he was being evaluated, perhaps to reward him, perhaps to denounce or punish him. Either way, the General held Flaum in thrall, full of both hope and fear, asking him pointed questions about doctrine and expressionlessly listening to Flaum's eager, precise answers. Then the General elicited similarly precise evaluations of Flaum's comrades in his party's apparatus, and Flaum ruthlessly exposed the flaws of his closest associates. None met expectations. All somehow were letting down the Party and the revolution. The General could not have had more control over Flaum if he had him on an operating table and was performing surgery on his brain.

I looked at Ryan and invited a comment, but he only tilted his head in that way that says 'it is what it is.' The craft needed to be perfect and perfectly applied because the stakes were so great.

The General could not rush this but he inevitably headed to where Flaum would tell him any and every secret, would reveal his most intimate details, and do so because this was why he lived. So that the revolution would choose him for a higher purpose and give him greater responsibility and power. It was painful to watch as pride and hope swelled in him, and I wondered where the General would finally leave Flaum.

At last, after about ninety minutes of this excruciating manipulation, the General got to the vital question. He went at Flaum with the accusatory tone that was the prerogative of higher revolutionary authority.

"What have you ever done, Flaum, for our great beloved leader of socialism in Korea besides invite yourself to bathe in his glory?"

"I have dedicated myself to advancing his legacy," Flaum replied.

"Just words. You have done nothing concrete to demonstrate your commitment."

"No," Flaum said, shaking his head slowly, "you are wrong about that. I have given selfless, tireless effort for our dear leader in Korea, and I have protected him. I sent a great fortune his way, quietly, without taking credit, because I know that the imperialist attack on him strangles his cause."

"More tiresome words," the General said. "You have done nothing. You merely feed off of the revolution, like a dog."

Flaum hit the table with a flat hand.

"No," he said, "you do not know. Do you see that pig police commissioner lying near death? We made that happen, but we did that for and by the honor of our beloved leader in Korea. We made a fortune available to him, and gave him the honor of arranging the murder of this pig."

The General leaned forward toward Flaum, his eyes spitting contempt.

"But I just spoke with our beloved leader about that great revolutionary act and he said nothing about you, Flaum."

Flaum jumped to his feet.

"You spoke with him? When?"

"Just hours ago," the General said smugly. "You were not mentioned."

"Of course not," Flaum said, "we sought no credit. Our satisfaction is in the revolution and in nothing else."

"You protected yourself, in other words."

"No," Flaum protested, "we protected our beloved leader, and we honored him. Nothing can be traced to him. We moved the money like an invisible gas, unattached to anything, with no trail. It didn't happen. It doesn't exist. But you still see the body of the pig police overlord crushed and dying."

Flaum's excitement was sexual. Even the lines of his perpetual smirk dissolved in his excitement.

The General looked at him approvingly now. He nodded at him slowly.

"Sit down, Flaum," he said. "Wait here." The General got up and left the interrogation room.

Ryan got up and left the observation room. Yael looked at me.

"You were right. Great work."

"The General did it," I said.

"It's not over yet," Yael answered. "We've got to know where that money came from."

Ryan came back in and just nodded at the television monitor, as if to say 'watch this.'

The General sat back down across from Flaum, who had regained his composure and showed now the pride of his humble service to the great revolutionary leader in North Korea. The General looked at him with the serious face of high authority about to announce its finding.

"We are sending you to Pyongyang, Flaum, to fill a position at the leader's side, subject to his direct authority."

Flaum reacted by straightening himself in his chair and increasing his calm. His face became expressionless. He surrendered to duty, to the revolution, again. He nodded almost imperceptibly at the General.

"Now," the General said, "the funds. How did you come by them?"

"We accumulated them. We have a global outreach. We have lists and lists of contributors. We slowly and inexorably accumulate them, from Asia and Europe, from South American, and from North America. With each imperial act taken by the United States the funds almost raise themselves, from rich and poor alike."

The General remained expressionless. He tapped his forefinger once on the table.

"Why did you choose the New York police commissioner as your target?"

"That wasn't our choice," Flaum said.

"Whose choice was it?" the General asked the question almost indifferently, as though he was bound to be unimpressed with whatever answer Flaum gave.

"It was the choice of our comrades within the capitalist power structure."

The General's face became heavier, a mixture of boredom and seriousness, he brought his hand to his chin and rubbed his upper lip with his forefinger.

"The name of the comrade who chose the target," he said.

"John Marshall Norton," Flaum said.

The General nodded, solemnly, approvingly.

"Who is John Marshall Norton?" I asked, turning to Ryan.

"A retired American diplomat, State Department lifer."

"And?"

"And apparently considered a brother-in-arms by this revolutionary," he said, pointing to the image of Flaum on the monitor.

28

We watched for another hour as the General carefully examined Flaum to determine if he had knowledge of a plan to attack New York. By this point Flaum was full of his sense of duty, believing that the General was his overseer and deliverer. It was clear that if he had known about a plan he would have been eager to brandish the knowledge. He already believed that his successful role in the attack on the commissioner had led, finally, to recognition and advancement in the ranks of the revolution. That he had never seen nor heard of the General and still had no name to go with the face he was seeing was unimportant to him. The General's authority was clear and overwhelming. His knowledge of doctrine impeccable. Flaum believed he had passed the test and was being invited to join the inner circle.

I had asked both Ryan and Yael who the General was and they both told me that I would have to ask the General that question. After watching him undo the mind of Steven Flaum the notion that I would ask the General that question froze me, giving me not just the sense that such a question would be hard to ask, but maybe impossible. Would my mouth be able to move the words out, I wondered.

When the General was satisfied that Flaum knew nothing about a plan to attack the city he left him alone again in the interrogation room.

"What happens with him now?" I asked Ryan.

"Flaum? Down to Pensacola. The interrogation there will pick up the thread. Flaum will be asked to evaluate all of the elements of the network of parties he works with internationally, as if his observations constituted life and death judgments, and that's how we'll get the rest of what he knows."

"And then?" I said.

Ryan looked at me, his mouth hard and flat. "That man is proud that he arranged for the assassination of the commissioner. He believes that has won him his advancement. Shouldn't he be advanced?"

"When is he going to find out that this isn't what he thinks it is?"

"I don't know," Ryan said, "but I hope I don't have to see that."

The General opened the door to the observation room, hesitated for a moment, as if he was about to call Ryan outside, but then came in and joined us. He scratched his temple with his forefinger and there was a faint smile attached to his mouth.

"John Marshall Norton," he said, and paused. "That man," he paused again and shook the finger that had been at his temple, "that man is someone I once played poker with and I wonder now whether he was a bad player or lost intentionally."

"Is that important?" I asked boldly.

The General pointed that same finger at me and smiled with his mad eyes.

"You," he said, looking over his finger as if it were a gun sight, "know how important that question is," and then he turned and left.

"John Marshall Norton and the General know each other?" I asked Ryan and Yael.

"They're acquainted, at least," Ryan said.

"Does that make a difference?"

"Only in the approach the General takes," Yael said.

"We're grabbing him?" I said.

"Oh yeah," Ryan said. "That's happening now"

John Marshall Norton had been a part of the Washington scene for fifty years. Ryan had a file on him, produced within minutes of Flaum identifying him as the man who gave the order to him to arrange for the assassination of the commissioner.

Norton was now seventy-five. He had been stationed at embassies throughout the Middle East during his diplomatic career but had done plenty of desk time at Foggy Bottom, the headquarters of the State Department. Now he sat on this and that advisory board and was A-listed on the Georgetown cocktail party circuit.

Ryan held up a sheet from Norton's medical records.

"Resting heart rate of 53 and his blood pressure was 110 over 69 at his last physical. Impressive. I think the answer to the General's question is that he lost intentionally at poker."

"And you get that from his heart rate and blood pressure, how?" I asked.

"His life," Yael said, "has been a life of deceit. Everything is a calculation from that. With him, up is down. In is out. Losing at poker is a calculation too, to avoid envy, to avoid being seen as a calculator. He's a confidence man with compounded deceptions. His heart rate and blood pressure show the calm physiological core needed to pull that off over a lifetime and still be at it."

"You're describing a psychopath," I said.

"No, not quite," Yael said, "the narcissist who becomes a revolutionary owns the world differently than the narcissist who becomes a psychopath. They are both indifferent to the lives of others, but the revolutionary believes he has a higher purpose, especially as he kills. The psychopath has no purpose higher than himself and unless he seeks power is less dangerous than the revolutionary.

"But less dangerous," I said, "solely on the basis of how much killing he is likely to do."

"Yes," Yael said, "the psychopath who doesn't seek power may never kill at all, even without a conscience to stop him. He knows that society puts a cost on killing that he doesn't want to pay. The revolutionary believes that killing is always the fault of the malformation of society. It's never the revolutionary's fault that people have to die. It's the fault always of a corrupt society and its illegitimate power structure."

Norton had also been a product of Ivy League universities, with a PhD from Princeton, and several turns as a visiting professor, including as well two ventures outside the Ivy curtain to Johns Hopkins and Georgetown.

"Flaum implied that Norton was one of his comrades in the power structure," I said.

"That's correct," Ryan said.

"So that's how many?"

"We'll find out," Yael said.

"From Flaum or Norton?" I asked.

"Flaum probably doesn't know," Ryan said, "or we would already have more names. He knows there's a network, but Norton is maybe his only direct contact with it. Norton, on the other hand, will know but he'll be much more difficult to open up."

"You really think so?" I said. "On paper he seems like a much softer subject than Flaum."

"No," Ryan said. "That's backwards. Flaum is the softer of the two. Norton is the kind of guy you can't beat the truth out of because the truth is a greater enemy to him than death. And Norton's vanity is his secret life as a revolutionary. He needs that secret more than his life. Opening him up is going to be quite a chore."

No one said after that, "But the General will do it," but that belief seemed to hang there in the air.

Ryan left the room, I assumed to confer with the General. Yael looked at me with concern and then hesitated.

"Go ahead," I said.

"Be prepared, Mara. The attack on the city," she said, "we have just the slimmest chance of stopping it. The commissioner always seemed to have the margin of error covered. The enemy clearly had that figured out. If the attack is already in motion even knowing the nature and mechanics of it might not help."

"Look," I said, "the commissioner might have been a mystic, but there are a lot of smart people in NYPD. They will pull together."

"I'm listening," she said.

"It's a big outfit but when all of that cop sense gets woven together, it's like it sees through walls and anticipates the bad guys' next move. You would be surprised. I've been around it for most of my adult life. And if they know an attack is coming and have some idea what they're looking for, then they can stop it. If the General can get them a sketch of what they're looking for, they can find it and contain it. I also believe that the commissioner, what he was, has been absorbed down into the department, down into the details, and that he made sure of that. So don't believe it's too late."

Yael smiled a little and nodded.

"You made a good call on the fringe party. You've got good insight," she said. "I'm more worried about the mayor than NYPD. The political people specialize in snatching defeat from the jaws of victory."

"That's true enough," I said, "but sometimes everything comes together when it has to. We have to do what we're doing and hope that even the politicians don't screw up their end of it."

She agreed and nodded.

Ryan returned and told us that we were flying to Virginia, outside of Washington. John Marshall Norton was being taken to a facility at the small airport we would use. The General wanted me to be the first to question him.

29

Being chosen by the General to take the first crack at Norton carried with it the sense that I was a chess piece being played in a strategy I didn't understand. On the flight to Virginia I expected Ryan to coach me, but he didn't.

"You're ready," he said.

"For what?" I asked. "What am I supposed to do with him?"

"Find out what he knows?"

"Yes, but who am I in that room?"

"You're nobody. You're a black box. He's been plucked out of his world. He's been seamlessly taken into custody, or maybe abducted. No one has spoken to him. He hasn't been harmed or mistreated. But the force used to grab him, in all its gentle precision, had the snap, crackle, and pop of real power. So you have his attention. He's going to want explanations from you, but he's the one that needs to talk. Get him to talk. Let him feel the comfort of the easy way you offer. Don't bring up the hard way, but let it sit there in the room with you."

"Do I bring up the hit on the commissioner?" I asked. That seemed to be an important item.

"He knows it's at least about that. The preference is to let him bring it up. But you're tangling with a willful, vain old diplomat who has lived a secret life. What does he know about an imminent attack on New York? That's the theme. Getting his confession on the hit isn't important."

It's impossible to know what other people really know or think about you. But if Ryan thought that I was prepared to do this and was leaving it much to my discretion, then I would do it my way. I only hoped the General and Ryan were ready for that.

The interrogation room at the Virginia facility had the familiar bookcase-lined library look. On the observation room's monitor I watched John Marshall Norton fidget with his wristwatch as he sat there alone. He had an austere patrician demeanor, written on a long, thin, grey face.

"How long has he been waiting?" I asked.

"His whole life." It was the General speaking. He had entered the observation room behind us and I hadn't noticed. He had not been on the same flight down with us.

"Go ahead," he said, "let him confess his humble heroism to you."

I shrugged and left and went into the interrogation room and sat down opposite the man who had ordered the hit on the commissioner. He greeted me with a haughty smile, a chirpy grin really, as though he were about to make bird sounds.

"And you are?" he asked.

In response I shot my 'that's not an appropriate question' smile back at him.

"Mr. Norton," I said, "you do understand why you are here?"

"No. Why don't you tell me and then we'll both know."

There was a clipboard with blank sheets of unlined paper and a pen in front of me. I slid it down the table to Norton.

"First thing," I said, "you can do it while we speak. Make a list of people, family members, colleagues, friends who you would want to see protected and kept safe. We're asking you to limit the number to ten."

I had surprised myself, and had no idea how I had come up with that, but it succeeded in moving my game into his head.

He looked down at the clipboard with contempt.

"What is this about?"

"In a matter of hours no one in the D.C. metro area will be safe. That's why you're with us now, and why we'll protect those closest to you."

He looked sideways at me, down his long patrician nose and with a now sour mouth.

"Fuck off, you cunt." He wasn't buying, but it was still an act. He was testing me. I laughed as though he had just told me a hilarious, naughty joke.

"It's all right, Mr. Norton. I understand that this has been a very impersonal process, but we had to pull you out of D.C. and we have to debrief you. If we can get you through that, then you'll be on your way to a safe and secure location, you'll have all the comforts, and if you give us your list of names, the people you care most about."

"What the hell are you talking about?"

"The terrorist attack on D.C., Mr. Norton. It's coming in a matter of hours."

"D.C.? I don't know anything about an attack on D.C."

I said nothing. I just smiled and looked at him very sympathetically. I watched him think. His eyes showed that he was running calculations. His guard was down. I wouldn't otherwise have seen that much. He softened his expression, trying a fresh mask.

"What do you want from me?"

"You understand that all of this had to be very compartmentalized," I said.

"All of what?" he interrupted.

"The attack on D.C.," I said, "and we need to bring it together now in preparation for the aftermath."

I was, you see, only his humble servant, like an airline ticket agent, just trying to get him on the next flight out, and if he would just cooperate...

"I apologize for calling you that awful name," he said. "It was my understanding that only New York would be attacked. I had no idea about D.C."

Now he was watching me, but I didn't offer any change in demeanor, just my helpful smile and ticket-agent understanding. I was in the revolution's customer service department.

"Again, it's compartmentalization, Mr. Norton. You're the sixth person I've debriefed today, but I assure you that we can get through this pretty quickly."

Now he seemed more comfortable as it dawned on him that I was merely an officious subordinate. Perhaps, after I got him through this, when everything was settled down, he could find out who I was and make sure I was put in my place. It was maybe starting to make sense to him.

"So what is it I need to tell you?" he said.

"Just a brief narrative."

He didn't like that. "Of what?"

"Of how your cell operated. Who did his or her job well, who didn't. How you got things done. Especially if there are loose ends."

"I really don't believe this," he said. "You need to bring your superior in here. I'm being trifled with. Do you have any idea who you are dealing with?"

"Yes, of course I do, Mr. Norton. I know about your service to the cause. I hope that one day I can be thought of by our leaders as highly as you are. And I assure you that I am not trifling with you. This is a matter of expediency and getting you on your way. I ask again for your cooperation."

Now Norton took on an affect of boredom, which I read as a luxury he allowed himself only if he was reassured.

"What do you want from me again?"

"Just a brief narrative of your part in the operation, your evaluation of key personnel, positive and negative, any loose ends you think need attention." I smiled. Norton was the customer and he was always right.

"Very well," he said. "Is this being recorded?"

"Yes, sir, it is."

"All right. The first thing I want to say is that I find this process repulsive. It's too corporate. But I understand I'm just a can of goods on a conveyor belt and I need to do my part and get out of the way."

"I understand," I said, beaming out a smile so warm and sincere that I could watch its physical effect on Norton. He was re-assuming the mask of the courtly, paternal gentleman. Perhaps he wouldn't even see to it later that I was put in my place.

"Be brief," I said. "There will be time later for the archivists to work with your more detailed account."

And so he began, John Marshall Norton did, to talk about a massive and brutal plan to attack New York as though it were a luncheon for the old boys club from Foggy Bottom. Poor Steven Flaum, he came in for the harshest assessment and was definitely a loose end who needed to be 'tied off.' But then he did have that essential doting relationship with the North Koreans, who were capable of anything.

When I left the interrogation room, telling Norton so politely to please wait there, I imagined the room filling with gas the instant I closed the door. It ought to be a gas that would dissolve him into his constituent atoms, sanitize the room, and then be exhausted to a place outside the earth's atmosphere. But that would still be a lighter sentence than the one John Marshall Norton had helped plan for New York.

30

In the corridor the General hurried past me. He nodded his head respectfully, even gratefully. I had done a good job. When he had passed by and I was about to open the door to the observation room, I heard him say, sardonically and for my benefit, *"Viva la revolucion."* That about captured it, or them, the wonderful narcissistic killers for the revolution. Their slogan, their prayer really, their after-dinner mint taken after murder.

Yael greeted me with 'well done.' Ryan was on his cell but looked over and nodded in acknowledgment.

Norton had described an insidious and barbaric three-pronged attack on New York's subway system that would sicken, maim, or kill at least a hundred thousand people.

"And if we get lucky," was the phrase Norton used, then the number would be two or three times that. In one rush hour, anthrax, sarin gas and explosives would be used in tandem to kill, to instigate mass hysteria and chaos, and to render New York helpless for weeks if not months.

It would be "a wonderful blow for justice," Norton said, "that would be heralded around the world. Much bigger and much much better than 9/11."

The biological, chemical, and munitions elements, coming together perfectly would be particularly deadly to the emergency responders, who would nonetheless unwittingly carry the biological element back to the hospitals to wreak havoc. The subways might be unusable for months, even years. The dead would pile up. The civil infrastructure would be pushed beyond the breaking point. New York would be the capital of fear and that would radiate throughout the United States.

No wonder Norton began to cooperate when he was told his own home city would also be attacked. He wanted no part of that and welcomed the recognition he deserved in being mysteriously pulled out ahead of time. He was happy for once not to feel like he was the only one doing his job and thinking clearly. And of course he would be needed to help handle things in the aftermath in all his grey eminence.

It had been that annoying overbearing police commissioner in New York who presented such an obstacle to any well-designed plan.

"The man was psychic. I'd swear to that," Norton had told me. So the commissioner was viewed as the head of the snake and had to be cut off.

"He was a danger to anything we might attempt," said Norton.

Ryan, briefly off his cell, said, "We're moving. The mayor has been straightened out. Good job, Mara," and then he was onto another call.

Norton had noted how the commissioner had thwarted an earlier biological attack that was to be launched by infecting the homeless population of New York with a contagion.

"He foresaw it," Norton shouted. "Like he had the devil whispering in his ear." One had to be impressed by Norton's capacity to invert good and evil. The devil was whispering into the ear of the commissioner to save the guilty anonymous New Yorkers from revolutionary justice. The only thing I understood about that, for sure, was that Norton didn't believe there was a devil.

This time, with the commissioner unable to work his demonic magic, just ten terrorists – "half the number used on 9/11," Norton boasted – would do the work of an army.

Anthrax casually spread throughout the subway lines before the rush hour would be tracked by riders everywhere. Canisters of sarin left in discarded coffee cups would be on timers set to discharge promptly at 7:45 a.m. the day of the attack. Newspapers left under seats and in the trash at stations would hide explosives that detonated at 8:20 as the ever efficient emergency response teams responded to the chemical attacks. The ten man team of terrorists would be in and out of the system for hours, carrying in their prepositioned weapons, casually placing them, and then leaving to retrieve more and return.

"No wasted effort or manpower," was how Norton saw it. "Get maximum productivity. That's why the suicide bomber, as delicious a concept as that is, has so little utility. You use it up in one shot. What is the point of that?"

All ten of the terrorists were Islamic extremists, all well-educated, middle-class, and established in the U.S., living and working or studying in New York. They knew the city inside-out.

Norton described the attack as a 'joint venture' between the radical jihadists and the solemn revolutionaries of the West, both sharing a hatred of the West.

"We are like the saucer, you see," Norton explained, "into which their hot cup of anger is poured and cooled to make it rational. And forget about all that Allah business. Learn to look past that and just appreciate the violence. We haven't had the capacity for that kind of violence since Che, maybe since Lenin himself, if you want to be pure about it. It's magnificent to have that again. Don't get hung up on the religious wrapper it comes in. These men are revolutionaries and they are maturing into that through this perfect capacity for violence."

I wondered how many years, or maybe centuries, it might take to untangle Norton's mind or the mind of anyone like him. Norton had never tested his ideas. He obviously had picked them up as a young man and then lived with them secretly, inside the 'power structure,' as Flaum had put it. It was still not clear how Norton and the network he was a part of had detached and nurtured itself apart from the Soviets when the latter collapsed at the end of the Cold War, but it clearly had. Even the old KGB network had found better things to do, so to speak. But for Norton the revolution was more alive than ever, at once vicariously through the violence of Islamic extremists and then by his own unrelenting inversion of values and meaning, and the accompanying narcissistic moral vanities it had taken to maintain dedication to the old cause that so many believed to be lost.

The price to the world for all that effort and dedication of course had to be mass violence and death.

Yael asked me what sitting across from Norton felt like.

"Like a medical examiner performing an autopsy and the corpse on the table is talking to you."

"You transformed yourself in there," she said.

"I kept saying to myself 'don't go deep, stay shallow,' because that man might be the shallowest human being I've ever confronted. The real effort was to remain superficial and let him assume command. I was a functionary subjecting a superior to an unfortunate but necessary process."

"You caught the implication of his response to that?" Yael asked.

"Oh, yes. That knocked me over. There's a whole hierarchical infrastructure that he's just a part of. It's mostly invisible, even to him, but he believed that was what grabbed him and what he was responding to. Flaum reacted the same way to the General's ploy, but Norton's vision of the hierarchy seemed much more luxurious. I mean, clearly he is part of something bigger than the names we're getting out of him."

"When I saw the way he responded once he accepted you as a representative of the official revolution," Yael said, "I started thinking about Randall Wolfe's description of the academic world. It's there where you see the background radiation, let's say, of the hierarchy Norton thought he was responding to."

"I think, Yael, when we get deeper into it, that we'll start to see some of that background radiation in ourselves, too."

"What do you mean?" she asked.

"Well, maybe I shouldn't include you, because your feet are hard on the ground. But I'm seeing Norton's hatred for ordinary society, much watered-down of course, reflected in some of my own patterns of thinking over the years. Some of the things I've heard many times from friends and colleagues, from my daughters, things I've said, seem almost like shadows from the minds of people like Norton."

"You're realizing that the culture has been polluted by the Norton's among us."

"Yes," I said, "and I'm not innocent. I've taken a lot for granted."

"We are imperfect people, Mara, living in an imperfect world. The John Marshall Nortons long ago mastered how to take advantage of that."

"By relentlessly condemning us by our own ideals while they speak as if with the voice of perfection," I said.

"That's it," she said. "John Marshall Norton is perfect, so he stands in judgment of our imperfect society."

"And all those condemnations, we take them up, incorporate them into our attitudes, and bash the living hell out of our way of life."

"And then thank our enemies for killing us," Yael said.

"Almost," I said.

"It has gone past 'almost,' Mara," she said.

31

"Let's go," Ryan said. We left the Virginia facility in a hurry. We needed to be back in New York.

On the flight Ryan told Yael and me that the Feds had identified seven of the ten terrorists who were to carry out the subway attacks, and had located two of them.

"The Feds have taken control?" I asked.

"Of locating and handling this cell, yes. Only NSA has the resources to find ten grains of sand on a beach. That's what they're good at."

"Seven identified, just two located," I said. "Are those two in custody?"

"Not in the conventional sense," Ryan said. "They're under a level of surveillance that's tighter than a bug's ass. That's their maximum value right now. Unless we got lucky and hit a weak link it would be useless to interrogate operators on this level. These are the hard tactical soldiers. If it comes down to the initiation of the attack, they will show us the way."

"The Feds can still screw this up," I said. "Remember how the commissioner always managed to keep them back, off city turf."

"Like I said," Ryan answered, "when you need NSA's capability badly enough, the whole family is going to come to town. But the good news is that NYPD has control of the ground game."

"But who is in control of NYPD?" I asked.

"Rob is," Ryan said. "The mayor has put him in charge for this crisis."

"Rob's just a lieutenant," I said.

"Not anymore."

"How did this happen?"

"Well," Ryan said, "the General knows a lot of people and he knows Rob."

The General gets around, I thought to myself.

By the time our flight landed and we were on our way by van back to Manhattan, Ryan told us that two more of the terrorists had been identified, making it nine of ten, and four more located, bringing that number to six. All ten had gone underground, meaning that they had disappeared from their normal routines, their jobs or classes, the regular living arrangements, and that meant that the attacks were imminent.

"Four of them are still out there, one of whom we don't know anything about," Ryan said.

"What worries me," I said, "is that we're going by what Norton knew. He was willing to accept the fact that he had been kept in the dark about a parallel attack on D.C. There might be a message in that and maybe we should look at it."

I knew I had hit something with that because Ryan and Yael both said nothing. They listened to my hunches and they understood what I was saying now, which was that our thinking might be too narrow and we might be underestimating our opponent.

We came up out of the Holland Tunnel into lower Manhattan almost precisely at midnight. A Monday was becoming a Tuesday. Dark and daylight had ceased to matter. Time had become events. Hardly noticing it, I had taken on the rhythms of Ryan and Yael. There was no such thing as a night's sleep. There were stolen naps. Minutes out before quickly snapping awake. No meals, just nourishment grabbed, a protein bar and black coffee. And the steady flow of adrenaline. I had done no exercise, other than stretching out on the run, but I had lost weight and could feel inside myself the aggression of a conditioned athlete.

"It's real," Yael said, when I described this new state to her.

"Not an illusion? No crash coming?"

"Everything crashes, in one way or another, Mara. It's how you manage the crash."

Our newest location was a second floor loft on the Bowery, just up from the Manhattan Bridge. It had surveillance monitors with views of every angle up and down the block and around the corners. There were laptops galore, a refrigerator with a single but fresh quart of half-and-half in it, a coffee maker, fresh clothes for the three of us, and a shower with authentic water pressure and really hot water. We had reached the promised land.

By the middle of the night the NSA had identified the tenth terrorist and the combined Fed effort had tracked down and located him and the three others whose whereabouts had been unknown. All ten terrorists were under heavy surveillance.

Ryan didn't seem pleased.

"What?" I said.

"I don't know. Something isn't right."

"You mean aside from a plot to murder a hundred thousand New Yorkers?" I said sardonically.

"You were right, Mara. Norton didn't know everything. There's more out there."

"Call Rob," I said. "Tell him that. Get his reaction. A lot of the commissioner rubbed off on him. He'll take you seriously."

Ryan took my advice. He was on with Rob for a quarter hour. When the call was done he said that NYPD intelligence division was pulsing its network of informants round the clock and what was disturbing Rob was that none of the ten terrorists identified by NSA had shown up on NYPD's radar. What that meant was that the terror plot had been so carefully designed that it didn't so much as ping the NYPD watch. NSA had plucked them out of the ocean of telecommunications only because of the leads we had gotten from John Marshall Norton.

"Rob agrees that we are missing something," Ryan said.

"Maybe we should grab one of the ten terrorists and see if he has a breaking point," I said.

"If we grab one of them that might act like a circuit breaker on the plot and the rest would not act," Ryan said. "The thinking is we need them to put the plan in motion so that they go to their weapons caches. Even once that happens and we intercede and stop them, we'll only have the first round of weapons. Remember that Norton said they would be in and out of the subway system from early morning on. We don't think that any of them will cooperate, easily at least, so there will be weapons left out there well after the initial plan is stopped."

"What if there's a second team," I said, "a group of operators who shadow the first team. If they exist, then they will restart the plot and use those weapons while NYPD and the Feds are back at the ranch high-fiving over having rolled up the attack."

"That's plausible," Ryan said, "but a dozen other scenarios could be just as plausible, some of them having nothing to do with these ten men."

Yael had been listening.

"Let's not overestimate the opponent," she said. "I don't mean his deviousness, but rather his resources. This was an excruciatingly tight operation. I think Mara has the right idea, that the ten would have shadows."

"How about more like understudies," I said, "like in the theater, actors who are ready to step in when someone in the cast is ill."

"Yes," Yael said, "and they would train together. The substitutes would train with the ten terrorists. They'll be right there somewhere in the everyday lives of the ten."

Ryan didn't hesitate. He was back on his cell immediately. Our theory predicting the existence of a shadow team behind the first ten terrorists would be tested right now. The power that the Feds had to scan through individual lives was disgraceful, but it had its place in the immediate threat of mass murder. It worried me sick that the terror threat had already turned us into a surveillance society and worried me even sicker when I thought of the potential for abuse inherent to it. But survival had its priorities, and here I had been for days in the middle of a survival exercise so outside of the law that it was now just the raw state of nature itself with no structure but right and wrong.

This was the pace of the new warfare. It was high-speed wireless death, where 'hand is quicker than the eye' deceptions cascaded outward from multiple nodes. Getting a breath in was difficult. Things like warrants and due process were like lighting a match in the dark and inviting the enemy to blow your brains out.

Back down on the streets the beautiful functions of civil society churned on, while a hidden world of cursed maniacs stood just beside it ready to poison and maim and kill. I knew that if we succeeded in taking the maniacs off the board that civil society would still want to take its revenge on us. That was how the frozen innocence of everyday life reacted to contradictions of its settled ways.

32

Toward dawn Ryan finished a call and told us that John Marshall Norton, after he had been moved to the Pensacola facility, realized that he had fallen for our ruse. Within minutes he had essentially lost his mind, got hold of something sharp, and cut open his jugular. He was dead.

"That was predictable and shouldn't have happened," Yael said. "People are getting sloppy. What did the General say?"

"He said *'c'est la vie,'*" Ryan answered.

"Norton had a lot of value," Yael said. "We needed him alive."

"Apparently he wouldn't shut up on the flight down and, thinking he was going to be an important player in some new emerging order, he went through a list of names of D.C. insiders who were part of his network, mostly to denounce them. The General said that some of the people Norton named were shocking, and I don't recall the General being shocked by anything."

"What did he use to cut himself?" I asked.

"A pair of sunglasses left on a table. He grabbed them, snapped one of the plastic lenses in half and went to work on himself," Ryan explained.

"Sloppy," Yael said again, "you never leave anything like that within reach of a prisoner. He could have just as easily done that to one of ours instead of himself."

"Did he name anyone a non-insider would know?" I asked.

"Would you recognize the name of a deputy chief-of-staff at the White House?"

"You're not kidding."

"No, I'm not."

"A deputy chief-of-staff with what kind of security clearance?" Yael asked.

"Not the highest, so she..."

"She?" I said.

"Yes, she," Ryan said. "She wouldn't be in on the President's daily intelligence briefing or anything deeper. But the General says that the White House is a leaky bucket when it comes to any kind of information, including the national security kind. That's why the agencies, as bad as they are, don't like to get into too much detail with the White House. But a deputy chief-of-staff can do considerable damage no matter what."

"What's going to happen to her?" I asked.

"The General thinks she'd go right down based on some bad habits she has."

"You mean she'd be forced to resign?" I asked.

"Yes," Ryan said.

"What are the bad habits?" Yael asked.

"Accepting gifts she never reports. It would be very embarrassing to the administration. She would have to resign."

"And then what?" I asked.

"Then, maybe, she takes a much needed vacation and meets one of our people on a beach. Hard to say right now."

"Did she know about John Marshall Norton's plan to attack New York?" Yael asked.

"Norton said that she did," Ryan said grimly.

"And why would he lie about something like that on his way to his new revolutionary nirvana," I said.

"Someone that close to the President knew about a plan to murder New York subway riders," Yael said, squinting to understand it, "and goes down for taking gifts. Please, let it be me who meets her on her much needed vacation."

"Things getting personal for you, Yael?" Ryan asked.

"Very personal," she said.

"Good," he said, "because it's all very personal for me."

"You mean you're not just a cold-blooded reptile, Ryan?" Yael asked.

And we all laughed. It was the only sane thing to do. In the midst of the least funny thing we had learned so far, we found some refuge in the absurdity of it. Yael's laugh being the most sinister because she sincerely did want to be the one to deliver justice to this woman.

"And what about Steven Flaum," I asked about another one of the guests in Pensacola, "is he still on the high road to North Korea or has his bubble burst?"

"No, he's still riding high according to the General, and he is an encyclopedia on the global network of fringe political parties of the Marxist kind. He knows everyone everywhere and he is not being easy on anyone."

"When will he get the bad news?" I asked.

"He's probably going to figure that out for himself," Ryan said.

"They had better make sure down there that no more sunglasses are left sitting around," Yael said.

"Yeah," Ryan said, "let's not do him any favors."

Flaum had been the one to orchestrate the payment to the North Koreans to arrange for the assassination of the commissioner. He had done that at the behest of Norton, but in his twisted mind Flaum was doing it as a reward for and homage to the North Korean regime as the keeper of the flame of true socialism. The regime could, after all, use the hard currency. The North Koreans contracted with the autonomous KGB remnant in New York, which in turn had the Stasi remnant from Buenos Aires come kill Janice and then Rolf Keller, one of its own, and then try to kill me because I sent Janice to look too deeply into Chelsea Fall, who was an operator for the New York KGB and whose mission was to use me to get close to Rob because he was close to the commissioner.

If that all struck me as impossibly complicated at first, it now seemed no more mysterious, or unlikely, than supply and demand at a corner grocery store and perhaps not even that complex. There were clearly people in the world who shared this thing, very alive and real to them, they called the revolution. Some of them were pathetic monsters like Flaum, who labored continuously at fringe fanaticism. Some were patrician narcissists like Norton, holding for a lifetime a secret fervor, and waiting and believing right to the end. They had never cared, any of them, when the hallowed Marxist regimes had committed mass murder in the past. And they knew that the United States needed a dose of that. It was only right.

But something about there being a White House deputy chief-of-staff involved, a venal woman who knew about the plot in New York, made me think that there was something more here than these hairline fractures of sanity. I had heard this woman's name, probably in the news, even though I didn't recall who she was and had no face to put with the name. But she was probably meeting with the President of the United States every day. She worked for him. White House secrets fell into her lap, by necessity. If this grotesque attack on New York went down she would likely sit in a meeting about it in the Oval Office and maintain a pretense of agony and anger, though she was complicit in the act.

That had brought my attention to a whole new level and I completely got why Yael took it personally. This was indeed no hairline fracture in a sideways world of narcissistic revolutionaries and cynical leftovers from beaten regimes. This was a gaping open wound. Rob had once said to me that D.C. was not what I thought it was, but he remained evasive and even tight-lipped when I asked him to explain what he meant by that. He probably thought I wouldn't believe him.

Norton had been a fixture in Washington for decades. This woman was inside the White House. The General said that Norton had produced a shocking list of names. I assumed that meant these people were spread throughout the bureaucracy. 'Comrades in the power structure,' was how Flaum had put it. Flaum was a true believer who looked to the purity of the last Stalinists in North Korea. But that wasn't where Norton looked. His sensibility was abstract, nearly amorphous. He placed his hope not in the last true socialists in the North, but in the purity of the violence found in Islamic extremism. That, however, was something utterly unpredictable. Norton was a madman.

Where did this woman working so high up in the White House look to? She had to be giving her loyalty to something more concrete than just the divine cloud of revolution.

"I don't think that Norton killed himself because his bubble exploded," I said to Ryan and Yael. "I think he did it because when he realized that he had been deceived he needed to protect the one thing he still hadn't unwittingly betrayed to us."

"I'm not following you, Mara," Ryan said.

"Norton was rhapsodic about the cause," I said. "His identity was entangled with the world revolution and he happily named names of comrades and subjected them to intense criticism."

"O.K.," Ryan said, "so what didn't he unwittingly betray?"

"He didn't betray," I said, "who he believed he was talking to, who he believed we were. He didn't tell us who he thought we represented because he assumed, of course, that we knew who we were pretending to be."

33

"When you questioned Norton," Yael said to me, "you took your lead from how the General questioned Flaum."

"Yes," I said, "I built on that."

"Both interrogations assumed that the subjects, Flaum and Norton, would respond to authority. Why?"

"In my case because I had seen the General pull it off and I just picked up on that thread, intuitively. Don't forget that I was thrown in there and left to figure it out for myself."

"My assumption," Ryan said, "was that the General was specifically projecting authority that was parallel to, on a par with, the North Koreans. He played directly on Flaum's devotion to that regime. But that's not what you did with Norton, Mara."

"That's right," I said, "I didn't invoke the North. I invoked an abstraction, an abstract authority that implied a hierarchy. Norton didn't buy right in. He tested it, and me. But he seemed to have some idea of what he was testing for."

"I assumed," Yael said, "that at his core Norton was a fantasist. That despite his network and his fervor he lived in a fantasy world and so he responded to a fantasy authority, which Mara successfully invoked."

"That's my point," I said. "I assumed that too. Then we all got caught up in the success of my deception and the information that began to flow from Norton. He gave us the plot and the strategies. Names. His network. He just kept talking. But we never got from him who he believed he was talking to, and we all wound up holding the assumption that he was responding to an abstract overseeing authority. Yael, you saw it as the culmination of Norton's fantasy life."

"But it wasn't anything of the kind, is what you are arguing," Ryan said.

"I'm saying exactly that," I said. "Norton wouldn't kill himself merely because he had been duped and outsmarted. His vanity would only compel him to get back in the game and avenge his deception. When he recognized our deception I think he realized that the thing he hadn't named and given up was *what he thought we were.* So he had one last thing to give to the revolution. He killed himself before we could get that out of him."

That was good enough for Ryan. He got on his cell to take it to the General. We had missed the forest for the trees. We had unraveled the attack against New York and broken open Norton and his network, which had planned it. What we had failed to grasp was the most obvious element in the whole thing: the authority behind it that we had mimicked to get Norton to talk to us. In theory it had to exist, but where and in whom?

Ryan's call with the General didn't last long.

"He agrees with you," Ryan said to me.

"That's all he said?" I asked.

"His exact words were, 'that damn woman is right; I knew there was a reason she's on the team.'"

"That's very flattering," I said.

"You have no idea," Yael added.

"What's the move?" I asked Ryan.

"The next move is in motion," Ryan said, his expression sharpening down to a look of uncertainty.

"What is the General doing?" Yael asked with a slight tone of worry that matched Ryan's uncertain expression.

"He's grabbing the White House woman," Ryan said.

"Shit," Yael said. "You can't be serious?"

"I know. This is going to explode in the media. It's going to change everything," Ryan said.

"Why?" Yael demanded. "Why take this risk when Norton gave us so many names that wouldn't kick up a dime's worth of media dust if we grabbed them?"

"I asked him exactly that," Ryan said.

"And?" Yael insisted.

"He said, 'she's the best bang for the buck.'"

"And what the hell is that supposed to mean?" Yael asked.

"He didn't explain."

Yael shook her head back and forth. She didn't like this.

"And Yael," Ryan said, "the General said that you're doing the interrogation."

Yael cocked her head, smiled somewhat perversely, and began to nod. This meant something I didn't quite get. But it had clearly balanced out the risks for her.

"Good," she said, "the General is a wise man."

"It's almost time for this woman to start her day at the White House, if she's not at her desk already," I said.

"We'll hear back from the General on that. If she's inside the White House compound already, he's going to find a way to lure her out. He wants this done yesterday," Ryan said.

"How is he going to do that, lure her outside of the White House?" I asked.

"She can be motivated easily enough. If she were an avid stamp collector, for instance, the General would find out which stamp she most coveted and if she thought she could buy it this morning she'd walk out of a meeting with the President himself so that she could have that stamp."

"So what does Allison Garvin like that much?" I asked.

"I don't know," Ryan said, "but if the General doesn't already have that information, he's just minutes away from having it."

"I'm curious to know what her equivalent of stamp collecting is," Yael said.

Ryan took a call and walked to the other end of the loft.

"We're moving into uncharted territory now," I said to Yael.

"No, you've got that reversed, Mara. We've been in uncharted territory, and that's where we are safest, because we know how to handle that. That's what we're good at. But when we take this creepy woman who works at the White House, we'll be in heavily charted territory where our range of options narrows considerably. No one can help us. We can't get winking cooperation from anyone. The Federal dogs will be out looking for her, which means they'll be looking for us, and the media will freeze it in place. The risk here is exactly because we're moving directly into the charts."

Ryan had finished the call and rejoined us.

"The General?" Yael asked.

"Yes. They're grabbing her mid-morning, around 10:00 a.m."

"What's the lure?" I asked.

"Yarn."

"What?"

"Yarn. She's a compulsive knitter or something, and she's a connoisseur of yarns. She's going to be pulled down to a shop that has just gotten a small shipment of exotic yarns."

"I would have bet on porn," I said. "I would have thought she'd want to look at porn while New York was being attacked."

"But she would be knitting instead," Yael said, knitting her brow.

"We're leaving, now," Ryan said.

"Back to the Virginia facility?" Yael asked.

"No, Pensacola. The General wants to be far away from D.C. He says it's a compromise to even keep her in the country."

"What about our unfinished business here?" I asked. "We're not sure we have the subway attacks bottled up."

"That's being managed. NYPD and the Feds have it. The General thinks you're right about why Norton killed himself and that the authority behind his network is the real core of the matter."

"And if I'm wrong?"

"Then we've taken this woman out of the White House at least. We'll get what we can out of her and know what she knows," Ryan said.

"And then do what with her?" I asked.

"I don't know," Ryan said, quite seriously, "drop her out of an airplane from ten thousand feet? I'll leave that to someone else to decide."

Our flight down to Pensacola would get us in ahead of the arrival of the deputy chief-of-staff of the White House. I knew that Yael handling the interrogation was going to be something different. I recalled that when Ryan stepped into the questioning of the Stasi officer he had shoved his nine millimeter in the subject's face and the answers came faster after that.

Yael had taken particular offense at the White House woman's betrayal of the country. Her reaction had been personal. I didn't get the sense that her approach was going to be either clever or subtle and that the General knew what he was ordering up because he knew Yael. In that sense, I didn't know Yael. From what I had seen of her mind at work she was brilliant, but not anyone who could take sitting at a desk. She was, like Ryan, addicted to action.

I had seen a glint of anger in her eyes that I hadn't seen earlier. Ryan saw it too, but it clearly wasn't new to him. He knew what was coming. I didn't.

34

"Isn't that too much?" were my words to Ryan as we watched Yael enter the interrogation room.

Allison Garvin was a petite woman with the pinched expression of a puritanical bureaucrat. Now her pinched face was pinned back in fear as she sat tightly shackled in a chair. She didn't know where she was, but standing just a few feet away was a thin, scowling woman wearing a Che T-shirt, dark glasses, and a beret. I thought that Yael's approach was almost comical, but Ryan signaled me to pay attention.

Yael stepped up scowling to the deputy chief-of-staff of the White House and just belted her across the mouth with the back of her hand.

"Traitor," Yael screamed at her.

Blood ran out of Garvin's nose and mouth.

"She's a bleeder," Ryan said.

Yael's T-shirt was tied at the bottom, exposing her abdomen. Her nine millimeter was stuffed into the waistband of her generic camo pants.

"What do you want with me?" Garvin asked, sniffling.

"You betrayed our military action in New York," Yael shouted in her face.

"No I did not," Garvin said defiantly.

"Liar," Yael shouted as she hit her again, harder.

I thought that Garvin was going out cold at first. Her eyes lost focus. She was bleeding steadily. But then the gristle that had helped her make her journey up the back stairs of national politics came to the foreground of her demeanor.

Yael had found what she was looking for.

"I betrayed nothing," Garvin said as if giving an order that she be believed. "Identify yourself," she barked.

Yael paused for a moment, allowing a wave of doubt to pass through her expression, and then stepped into another ferocious backhand across Garvin's face, which was swelling and darkening.

"Do you have any idea who I am?" Garvin spit out.

"You are the whore who betrayed our attack on New York," Yael said. "Here, look at what has happened to your fellow traitor."

Yael took photographs from an envelope and spread them on the floor in front of Garvin. I looked at Ryan.

"Norton's body," he said.

"I know him," Garvin said, apparently unmoved by the sight of Norton's slashed throat.

"Of course you know him," Yael shouted.

"So what?" Garvin shot back. "Whoever you are, when this gets straightened out, you are going to beg me to kill you. You are a nobody. I can tell that for sure, with that absurd revolutionary get-up of yours. Believe me, when you are in this chair and I'm standing where you are, you are going to know what real suffering is."

Yael hit her again, this time so hard that one of her eyes swelled shut.

"So," Yael said, "are you through running that mouth?"

"Listen to me. I told no one, no one, about the New York plan. Whoever is blaming me is wrong. If John Norton named me he was only trying to save himself. Who authorized you to abduct me?"

"You are a prisoner of the revolutionary council," Yael said.

"The who?" Garvin answered. "Never heard of it. Do you understand how important my position in the government is? How many years it has taken to get me in that position?"

"You are a traitor," Yael said.

"I am not a traitor. I helped create the New York plan. John Norton was my subordinate. You don't understand what we do. This is...you are making a huge mistake."

"Shut up, you disgusting liar," Yael shouted, but without delivering another blow. Garvin was already sufficiently beat up and not far from passing out.

"Look," Garvin said, "get in touch with Charles Spencer. I'll give you an email address."

Ryan, hearing that name, was on his feet and out of the observation room. I had no idea who Charles Spencer was.

"Why would I contact him?" Yael demanded.

"He is your own commander," Garvin said without arrogance as she began to fade.

"I've heard his name," Yael said. "I've heard favorable things. But he's not my commander."

"Yes, you will find out that he is," Garvin said weakly.

Yael watched Garvin fade into semi-consciousness and then left the interrogation room.

My guess was that Garvin had given up the name she believed could get her out of this. It would have to be someone with sufficient clout within the hierarchy to straighten out the zealots who had determined Garvin was a traitor. Garvin didn't know who Yael was, but if she believed she had one shot at escaping Norton's fate, she'd probably go with a leader high enough to know the branch of operations Yael belonged to and how to control it.

Yael joined me in the observation room.

"You were tough on the witness, counselor," I said.

She clenched her teeth and nodded slightly and rapidly.

"I had to get her to buy. We are on the same side, and I am falsely accusing her. She's not a traitor. She needs to go to someone big."

"Who is Charles Spencer?" I asked.

"He's big," Yael said. "Born in the U.K. Naturalized American citizen. Made billions in currency trading. Heavy financial ties with the Saudis and the regime in Venezuela. The General knows him."

"The General?"

"Yes."

"How well?"

"I don't know. I don't think it's a friendship. More like a same circles sort of thing."

"Did you enjoy that?" I asked, pointing to Allison Garvin on the monitor.

"Eh, it was just business. That she was going to sit in the White House and let a hundred thousand Americans die didn't make it any harder for me."

"So you didn't really take it personally," I said.

"No, I did," Yael said and flashed me a quick smile.

"How long before she finds out that it's not the revolution that has her?"

"I think we keep this one going for a while. Either way, this woman has paid attention. She attends to details. It's funny how when we were looking for answers from those KGB stiffs we were seeing into the past. Even when we had the thoroughly modern Chelsea Fall, it was such old-fashioned business. Here, with this hideous woman, we have the real future. The new, updated, forward-looking revolutionary, the postmodern power bureaucrat whose job is to play the President of the United States for a fool and then sleep soundly on the good conscience of a job well done and mass murder that goes down like clockwork."

"Is this something new," I asked about the sheer treachery of it, "or something very old?"

"It feels like history catching up with us. America was a step away from history, a step ahead of it. This feels like, maybe, we've lost that little margin. Maybe Ms. Garvin there got her start in a school where the American story is taught as all bad, the narrative of America where all the good parts are left out. So she's enlightened, maybe. Her America needs to be punished, big time. People like you and me, we need to get out of the way or die, Mara."

It was a good question right now, just who were people like me and Yael? She and I could have been strangers passing on a street, with seemingly nothing in common. Now we were comrades in arms. And that's the least we were. We were really sitting on the edge of history, watching the bad guys try to kill us.

Ryan returned and sat down with us.

"What about Charles Spencer?" I asked.

"The General believes it is impossible to grab him," Ryan said.

"We just grabbed a White House deputy chief-of-staff," Yael said, "what's the big challenge with Spencer?"

"Massive security. He's paranoid times five," Ryan explained. "It would be like grabbing the President."

"Then arrest him first," I said.

"Talk to me," Ryan said.

"Arrange to have this man Spencer arrested and then take him while he's in police custody," I said. "It won't be half as hard. The police will treat it as a routine arrest, if a little on the upscale side. It won't be anything like taking him out of his own security bubble."

"We don't interfere with cops, Mara. That's one of our rules," Ryan said.

"If it's a choice between breaking that rule and not getting hold of Spencer, I'd say a temporary suspension of the rule is called for," I said.

"I'll take it to the General," Ryan said.

35

The General walked into the observation room, followed by Ryan, and sat down next to me. He leaned back and looked me over.

"No," he said. "Your thinking has turned reckless. That makes you dangerous."

I shook my head and shrugged to express my dismay.

"Let's see. Have one of the wealthiest men in the world arrested and then kidnap him, presumably at gunpoint, from a police agency? Why don't we just edit that down to shooting ourselves in the head so that we cut out the middle work?"

"I'm sorry," I said, "but isn't that woman with the swollen face the deputy chief-of-staff of the White House?" I pointed to Allison Garvin on the monitor.

"Yes," the General said, "and she disappeared without a trace from a street in a D.C. suburb. No one has any idea what happened to her. She wasn't pulled at gunpoint from a presidential motorcade."

"I take your point," I said.

"Good. Sloppy thinking kills," said the General.

"It was a bad idea," I said.

"Bad ideas kill," he said.

This was the first time that the General had really let me see him. He was serious but he wasn't angry. I was being warned to be more careful in my thinking. He wasn't just concerned that I had a bad idea, but with the shape my mind was in. He knew stress, adrenaline, and fatigue. Maybe he was considering returning me to civilian life.

"So, am I out?" I asked.

He laughed.

"No, you're on the team," he said.

"The team doesn't exist," I said.

"That's right," he said.

"So where do we go with Charles Spencer?" I asked.

"Spencer is outside our reach," the General said. "He lives in a top to bottom buttoned down world. There are heads of state who don't have that level of security."

"But here's my question," I said, "in theory, if we had him, he would tell us everything we need to know?"

"Such as?"

"Such as who runs the network that the Garvins and the Nortons belong to. Such as where all that comes down from, who ultimately calls the shots."

"Well, you know Miss Rains..."

"Please, call me Mara."

"You know, Mara," the General said, "that if we found all that out it's almost certainly going to be more than we can handle. You already know that, don't you?"

"I don't need to know that, do I? Why not find out before reaching any conclusions?"

"Would you," he said, "be able to stand the burn of knowing without being able to do anything?"

"I already can't stand the burn of not knowing," I said.

"Your old life is gone," the General said.

"No," I said, "my old life is perfectly intact. When this is over I'm going back to it. I know who I am."

"Indeed you do," the General said.

"And while you're here, sir," I said, "have you forgotten that we've never been formally introduced and that you have me at a disadvantage?"

It was an inescapable fact. I didn't know who the General was, and when I had asked about who he was I was told that I'd have to ask him that question. So now I had asked him.

"I don't exist," he said and pointed to Allison Garvin on the monitor. He smiled and got up and left the room.

"Did he just imply," I asked, turning to Ryan and then Yael, "that I might find myself in that position?" I gestured toward the monitor.

"I think so," Yael said.

"Yeah," Ryan agreed.

"And that I would give the General up if I knew who he was?"

"Yes," Ryan said.

"But I could just describe him if I was under that kind of duress."

"Right," Yael said, "but what else do you know about him?"

"That he once played poker with John Marshall Norton and belonged to the same social circle as Charles Spencer. That he knows Rob."

"You know," Ryan said, "that Rob was in a room with him and called him 'General.' You saw and heard that. But the other facts, about him knowing both Norton and Spencer, those might be disinformation."

"You're telling me that the General might have deliberately planted me with disinformation about himself?"

"Yes," Ryan said.

"Well, which is it," I asked, "did he or didn't he?"

"We don't know," Yael said.

"But you two do know who he is, don't you?"

"No," Ryan said, "we don't."

"You didn't serve under the General, Ryan?"

"No," Ryan said.

"Then you don't even know if he's an actual General?"

"No," Ryan said.

"What the hell?" I said.

"You're beginning to get it, Mara," Ryan said.

"Get what?"

"Just how serious the non-existence of the General is," Ryan answered. "I couldn't just explain it to you because our camaraderie depends on an assumption that we are all tight with one another and that the General is one of us, the head of the team, and in time you will know him the way we know him. But we don't know him either, Mara, not in the personal sense of knowing who he is or what his background is."

"Then how can you trust him?" I said.

"The trust is in the work," Yael said. "You've seen the work. Have you seen a false move, a move that wasn't right?"

"No," I said.

"Then you get that the General is protecting the work, not himself," she said.

"I do get that," I said.

"That's what we know about the General," Ryan said, "and that's the source of our trust."

"But you two didn't just get assumed onto the team the way I did," I said.

"We didn't?" Yael said.

"You mean you did?" I said.

"Let's leave that for later, Mara," Ryan said.

"O.K.," I said, "that's fair enough. I'm feeling like you're all a bunch of damn phantoms now, and I'm becoming one too."

"Like you said, Mara," Ryan gestured back to a few minutes earlier, "when this is over you'll go back to your real life. Meanwhile, we have a White House deputy chief-of-staff to deal with."

Suddenly that real life of mine did look impossible. I knew too much. And once you knew too much, you couldn't very well walk around Manhattan, go out for a regular lunch, meet old friends for drinks, or could you? Wouldn't I risk spilling some incredible bit of information if I resumed my normal active life? As an attorney I understood confidentiality, but client matters were easily compartmentalized. Compartmentalizing the enduring peak experience I was living through minute-by-minute right now would be another thing altogether.

When I asked Ryan and Yael who the General was they told me I had to ask the General that question. When I finally had my opportunity and asked the General it was as if my perspective was then deliberately uprooted by him and shifted ninety degrees and then another ninety degrees by Ryan and Yael, leaving me each time looking at all this not simply from a new and unfamiliar perspective, but from an alien and bizarre perspective. Then Yael focused me back on the work, and that was the thread that made sense. The work was true. As wild as it had gotten, it all fit together and made sense.

The door to the observation room opened wide and a tall, muscular black man who I had never seen before leaned through it.

"We're blown," he said with a British accent and disappeared back into the hallway.

"Shit," Ryan said.

"What does that mean?" I asked.

"That we're done with this place right now," Ryan answered. "Yael will take you to the tunnel."

On the monitor the black man who had just been at our door was giving Allison Garvin an injection in her arm. He unshackled her and carried her out of the interrogation room. She was unconscious.

Yael indicated that I should follow her and we left and took the corridor to a stairwell and went down one flight to a utility room where we followed some other personnel I'd never seen into a dimly lit tunnel. It seemed to run for a few hundred yards with one forty-five degree turn. At the end of it we came to a flight of stairs that took us up into an airline hangar.

Yael pointed to a small executive-style jet that was getting ready to taxi out of the hangar and we boarded it together. Ryan came on board a few seconds later.

I finally asked Yael what was happening.

"Not to put too fine a point on it," she said, "we're running, like hell."

36

As the jet gained altitude I saw a fire raging on the ground. It was the facility. I looked at Yael. She pointed off in the distance. A cordon of vehicles, lights flashing, was racing in the direction of the burning facility.

"Fire trucks?" I asked.

"No, police, probably military."

"After us?"

"You got it."

"Because of Garvin?"

"That would make sense."

"We should find out," I said.

"That," Yael said, pointing, "is not going to be on the news."

"Do they know who we are, our names, what we've been doing?"

"Very unlikely."

"Then what? Why are they going to the facility?"

"From time to time locations get blown. We find things. They find things. Sometimes they find things for us. Sometimes they find us. When they do, we leave, and in this case they find a building on fire."

"How," I asked, "do we know in advance that we've been blown?"

"They tell us," Yael said.

"They do?"

"One way or another, yes."

"What happens if we don't know they're coming?"

"Shooting happens," Yael said, touching her neck wound.

Ryan, who had been in the jet's cockpit, joined us in the passenger cabin.

"We're going to set down in Mexico, at a strip in the Yucatan," he said.

"Explain the meaning of that," I said, sensing something was different.

"The attack on New York has been thwarted," Ryan said matter-of-factly. "The primary ten-man team and its back-up, all of them are in custody. Most of the stashed weapons have been recovered. Not a word has gotten out to the media about it. Instead, everyone is buzzing about the disappearance of Garvin. The President has made a statement vowing to find her using all of the resources at his disposal."

"Does he know that she was in on the New York plot?" I asked.

"Not so far as I know," Ryan said. "I think only we know that, along with her own network, of course. Unless the Fed agencies have turned something up on her since she disappeared. Their suspicions are always aroused about people who disappear. On the other hand, she did get through the security clearances at the White House."

"Are you not telling me something, Ryan? You have an odd look."

"I'm always not telling you something, Mara. It's always need-to-know."

"I'm not talking about me being kept in the dark generally. There's something specific. I'm reading it in your tone."

"How about," Ryan said, "the President is meeting today with Charles Spencer? Could that be it?"

"You're joking?" I said.

"No," he said.

"Makes perfect sense," Yael said, "Spencer pays a lot of money for political access and he's going to want to pump the President for the story on Garvin. She was Spencer's agent in the White House. He needs to know what's going on. He's a meticulous paranoid."

"It's crazy," I said.

"That Spencer can get in to see the President just like that?" Ryan said.

"Yes," I said, "why don't we tell the President about Spencer?"

"Way too early for that," Ryan said.

"He's the enemy we just stopped in New York," I said, "and he's going to have coffee with the President of the United States."

"As worlds go," Ryan said, "this is a pretty funny one. But old Yasser Arafat, who had a hand in killing a lot of Americans, got some good face time in the Oval Office when he was still alive."

"But everyone knew what he was," I said.

"Are you saying that made it better?" Yael asked.

"I'm saying that not knowing that Charles Spencer is the enemy is more dangerous."

"Are you sure about that?" Yael asked.

"I get your point," I said. "It's just that I haven't spent as much time on this side of the looking glass as you two have and I think of the Presidency as hallowed ground."

"The question the General wants an answer to," Ryan said, "is whether or not Charles Spencer is a good faith revolutionist or if he's operating on some other motive."

That threw me off.

"What is a good faith revolutionist?" I asked. "Someone who hums the Internationale while murdering thousands of New York subway riders?"

"That's a good way of defining it," Ryan said. "Yes, the General sees that as a crucial question. Revolutionary motives or ulterior motives. We saw the KGB in New York had gone into business for itself and was no longer serving the revolution."

"Where's your money?" I asked Ryan.

"I think Spencer's a true believer," he said.

"Yael?"

"True believer. Revolutionary. And you, Mara?"

"I think he's a mental case and a murderer," I said.

"Spoken like a true New Yorker," Yael said.

We landed on a long airstrip in the middle of the Yucatan nowhere. There was one large hangar near the end of it and our pilot taxied the jet inside. There were two other small jets but not a person anywhere. We stepped out of the plane and took refuge in the now customary glass booth office. There was a full bank of communications equipment, radios, radar, internet-connected laptops, surveillance cameras, all of it up and running without any evidence of a human hand in it, not even a styrofoam cup.

"No ground crew at this airport?" I said.

"We are the ground crew, "Yael said.

"Who runs this equipment?" I asked.

"The ground crew," Yael said, stifling a laugh.

"What's the plan?" I asked.

"Watch this," Yael said, tapping the radar screen with her finger.

"What am I looking for?"

"The next flight in. Allison Garvin is on it. We're not done with her."

"That was pretty brutal, back in Pensacola. Are you up for more of that?"

"No. Ryan is going to talk to her now and lay it out in life and death terms. She gets to choose."

"What do you mean?" I asked.

"Outthataways," Yael said, pointing, "through the jungle, we've got some buildings, nothing fancy like the one we just burned to the ground. We're going to march her out there, and then Ryan will sit down with her and lay it all out. If she cooperates all the way, in every detail, she lives."

"And if she doesn't?"

"I'm sure she will," Yael said. "She knows she's not in Kansas anymore."

"No more of you pretending to be Tonya the revolutionary?"

"Nah. Enough of that. I think that the change of perspective is going to be good for her. You're used to being around Ryan. She'll be meeting him for the first time."

As we spoke the radar screen showed an approaching aircraft. As the plane got closer we went outside the hangar and watched it land. Then it taxied inside and the tall black man carried the still unconscious Allison Garvin off the plane and laid her down on the surface of the hangar. She had a full hood covering her head and her hands were cuffed behind her back.

"How are her vitals?" Ryan asked.

"Vitals are good," her minder said in his crisp British voice.

"Bleeding?"

"Stopped."

"She'll live then," Ryan said.

"She will live," her minder said.

"Get her awake, then," Ryan said.

The minder retrieved a kit from the plane and broke open a small ampoule and held it at Garvin's nose through the hood. It jolted her awake, but even without being able to see her face I could tell she was a groggy mess.

Still, her minder encouraged her and got her to her feet and moving. Ryan led the way and we left the hangar, crossed the runway, and took a path into the jungle. About a half-mile in we arrived at the site of a few metal buildings, all of them windowless. Ryan took us into one and it was much better inside than I expected, finished, with a tile floor, and air-conditioning. There was a lounge area and a kitchenette. I went in search of coffee and found some and started a pot.

Garvin's minder sat her in a chair and shackled her and then removed her hood. She was fully awake now. She looked around and took note of all four of us. She was possessed with an air of authority and power even under these conditions. The attitude was natural to her. She must have been born with it. She turned her head and focused on me.

"I know you," she said.

37

"I met you at a party in New York. You're married to a cop. It was five years ago."

She had found a friend in the room. I didn't respond and looked to Yael. She nodded at me, indicating that I should go ahead and run with it.

"I don't recall meeting you," I said coldly. I was telling the truth. I might have been introduced to her and several other people and had five other things on my mind. She must not have made an impression.

"It was my friend Jenn Marcus who introduced us," she said.

That sent a jolt of anxiety through me. I didn't like it that Jenn knew Garvin, and it was revolting that Garvin recognized me from such a familiar context.

"How did you get mixed up with these people?" she wanted to know.

I didn't know the right way to play it. Continue with Yael's revolutionary spiel or just cut the crap, and go straight at her. I looked to Yael, who knew exactly what I was thinking and signaled that it was my call. I went with playing it straight.

"You've implicated yourself in a plot to kill thousands of New Yorkers with biological and chemical weapons, Ms. Garvin. You are not being held by a faction of your own revolutionary movement. These are the people who uncovered the plot and stopped it. You are not going back, indeed you cannot go back, to your life. If you cooperate, however, they might let you live."

She looked at me, squinting, with an expression that let me know she was sizing me up and that once she was done she would have me.

"In that case," she said, "I would like to see an attorney."

I couldn't stop myself from laughing.

"As far as you are concerned," I said, "all the lawyers are dead."

"This is an extra-judicial proceeding," she said. "When the President hears about this you'll all get what you deserve?"

"You have no idea just how extra-judicial it is," I said. She thought that the group was from somewhere inside the government and was exercising power outside the law. She hadn't conceived yet that it might be beyond even that.

"The President is no friend of your kind," she said.

"And what would he think of you, Ms. Garvin, if he knew what you were up to?"

"He would still insist that I be treated fairly, that I get all the rights and due process I am entitled to as an American." She was suddenly a proud American again, entitled to her rights.

"Well," I said, "we're not caught up in the details of due process right now. Let's say that you'll get the same due process that you were prepared to give subway riders in New York. Your choices right now come down to talking to me, as a friend of a friend, or continue the interview with my rough colleagues. They don't speak cocktail party."

She wanted to know what good it would do her. I told her that she could clear her conscience, if she still had one, and that down the road there was some hope. She wanted a guaranteed deal.

"O.K.," I said, "my associates will drop you into the jungle from an airplane at ten thousand feet if you don't search every corner of your mind for every detail you know about your revolutionary terror network. That's the deal. It's not negotiable."

"And in exchange I get hope? Hope for what?" She asked.

"Hope for mercy," I told her.

"Who are you people to give yourselves that power?"

"Why, we're the good guys, Ms. Garvin, and you are one of the bad guys, and we caught you being very bad."

"I was only seeking justice for the oppressed people of the world." She was starting with the song and dance of the revolution.

"By murdering tens of thousands of people on their way to work?" I said.

"Everyone who works for the machine is complicit with the machine and shares the guilt."

"Without due process? Guilty without due process?" I asked.

She had tried another run at the circle and I finished it for her. She was ready to give it all up now. The mood in the room became relaxed. I needed to get everything she had on Charles Spencer.

"Is Charles Spencer the leader of your revolutionary cause in the United States?"

"In North America," she said.

"Take me up and down from there," I said.

"Charles belongs to the supreme world soviet."

"Really?" I said. "I've never heard of that."

"Why would you have heard of it, it doesn't exist."

"You mean its existence is hidden?"

"Yes."

"Who is Charles Spencer's second in command in North America?"

"There is no such thing. After Charles there is the chamber of deputies. There are supposed to be thirty members, but that's an ideal. There are only eight right now for North America."

"And you are one of these eight?"

"No, I am below that."

"Do you know all eight?"

"Yes."

"I asked for the names and she rattled them off. I didn't recognize any of them."

"Who among that group most covets Spencer's position?"

"That would be Franklin Beers. He and Spencer are at odds."

"Over what?"

"Over revolutionary violence. Beers wants there to be much more of it. Spencer believes it should be sporadic but intense. Beers wants a constant flow of violence, always increasing."

"Who do you side with?" I asked.

"I agree with Beers, but I understand Charles. He believes in people, that they can be changed. Beers doesn't.

"How much support does Beers have?"

"Lots. I thought that bitch who was beating me up earlier was from a faction financed by Beers. He likes that sort of approach. Very rah rah."

"But you agree with Beers?" I said.

"Yes."

"But you recognize Spencer's authority."

"Yes."

"How did Spencer get his position?"

"Eliminated his competitors," she said.

"Killed them off?"

"That's what a strong leader has to do. Eliminate uncertainty to create unity."

"Why is Beers still around then?" I asked.

"Beers is old, almost eighty. He'll die soon enough. And Charles likes him. Beers has more wealth than Charles and he feeds it without hesitation into the cause. Every revolutionary handbill, pamphlet, website, lecture you see has some of Franklin Beers' money in it. So Charles is very wise to tolerate his dissent."

"What else does Beers feature besides money and a belief in total violence?"

"Sex," she said.

"Even as he nears eighty?"

"Yes."

"You've had sex with him?"

"Many women in the cause have."

"So that's a 'yes'."

"Yes."

"Why is that?"

"He exudes power. He's handsome. He wants sex. You give it to him."

"And that's no violation of your revolutionary principles?" I asked.

"What world are you living in," she said.

"Just asking."

"That sort of thing is nothing more than a coffee break. Franklin Beers pays for the movement. He wants sex. It's the least you can do for him."

"I hear you," I said. "Does Beers know that you take sides on the violence question?"

"Yes."

"Have you ever discussed removing Charles Spencer from command with Beers?"

"Not in so many words. You have to be careful. Beers likes to hear you support his view, but he's suspicious of anything that smacks of a challenge to authority."

It was baffling to contemplate someone who believed in unrelenting revolutionary violence but was wary about challenges to authority. But I suppose that if you had enough money you could be as nuts as you wanted to be.

"So people like Beers and Spencer supported you, cultivated you, and pushed you on your path in, what shall I call it, normal politics?"

"Yes, but I worked hard. That's what attracted their support. My hard work, my commitment, my intelligence."

"That package got you all the way to the west wing of the White House?" I said.

"It did," she said, "I gave my entire life to climbing that ladder."

"And Beers and Spencer backed you when you needed it?"

"They backed me all the way," she said. "I owe them everything, all of my loyalty."

"And what about the President? What did you owe him?"

She threw her head back with a snide little laugh.

"Nothing," she said.

38

"And who backed Beers and Spencer all the way?" Ryan asked Garvin, stepping in front of her.

"Come on," she said, "they're old-time communists, secret members of the U.S. party when that meant something. They took their orders from Moscow in the old days, but they always paid their own way. Their money paid a lot of ways."

"Who did they turn to when the Soviet Union collapsed?" Ryan spoke in a calm but insistent tone.

"To Marx and Lenin and Fidel and Mao, for their inspiration and authority," she answered. "That's where they turn when they need answers on how to proceed."

"Fidel survived the Soviet collapse. Did he run Spencer and Beers?"

"No," she said shaking her head emphatically. "They turned to the early Fidel, Fidel the revolutionary. They idolized that Fidel but saw the later Fidel as a weak, groveling welfare case, a con man looking for their money. That Fidel was for Hollywood types."

"What about the North Koreans?"

She laughed. "Crazy dirtbags looking for a handout."

"The Chinese?" Ryan continued.

"Sell-outs. Confused. Charles used to call them 'Nixon communists' and then he just stopped talking about them."

"So Spencer and Beers see themselves as the last pure Marxist-Leninists on the planet?"

"Not in so many words. What they believe is that history is stuck. That it is not moving forward according to the science of socialism, and the way to get it unstuck is revolutionary violence."

Garvin was now taking on the affect of the expert, perhaps in an effort to restore her own pride. She was bouncing off the bottom. Ryan was happy to oblige her renewed sense of authority.

"And their belief in violence," Ryan began, but she interrupted.

"Their belief in revolutionary violence," she corrected.

"That belief," he continued, "is what attracted them to Islamic terrorists?"

"Yes, is the short answer," she said.

"And what is the long answer?"

"That they were, that the jihadists were historical instruments of destruction who could and would facilitate the annihilation of the remaining bourgeois infrastructure of the West including, especially, that of the United States."

"So," Ryan said, "how did they justify the fact that Islamists want nothing to do with Marx and Lenin?"

"That it doesn't make any difference. It will all come out in the wash," she said.

"And the wash is the violence?"

"Yes, more or less," she said. "In their understanding, which I share of course, Islamic violence is a response to the decay of the bourgeois West, and its historical purpose is to get history moving again in accordance with the laws of socialism."

"It makes no difference then," Ryan pressed, "that the Islamists see their purpose differently, see it as a religious purpose?"

"Not a whit of difference," she said, "because if history is moving it can only move in accordance with the laws of socialism toward socialism."

"And that's what you believe also?"

"I believe it because it is true," she said.

"Your certainty is impressive," Ryan said. "It allows you to justify your faith in mass murder."

"It's not murder," she said, "when the violence is justified by the revolution. The bourgeois regime being attacked is criminal and inhuman and all who are obedient to it are complicit in its interminable violence. In acts of revolutionary violence against the enemy anyone complicit with the enemy who is killed is guilty of the crime of the enemy. It is not murder."

"So, riding a subway train to work," Ryan said, "is a criminal act punishable by death?"

"When seen in true historical context, it certainly is," she said confidently.

"Everyone on the subway is equally guilty," Ryan suggested.

"No, not if you go person by person, a maid or janitor is not carrying the same level of guilt as a stockbroker or corporate executive, but revolutionary violence sweeps with an inclusive broom. The statement it makes is bold and absolute and is a warning to all."

I thought that I could hear Ryan's teeth clenching in the silence he let fall in the room. He looked at her with a flat, calm expression, as though he had met his final opposite, the person who negated everything he was as he negated everything she was. She saw her opening.

"And what do you believe in, soldier boy? Gawd?"

"In the individual and his liberty," Ryan said, rising to the bait.

"Oh, dear, an American. You people are so charming, so quaint," she said, "always the perpetual football players running onto the field to the roar of the crowd and the bouncing breasts of the cheerleaders."

"You're an American, aren't you, Ms. Garvin?" he asked.

"Ah, no," she said, "I stopped thinking of myself as that, as an American when I was a teenager. That's what we call 'the normal maturation process' these days, soldier boy. Sorry you missed it."

"So you're not an American," Ryan said. "What are you?"

"I'm a citizen of the world," she said.

"That's a big concept," Ryan said.

"It's basic," she said. "You must have missed it while you were attending your ROTC meetings."

"I guess I did," Ryan said. "That would explain why I'm still just an American with a silly belief in freedom."

Garvin laughed.

"Freedom? You think this America is free? You've got ninety percent of the people glued to their couches gazing like zombies into their televisions and eating non-stop. And then they jump up off their couches for five minutes of history when a couple of tall buildings are knocked down in New York. That's the America I see. That's the America the world sees. That's the America the revolution sees. This freedom thing you believe in, soldier boy, is a fairy tale, just like Gawd. History is unfolding right before your eyes and you're running in the opposite direction after the fairies of freedom and the goblins of terrorism. You should run in the direction of revolutionary violence, all of you should, get out in front of it, and get off this America thing, because it is dead, a thing of the past. America no longer exists. You just haven't realized it. None of you have."

So spoke the White House deputy chief of staff. And I had no doubt that she meant and believed every word of it. What was worse, I knew a lot of people, close friends even, who would have agreed with most of it, quibbling, maybe, about whether they deserved to die for their complicity in the machine of bourgeois decadence. I knew a lot of people who said 'Gawd' for 'God' when they thought they were in safe company and most certainly shared Garvin's sentiments about how passé being an American was.

It was more than sobering to get this close to the ideological source of what had become casual disdain, in polite company, for American culture and ideals. Garvin was a furnace in which everything was burned for the revolution. People could be killed for going to work. Invoke their freedom and it was laughed off. They were slobs who watched television and ate. Garvin burned everything. The good parts had been burned a long time ago for her. Now it was just the ugly remains. America was a nation of burping couch potatoes that had already been to the gallows and was only waiting for cremation.

It wasn't really her affair, though. She'd been awake, always working, and was a citizen of the world. America was gone from her and she from it. She had moved on.

"What you people refuse to understand," Garvin said, jumping into the silence that had fallen over the room, "is that this freedom of yours is no more than pitiful self-indulgence at the expense of others. What the revolution does is take the anger and frustration of those who hunger for justice in the world and shape that into purposeful violence. You try to deny that by calling it 'senseless violence' and 'mass murder,' but I'm looking at your faces now and I can see those old defenses and the lies that support them draining out of you. You all look like children who have just been told that there is no Santa Claus, and you had really known that all along. You just needed an adult to make it official for you. Well, here I am kids, giving it to you straight, what you already knew."

The door to the building opened and the General came in. He was by himself and he looked as though he had been watching the whole thing. I noticed that he was carrying a nine millimeter in his hand, hanging at his side, and I thought he was going to threaten Garvin with it, possibly because he'd found a problem with her statements about Beers and Spencer.

His mouth was tight, and he shot only a quick glance Ryan's way, not looking at the rest of us. He walked straight to Garvin and she looked up at him.

"You," she said, with shock in her eyes.

"Yes, me," the General said, "let me shape some purposeful violence for you."

He raised his nine millimeter about three feet from Garvin's head and pulled the trigger. The bullet entered above her left eye and exploded out the back of her head.

"God forgive me," the General said, "lowering the gun.

39

No one said a word. All eyes were on the General standing in front of the slumped body of Allison Garvin. I wasn't thinking about it, just replaying the final seven seconds in my mind.

The General broke the silence.

"Tony," he said to Garvin's minder, "wrap her up. We'll drop her in the Gulf."

He looked around at us.

"We just stopped a terrorist attack on New York." He pointed at Garvin's body. "She was an agent for the sponsor of that attack and she worked in the Executive Office of the President. She confessed. She's been executed in the field."

"Sir," Ryan said, "did she have more value to us alive?"

"Maybe," the General said, "but if she had been rescued she would have destroyed us and gained more power in D.C. We've got fifteen minutes to get off this base. If they catch up with us I can die knowing that that diseased, corrupt monster is off the board."

He convinced me. Especially the 'diseased and corrupt' part. Ryan seemed satisfied. Yael helped Tony get Garvin's body onto a tarp.

"Let's move," the General said, "we're burning this base." He left.

The situation unfroze. The pace kicked back up. Garvin disappeared into the rolled-up tarp. Tony hoisted her over his shoulder and headed out the door.

"Mara, we have to go," Yael said, touching my elbow and giving me an 'are you all right' look.

"Yes," I said to her wordless question, "I'm fine. Let's get out of here."

It became obvious that we were on the run again, from the swiftness with which we moved back through the half-mile stretch of jungle to the airstrip. The buildings we left behind us burst into flame. In front of us one of the jets was racing down the runway on takeoff. I guessed the General was onboard.

Ryan joined Yael and me on the jet we had arrived on and the pilot took us quickly into the air. Tony had carried Garvin's body onto a third jet, which was ready to follow us on the strip.

"How much damage do you think she did?" I asked Ryan about Garvin.

"We'll never know for sure now," he said, "but if we start by assuming maximum damage we can always revise downward."

"I know plenty of people who would agree with how she viewed America," I said.

"That's New York," Ryan said.

"Yes, that's New York."

"We just stopped an attack there," he said. "Would those people still agree with Garvin if they knew?"

"I don't know," I said, "they might just as easily pick up on her 'goblins of terrorism' theme and sniffle about 'another attack that didn't happen,' and then focus on the 'legitimate goals of the terrorists'."

"That's the uptown view, Mara," Ryan said. "The everyday subway rider might have a different take on it."

I thought about that for a moment.

"I want to believe that, Ryan. It was true once. But in New York, Allison Garvin's ideas have penetrated. People hear it constantly and they repeat what they hear."

"Well, we still protect them, whatever they think."

"I know you believe that, soldier boy."

That got him to crack a smile.

"Was she getting to you with that?" I asked.

"No," he said, dismissing Garvin's taunts.

"Did she get to the General, you think?"

"I would have to say, I think that she rubbed the General the wrong way," Ryan said, suppressing a grin.

"She argued powerfully," I said.

"Mara," Ryan said, "she was insane. I mean clinically insane. She was arguing that killing thousands of people was justified because they were complicit in bourgeois decadence. That is insane, no matter how she got there."

"I'm not disagreeing, Ryan. I'm saying that her argument resonates in the world. She was certain and that conviction gave her power."

"I suppose you're right," he said, "but what she said was meaningless to me. It was gibberish. I know people are susceptible to that sort of thing, but that's not my department. I'm a tactical guy, not a Psy-Ops person."

"You're not a Psy-Ops specialist too?" I said. "You could have fooled me, with the way you manipulated the New York KGB network and turned them against one another."

"Point taken. But that was still tactical. Not a public propaganda campaign," he said.

"Well, you ought to start thinking about expanding your horizons, Ryan," I said, "because breaking the back of Garvin's propaganda might be the real battlefield. I'm serious."

Ryan understood that better than I ever would. I was just reminding him of what he already knew.

We flew low over the Gulf of Mexico. I had no immediate sense that we were in danger, but the buzz of running away from something was in the air. Yael and Ryan, I knew, always had the taste of death in their mouths but I wasn't quite there yet. I think they appreciated my relative innocence and tried to protect that, the way a parent tries to protect a child's innocence. In my case they were trying to maintain my outsider's viewpoint. It had value to them, even as it faded. I was still able to see things with relatively fresh eyes and it helped.

"Are we heading somewhere," I asked, "or just out for a ride?"

"We'll land in Guatemala. We've got to get off this plane and onto one with a legitimate flight plan so that we can get back to the U.S.," Ryan explained.

"And?"

"And Franklin Beers isn't the paranoid security-obsessed type that Charles Spencer is. We're going to talk to him," Ryan said.

"That sounds different," I said, "'talk to him'?"

"He's seventy-eight. Rough stuff might kill him. We need to break him on his soft side."

Yael picked up on that theme.

"He's a sex addict," she said.

"That could kill him too," I said.

"One can only hope," she said.

"Only hope which," I asked, "that it doesn't kill him or that it does?"

"Both," Yael said.

"So is this going to be a honey trap sort of maneuver. If so," I said, "don't be lookin' at me."

"Allison Garvin made it with the old boy, Mara," Yael said, "for her cause. Are you saying you would do less?"

"Don't even joke," I said.

"I'm not joking," she said, but she was.

On the switchover we boarded another jet that would take us back home. We were heading to Omaha, where Beers maintained an estate. I had never heard his name before Garvin brought it up, but from the brief Ryan had on him he was indeed incredibly wealthy. He was old money and had scrupulously avoided attracting any attention to himself. He knew how to keep his name off of any lists of the wealthiest people.

Like most serious old money Beers was invested everywhere. He sat on top of a diversified wealth machine and didn't appear to give a thought to how the wealth came in. Financial managers handled it. Nor did he live lavishly. He had the requisite high-maintenance mansion, but it was nothing compared to what he could afford. Beers spent his money, lots of it, just as Garvin said, on the revolution.

We had a record of what he spent publically, and it added up to over four hundred million for the past decade. What was unaccounted for might be twice that. Among the public expenditures was fifty million dollars to front groups for Steven Flaum's Stalinist fringe party. It was a small world, getting smaller.

By the time we landed in Omaha I felt like I knew Beers, all the way back to his puritan ancestors. He had picked up his Marxism while studying in the U.K. at Cambridge University and brought it home like a contagion. He had indeed been a secret member of the Communist Party of the United States, something that most people these days would view as quaint and amusing, and if Beers was anything, he was quintessentially quaint and amusing. Were it not for his desire to instigate relentless revolutionary violence maybe it could be left at that, an eccentric old Marxist who spent lavishly on the dying embers of the old cause.

But the old man was wearing Joseph Stalin's shoes. He didn't care how many people he killed.

40

We were met at the airport by Callista Langois, a twenty-seven year old Filipino-French woman raised in the United States. She spoke six languages, had test scores in the upper reaches of the top one percent, and was drop-dead gorgeous. My first thought on seeing her was that she might in fact cause Franklin Beers to do exactly that: drop dead.

There was no question that she would melt him like a stick of butter in a hot pan. I was thinking that she would also kill him, or kill him too soon.

Ryan briefed Callista on Beers but she knew her job without any need for coaching. As confidence levels went, hers hit up around the maximum. We needed someone who could walk right into Beers' life on the strength of hypnotic sexuality and sheer chutzpah and she was it.

Ryan fit her with a pair of glasses with an imbedded camera and audio. Her first job was to get inside his mansion and give us a look around at the layout and security. Ryan's preference was to deal with Beers entirely inside his home.

"This is high risk," he said as we watched Callista approach the front gate of the estate. We were in a van parked down the block. All she did was hit the front buzzer, stand in front of the security camera, and say, "I'm Roberta and I'd like to meet with Mr. Beers," and she was in.

She walked up the long driveway and we could see her approach the entrance and then we watched Ryan's laptop and saw what she saw. We expected a security person to greet her at the door but instead it was Beers himself who met her. He was wearing just a silk robe, open at the front with nothing underneath. His mouth hung open as he took a close look at Callista.

"Close that up, Mr. Beers," she said, taking charge of his robe and tying it shut.

"Must I?" he said.

"For the moment," she said teasingly, and that made the old fool giggle.

"Are you here to make love to me?" he asked coyly.

"I'm here to change your life," she said. "What a gorgeous house you have."

The place was an absolute mess. Callista gave us the panorama and it was pizza boxes and half-dressed young women draped across chairs and couches. It was a permanent orgy.

"Maid's day off?" Callista joked at Beers.

"Those people," he said with a foppish wave, "don't come unless I call them. Such insufferable bourgeois tools. I can't take their vacuuming or their disapproval. I want to see your body."

We could see Callista slap his hand away as he reached for her belt.

"Experience the joy of anticipation, Mr. Beers," she said. "I will let you into the temple when the time is right. But first I want to talk about the revolution."

"Oh, that," he said. "You're a thinker, are you. Let's go to the library for that. It will calm me down, and we can have a drink. What's your interest in the revolution?"

"To serve it," she said.

"Aha," Beers answered, "if you serve me my dear, you are serving the revolution."

They were alone in the library and Beers was pouring scotch into dirty glasses.

"I know about the failure in New York," she told him.

"You do," he said. "Well that was something Charles cooked up and I said, not to him of course, that it was bound to fail. You're not the FBI are you?"

"Certainly not," she said.

"CIA?"

"Do I look like a whore?" she answered.

"In fact you don't," Beers said.

"We cannot keep failing," she said.

"Who are you with?" he asked, taking on a more sober affect.

"I am a member of the Women's Latin American Support Collective," she said.

"Do I support that group?" he asked.

"Indirectly, yes, and we are grateful. We believe in the tactic of continuous revolutionary violence. I believe something must be done in the wake of the failure in New York."

Beers was now focused and momentarily out of his sex mode. He was looking at Callista with suspicion.

"Who are you?" he asked.

"Roberta M," she said, "and I am prepared to die for the future of the world."

"Are you really?" he said. "Well there's no need for that. You're too smart for that. I'll give you a few million dollars, you go hire someone to blow up anything you like, and we'll blame it on the Islamic radicals. They're only too happy to take credit anyway."

Beers slumped back in his chair and let his robe fall open. He sipped his scotch.

"Close that robe," Callista ordered, "and don't open it until I tell you to."

Beers appreciated her authority and followed orders.

"Such a serious girl," he said.

"I believe that the Charles Spencer era has passed," she barked.

"Has it ever," Beers answered. "Are you suggesting something?"

"That he be removed," Callista said.

"He would have to be killed in that case," he said.

"Would you object?"

"Not in the least. Charles is inept. I've always said that. He's repulsively bourgeois in his thinking. The revolution has decayed continuously under his command."

"His security is impenetrable," Callista said.

"Oh, yes. His security. He does seem to think that his life is of immeasurable value. He is so anal with all that security of his. It would be amusing to see him blown up."

"But he would need to be questioned first," Callista insisted. "He cannot be allowed to die with his secrets. Those belong to the revolution."

"You are quite the tiger, young woman," Beers said. "You remind me of the early Mao. Heartless about everything but the revolution. It arouses me."

"How will we get to Spencer? Callista said. "And how will we break him before his execution? What is his weakness?"

"The only weakness that Charles has is that he is weak," Beers said. "That's it. He is weak in the revolution. He is a gradualist, gradually getting nowhere. You see, look around, I spend nothing on security and I am perfectly safe because I live and breathe the revolution. I have no impurities or ambitions. Charles wants influence and power. I ask, influence and power over what?"

"We must remove Spencer from command," Callista reiterated, then dropped the next shoe. "I believe he had our sister Allison Garvin executed to protect himself after the failure in New York."

Beers sat up and made an angry face.

"Yes, that makes sense. And he must have known that Allison favored me. It must be Charles who is responsible for her disappearance. I'll kill him myself."

"But he must be interrogated," Callista said.

"You excite me so," he said.

"A plan," she said, "we need a plan. Can you get Spencer to come here?"

"Charles wouldn't come here unless I had something he wanted."

"What would it take?"

Beers began to calculate exactly that.

"Yes," he said, talking back to his own thoughts, "that's exactly it."

"And it is?" Callista followed.

"It is a painting, a Turner I bought off the black market, not because I wanted the damn thing but because I admired the industry of the thieves who stole it. Charles was very jealous when I told him and he's tried to buy it from me on several occasions. He's an art lover, the fool."

Callista coaxed him. "What shall we do?"

"I'll call the poor slob and say 'Charles, come get the Turner, it's yours,' and I'll insist that he come secretly with no more than two guards, and we'll kill them all. You know how to do that part, I assume?"

"Yes," she said, "I will handle that. Are you sure he will come?"

"For that painting he will kiss my feet. I knew it would serve a purpose someday."

"And you will take command of the revolution in North America," Callista said.

"Treat me right," he said, threatening to loosen his robe, "and you will see to the day-to-day details of that."

"When the time is right," Callista said, "I will give you an experience that is beyond imagination."

"You are a fever," Beers said.

"I am the fever of death itself," she said.

"I know," he said. "You and I could kill half the world together."

41

Ryan looked at me, then at Yael. "Beers is serious," he said. "That skinny, half-naked little man would leap to support a plan to kill half the world. Bring him a plan to spread a genetically altered plague virus around the world to which there was no immunity and he'd jump at it."

"Maybe that is what we should do," Yael said. "Bring him a plan like that, get him excited about it, and then use that excitement."

"Use it for what?" I said.

"To somehow dismantle that revolutionary infrastructure he supports," Yael said, "before it really does get a shot at killing half the world.

Ryan stared at the image of Beers on the laptop as Beers plotted with Callista to bring Charles Spencer to Omaha.

"This lunatic had a devoted follower in a top position inside the White House. And she was part of a network in D.C. that included John Marshall Norton. Norton gave her up. But he protected the next level up. That level is run by Spencer, not by this old fart. He's a lone wolf of sorts. The inspired eccentric revolutionary who just wants to kill."

"And like Beers said," I added, "Spencer is the one who develops influence and power."

"It's more complicated than that," Yael said. "The role that Beers plays, the way he spends his money, his purity, as he called it, that's something Spencer doesn't have. It's something that he needs and fears. Beers is the sugar daddy of the revolutionary élan. He's the gothic degenerate who doesn't care whether he or anyone else lives or dies, just so long as the revolution survives. Charles Spencer is a bloodless technocrat by comparison."

"So," Ryan asked, "is it a two-way street? Does Beers need Charles Spencer or is he serious about killing him?"

"I think he really wants Spencer dead," I said. "Remember, Allison Garvin agreed with Beers on violence and he knew it, and Callista has hypnotized Beers into believing that it was Spencer who disappeared Garvin. Beers would kill Spencer over that, no question. It becomes a matter of warped revolutionary etiquette. Garvin was a Beers protégé. He thinks Spencer killed her. Spencer has to die."

"And then, Beers believes, he will take the reins of the revolution in North America," Ryan said, "with Callista, who came to his door an hour ago, as his chief lieutenant. Hello?"

"I know," Yael said, "it has all the logic of a dream. But what it boils down to is that Spencer and Beers both have the big money it takes to be the top revolutionary dog in America."

That got us laughing, but it was true. Behind the revolutionary infrastructure were two top beneficiaries of the capitalist wealth machine. Even the revolution to overthrow capitalism depended on capitalist prosperity to finance it. No great revelation.

As we sat there in the van a local police cruiser came down the opposite side of the street. The two cops in the car decided they didn't like something about us, put their flashers on, and pulled across in front of us. One of the officers was getting out to talk to Ryan, who was behind the wheel, while the other one ran our plates.

The cop at Ryan's window, peeking down to get a look at all three of us got as far as 'license' of 'license and registration' before Ryan had an identification card in his face that stopped him.

"This stop never happened," Ryan said to him. "Make sure of it."

"Yes, sir," the officer said. "Have a good day."

"Same to you," Ryan said.

As the cop turned back toward his cruiser Ryan and Yael, who was in the front passenger seat, moved so quickly that I reflexively held my breath.

Ryan had the cop who he had spoken to on the ground with a move that involved the cop's wrist, elbow, and a knee. Yael had her nine millimeter at the head of the cop in the cruiser and was carefully pulling him out from behind the wheel. She put him down on the pavement between the cruiser and the van.

Ryan was on his cell, briefly, and in less than a minute another van had pulled up, two men and a woman got out and cuffed the two cops on the ground. Ryan and Yael helped them get the cops into the back of the van. The two men got back in and drove off. The woman got into the police cruiser and drove it away.

"What just happened?" I asked Ryan and Yael as they got back in the van.

"They weren't cops," Ryan said.

"How do you know?"

"When I show that card to a local cop he has to give me a countersign," Ryan said.

"Which is?" I asked.

"Which is classified," Ryan said, flashing a grin.

"Well who were they if they weren't cops?"

"That's what our friends are finding out right now, but I don't think it's going to be good."

"So Beers does have security," I said.

"Probably not Beers," Yael said.

"Then they might work for Spencer," I said.

"That's a reasonable guess," she said.

Ryan's cell rang. He answered and listened.

"They're an unregistered security outfit," he said when he got off. "Ex-cops. They were hired by a shell operation to keep an eye on Beers' estate."

"Who set up the shell?" Yael asked.

"Still working on that," Ryan said, "but I think it leads to a dead end. That would probably mean it's Spencer."

"Then Spencer probably has someone inside the house as well," Yael said. "One of those girls."

"At least one of them," Ryan said. "The good news is that there hasn't been any communication out of the house since Callista went in."

"How do we know that?" I asked.

"They're being monitored," Yael said.

Ryan touched a small microphone attached to the cuff of his shirt.

"Callista," he said and waited for her to nod so that the shot from her camera bobbed up and down. "One or more of the girls in the house is likely a hostile." The camera shot bobbed again in acknowledgment.

"Shouldn't that cop, that ex-cop, have known he needed to give you a countersign?" I asked.

"He did know," Ryan said, "that's why he tried to beat it back to the cruiser like that. He was hoping I would let it slide."

"Why didn't he have the countersign?"

"It changes, Mara."

"How often?"

"Classified," Ryan said.

"Hey, I'm on the team."

"Need to know," he said.

"Why couldn't that cop, as an ex-cop, have access to the current countersign? He must still know plenty of cops."

"That's right, but for an active cop to give up that countersign is a one-way ticket to hell. Because someone like me is going to come around and collect on that bet."

"That serious?" I said.

"That serious," Ryan said. "Remember the fake cop who blew up the townhouse? That serious."

"Rob was mortified by that," I said.

"Yes he was," Ryan said. "It's a basic terrorist ploy and preventing it is basic to counterterrorism."

Ryan's attention was distracted to the laptop. Beers had grown weary of revolutionary plotting and had thrown open his robe. Callista was barking at him to behave.

"You are so dreary, my darling, so serious," he said, "all revolution and no play makes Franklin a dull boy. Surely you can take pity on me."

Had Callista had real pity on Beers she might have snapped his neck for him, but instead she used her revolutionary authority to again successfully order the closing of the robe.

Mao himself had been a filthy murdering degenerate. Beers claimed to have met him, and I didn't doubt that. Perhaps it was straight from Mao that Beers had acquired his casual taste for mass violence. I remembered the sanitized image of Mao that some of my radical friends had during my college days. Five minutes worth of facts could have disabused them even then, but the revolution specializes in not listening, not even for that long.

I flashed on the General entering the building at the Yucatan airstrip and executing Allison Garvin. I thought that he did that because she had enraged him and she had enraged him because she dismissed all meaning outside of the revolutionary cause.

Beers had done the same, even more so. It had probably been fifty years since he had given a thought to anything but the revolution, or his addiction to sex.

42

Charles Spencer had a flat, soft British voice. His tone with Beers was that of a doctor barely restraining himself with a hypochondriac patient who called several times a day. We listened in the van to their conversation. Callista had put a device on Beers' land line.

"I'm rather pressed, Beersy," Spencer said wearily as he took the call after Beers had insisted to a chain of assistants that he needed to be put through.

"I have something for you, Charles. It's going to make your day," Beers said.

"Go ahead, then," Spencer said.

"My Turner, it's yours."

"Say that again," Spencer said, his tone more friendly.

"I want to give you the Turner. I know you like it, and I want you to have it, for all you've done."

"I don't quite know what to say. That's just so lovely of you, Beers."

"One condition," Beers said. "You come by to pick it up, so that I can see you and we can chat about a few items."

"I can do that, of course," Spencer said.

"How soon?"

"I can fly out there tonight. For the Turner, and you of course, I'll cancel whatever."

"One thing more, Charles. Could you please limit your private military guards to just two. The last time you were here I had nightmares for a week."

"That's perfectly reasonable, Franklin. I do get carried away with the security," Spencer said.

"They might have a pill for that now, Charles," Beers joked.

"I'll see you later, then, tonight. Expect me, and thank you so much for this gift. Really, Beers, it's dreadfully kind of you." Spencer sounded sincere.

The call ended and Beers immediately began to cackle about it to Callista.

"See, see, I told you, my sweetest darling. See, I know where Charles is weak. I knew he'd be a kitten over the Turner. I'm the only one in the world with the key to that steel heart."

"But will he like me?" Callista asked.

"Charles? That's a very good question. I think any man should like you. But Charles's mistress is money and power and his stick-up-the-ass pedantic idea of the revolution. Could you attract him away from that? I don't think so, darling. That's what the Turner was for. But, wait, will he like you? I remember once seeing him around with a gorgeous actress. She was a revolutionary, of course, such as it goes. Don't know what happened to that. Yes, though, you give Charles your full frontal revolutionary self and he might relax with you. But don't get into the bourgeois excess of the Turner. Don't call him on that. You'll infuriate him. Remember also that he has just had the huge failure in New York. Don't let on you know about it."

Beers went on in a stream of consciousness, eventually discoursing on how he and Charles Spencer had once teamed up to denounce a third wealthy revolutionary they knew. It all began as an effort to get him to shut up a bit, but led to him being assassinated by a younger zealot who took to heart their accusations that the wealthy comrade was a counter-revolutionary.

Ryan got a call in the middle of that. It was about the rogue security outfit whose fake cops we had taken down.

"They don't belong to Spencer," Ryan said.

"Who then?" Yael asked.

"To Beers, but the outfit doesn't know that. We found it out."

"My question is, does Beers know it himself?" I said.

"That's a good question because the job was contracted for several years ago, was never cancelled, the outfit gets a routine quarterly payment, well into six figures. But there's no other activity. They don't file any reports."

"They just ride past the estate and collect their money?" Yael said. "I'm not ready to buy that."

"Maybe Beers had an attack of paranoia," I said, "hired them, and forgot about it. He doesn't attend to his own finances, and his money people wouldn't quibble about a security expense."

"Does this outfit have anyone inside the house?" Yael asked.

"No," Ryan said, "but that doesn't mean that one or more of those women in there doesn't work for someone."

"With Beersy's eye for purity, maybe they are all there just for him," I said.

"There's that, the pure purity of it," Yael said.

"It's good news the fake cops weren't Spencer's people," I said.

"Still doesn't feel right," Yael said.

"I'm blank on it," Ryan said. "But why would Beers hide his own interest in the surveillance of his house from the security outfit he hired to do it?"

"He was paranoid that his paranoia would damage his reputation as the totally carefree revolutionary," I said. "He didn't want it to get out that he was concerned for his own safety. It would spoil his image."

"Not buyin'," Yael said.

I trusted Yael's instincts. Ryan said we would leave it as an open question and focus on the arrival of Charles Spencer later that night. It was already twilight in Omaha.

"He's not coming with just two security people," Ryan said. "That's how many he'll take inside with him. He'll bring an army and leave it out here in the street. The General wants zero violence."

"Beers expects Callista to kill Spencer and his guards," Yael said. "Once that bubble bursts for him, he'll be unpredictable."

"And regardless of the fact that Spencer is only taking two men inside with him they'll be wired to the team outside," Ryan said.

"We're backed into a corner," Yael said. "We got ahead of ourselves. There's no opportunity here."

"Opportunity?" I asked.

"To do anything with Spencer, grab him, or control him," Yael said. "We've jumped the gun."

"We're using what we had and what we could develop out of it, Yael," Ryan said.

"I understand," Yael said. "But Spencer is a contingency freak. We're not cracking that or catching a break on it."

"We'll have him inside the house," Ryan said.

"With his army just outside," Yael said.

"We'll take them out," Ryan said.

"How," she asked.

"Spencer travels with a contingent of three corporate jets. His personal jet, with aides and immediate bodyguards. A jet with his surrounding security team. And a jet with his advance team that will arrange for all surface transport and will show up here to check things out in a few hours. Unless they give the O.K., Spencer won't come here. So there's no point in us having an operation set in place right here because it will get made by them and they'll have Spencer cancel his visit."

"And if we move in after Spencer gets here," Yael said, "the thing blows up. Where are our options?"

"We need to put Spencer's men out, put them to sleep," Ryan said.

"Ryan?" Yael said skeptically.

"I'm thinking," he said.

"Well think fast," she said.

"The vehicles," Ryan said. "We'll get to the vehicles they reserve for ground travel and we'll..."

"We will what?" Yael said.

"We'll make them, we'll make it so there's something in the vehicles that will put them out."

"Something they won't turn up when they inspect and search the vehicles," Yael said.

"Of course," Ryan said.

"Because they will find any sort of container, anything like that," she said.

"I know," he said, "but they won't find something that's just sprayed inside the vehicles."

"That does what?" she said.

"That puts them out."

"When? How? If we can't control when it happens, then it's useless," she said.

I hadn't seen the two of them like this before. She was flogging him with her skepticism, but the purpose was to push him. He was the tactical genius. She was telling him he had nothing. He wouldn't accept it.

I had no idea how Ryan would make it happen, but I wasn't a skeptic. He was one of those guys who if you gave him a strand of wire he'd find a way to turn it into a water purification plant.

He got on his cell and began describing exactly what he needed to someone on the other end. It was basically a colorless, odorless liquid that could be sprayed on the interior surfaces of vehicles that would outgas at levels that would make human beings unconscious when heated with infrared waves or microwaves. Could he please get some of that right now.

43

It was near the end of twilight, not yet dark, when I excused myself to the back of the van. Yael had arranged squares of folded blankets to create a lounge chair on the floor. It elevated your head and your knees. I was going to grab ten minutes.

When I woke up I checked my watch. I had been out for fifty minutes. By our standard of time the world had been around the block eighty times. It was dark and the van was empty. Ryan and Yael had stepped out. I moved into the front passenger seat and poured myself a cup of coffee from the tall thermos we kept.

We were no longer parked where we had been. I guessed we were several blocks away, out of any reasonable range of interest of Charles Spencer's security. There was an SUV parked in front of us, with heavily tinted windows. I guessed that Ryan and Yael were inside it, meeting with other team members. If they had needed me, they would have called me out of sleep.

I sat there drinking my coffee in the dark, staring blankly at the darkened rear window of the SUV. My mind's edge was coming back, like a lost dog finding its way home. There was heavy movement inside the SUV. Then two flashes of light, one right after another. It felt like gunfire, silenced. I waited.

Ryan got out of the SUV first, then Yael, then the General, who was wearing a tan raincoat over his suit. The SUV pulled away, and I moved with my coffee to one of the rear seats. Yael got in next to me, Ryan got behind the wheel, and the General took the front passenger seat I had just vacated. No one said anything, not a word. The usual rush of questions filled my head, but I knew better. Something had just happened that wasn't going to be discussed.

A few minutes passed. Another SUV pulled up alongside us, and the General got out of our van and into the SUV and it drove off.

In the van we continued to say nothing. We weren't even looking at one another. Ryan took the thermos and poured some coffee and handed it to Yael. Then he turned and refilled my cup. He poured a cup for himself. In this long silence I could feel the grim, calloused, solitary anguish of both of them. I knew they would never tell me what had just happened, and if I asked they would deny that anything had.

Ryan opened a laptop to a series of camera views. They covered the outside of Franklin Beers' mansion and the street out front. The shot from inside, via Callista's eyeglasses, showed Beers still going on with great animation, trying to fascinate, or simply reflecting his fascination with, Callista.

My eye for surveillance shots had improved. I pointed at the screen and broke the cold silence.

"Spencer's advance team?" I asked, referring to two black vans parked on the street.

"Yes," Ryan said, without a hint of anything but his usual straightforwardness.

"When is their master set to arrive?" I asked.

"He's in the air. We're expecting him here in about ninety minutes."

"So," I said, "what's the plan?"

"The General," Ryan said and then paused to sip coffee, "has changed his mind and wants Spencer taken, under whatever circumstances."

"You mean the 'no violence' order he gave..." I started.

"Has changed," Ryan finished.

"What changed it?" I asked.

"The General learned that Spencer has accelerated plans for more attacks. That's been his response to Allison Garvin's and John Marshall Norton's disappearances. Since they went missing, and with the thwarted attack in New York, Spencer has come around more to Beers' view on violence. He's also feeling cornered, so he wants to shake things up, put a fresh face on the cause, as if American society was some company that he owned."

"So we're grabbing Spencer?" I said.

"And Beers," Yael said.

"That's special," I said, unable to think of anything else.

"But with these security teams of Spencer's," Ryan said, "we're looking at a potential level of violence that will attract attention and because it involves Spencer, make world headlines."

"That's bad," I said.

"That's unacceptable," Yael said.

"But the General says it's now or never," I said.

"Exactly," Ryan said.

"What about your plan to put Spencer's security out inside their vehicles?" I asked.

"In place, but untried and untested. High probability of failure," Ryan answered. "In a perfect situation they go out and don't wake up until we've left the scene with Spencer in hand, then they waste time dithering about what happened. But the consensus is that it won't work like that and there will be combat. All of Spencer's people have Special Forces level capability. We know what to do with them, but these people are trained to survive and turn it around."

"Are you saying that we would lose to them?" I asked.

"I'm saying," Ryan responded, "that they could prolong the operation long enough to bring all the locals in around us. Then the public spectacle and the behind-the-scenes arrangements we have with the locals come crashing into each other, and with Spencer involved it's a mess that can't be untangled."

"But it's less of a mess, much less, than if any of Spencer's planned terrorist attacks succeed," I said.

"That's the point the General's decision turned on," Ryan said.

"We just can't lose Spencer," I said.

"No, we can't," Ryan agreed, "and if we can't take him, the General wants him dead."

"But that's a huge loss for us because we need Spencer to give us his whole operation," I said.

"Yes," Ryan said.

Ryan tapped a key on the laptop. He enlarged the window with the shot from Callista inside the house. Something had caught his attention.

Beers was pacing back and forth in his library, wildly waving his arms. With the volume up we heard him denouncing Charles Spencer as a weak revolutionary without nerve or guts.

"Charles is nothing more than a pussy," Beers kept shouting, "and when you kill him my dearest I am going to reward you. In fact, you'll have anything you need and on top of that I'll make you my sole heir. My kingdom for the head of Charles Spencer. And then you and I will show them the true face of the revolution!"

He had been going on like that for hours, but it was beginning to look less like a rant and more like a psychotic break with reality.

"If that delusion is fixed," I said, "maybe we can ride it."

"I don't get what you're saying," Ryan said.

"Beers sounds like he's offering to give Callista control of his fortune," I said, "so that with Spencer out of the way she can prosecute the revolution, or is he just not serious?"

"Well, if he is serious," Ryan said, "you're saying we could leave Callista in place and, what, gain control of his billions?"

"At least," I said.

Ryan focused on it. As he thought about it, I regretted raising the question. Beers was just unstable and manic. It would be a loose bet, at best, to try to use Callista to work the situation beyond tonight. I needed to start thinking more before I spoke.

But Ryan continued to mull it over. He got out of the van and made a call on his cell.

"You could be right, Mara," Yael said. "If we take Spencer and Beers thinks he's dead and that Callista arranged it, he'll worship her. We can get effective control of his money."

"But then he'll want results," I said. "He'll want Callista to orchestrate relentless revolutionary violence."

"Well," Yael said, "by the time he becomes dissatisfied she's already worked her way so deep into his situation that we can just medicate him out of the picture, or something."

"Right," I said, "or something."

Ryan got back into the van.

"The General likes it," he said. "He said to tell you that you lift his spirits, Mara. He likes the way you think."

I looked at the shot of Beers, still ranting, on the laptop.

"Are you saying that I inspire the General..."

"Don't even say it," Ryan said, smiling for the first time since the incident in the SUV.

44

Charles Spencer arrived at the Beers mansion in a motorcade of three black SUVs. Only the one carrying Spencer drove through the gate and up the driveway. The other two parked on the street along with the two SUVs that had arrived earlier with the advance team.

From observers at the airport we knew that there were five men in each of the four SUVs parked on the street. The SUVs were heavily armored vehicles with bulletproof glass, and the men inside wore body armor and had a variety of weapons available to them. In Spencer's SUV there were, besides Spencer, his two immediate bodyguards and the driver. The two bodyguards, as Beers had requested, would be the only security who would accompany Spencer into the house.

The twenty-man team back on the street could respond in seconds to a call from the two bodyguards inside with Spencer. From a military point of view, Ryan had explained, the twenty men in the SUVs, as well as the two guards with Spencer and his driver, were at Special Forces level in training and experience, many of them recruited from the British SAS. They constituted a small, lethal army and would be the good bet against a much larger contingent of conventional soldiers.

Ryan had guessed correctly that the men in the SUVs would stay in the vehicles until and unless they became alert to a threat. They weren't looking to attract any attention and stretching their legs was not going to be a high priority. As long as they remained in the vehicles they were sitting ducks for Ryan's plan.

These vehicles were rented for the duration of Spencer's hours on the ground while he completed his visit with Beers and returned to the airport for the flight out. Our people had gotten to the vehicles beforehand, at the garage of the rental agency. The interiors were sprayed with a chemical. When Ryan gave the word a helicopter would make a pass over the street and blast the vehicles with microwaves. The men inside wouldn't be cooked, but their skin would tingle and they would feel uncomfortable. Before they could do anything about that, or so went the theory, the dried liquid would outgas a vapor that would render them unconscious.

"What is it?" I asked Ryan.

"The gas? I don't know. They wouldn't tell me," he said.

"Why not?"

"They didn't want me to know," he said.

"Do you think it will work?"

"No, not really. It might make them angry, though, which won't help us."

"But it was your idea. You asked for it and the tech people delivered," I said.

"I know," Ryan said.

"Now you've lost confidence in it."

"No, I'm just being realistic. Bright ideas usually aren't that bright. Fortunately, most of them aren't tried. But we needed something here to avoid the inevitable."

"The inevitable?" I said.

"Yes. We're going to light them up if that gas doesn't work."

"We're going to kill them?"

"Yes, Mara, we're going to kill them."

"And with Spencer grabbed," I said, "that's a world terrorism headline. If they're all asleep, it's just a mysterious disappearance. Big difference."

"Yes," Ryan said, "big difference."

Charles Spencer waited in his vehicle for a few minutes and then got out, one of his guards opening and holding the door for him. Spencer was medium height with the posture of an arrow. He was boyishly thin. But he had a face like a straight razor. It was sharp and threatening.

Franklin Beers greeted him outside the entrance. Beers had exchanged the silk robe for trousers, shirt and tie, and a jacket. Callista wasn't with him so we didn't hear the conversation outside but it didn't become involved. The exchanged greetings appeared warm but they were brief, and the two men went directly into the mansion, Beers taking Spencer by the arm. The two guards followed.

Beers had sent his team of half-dressed women to the nether regions of the mansion and called in the housekeeping staff. They had put the place in order for Spencer's visit and also provided the means for our people to get inside. Among them was Tony, who had been Allison Garvin's minder during her brief stay as our guest.

Our view of Spencer got a bit sharper as he was introduced to Callista. Spencer turned out to be just another man after all, as he disintegrated at the sight of her. It was obvious that Spencer now wanted more than the Turner from Beers.

Callista gave us a view of Spencer's guards, who were positioned in the entry foyer, where they could look in on Spencer as he sat with Beers and Callista in the main room. Their fatal mistake was taking it for granted that the house was safe for them and for Spencer.

"Charles," Beers said, "I want you to know something about Callista. She is not just another pretty face."

"Certainly not," Spencer said, glowing even hotter.

"No, listen to me," Beers said, "she more precisely embodies our way of thinking than anyone I've met in fifty years. I compare her to the early Mao. She has a steel heart for the revolution."

"Is that so, Callista," Spencer asked, "or has Beers gotten carried away?"

"I'll say this much," Callista said flatly, "if I had a hand in the matter, your miserable failure in New York would not go unpunished."

"Oh, dear," Beers said, "see, Charles, she's a lioness."

Spencer's face froze and went numb.

At that moment I heard the roar of the copter overhead. Ryan had given the order and it was sweeping above the street.

"You impudent piece of trash," Spencer spat out at Callista. She gave us a view of Spencer's guards. They were looking in with concern at the harsh tone of their master's words.

The copter had completed its sweep. The men in the SUVs should be unconscious. On the monitor the rear door of one opened and one of the men stumbled out, fell to the pavement, and appeared to go unconscious.

Callista's view of Spencer's guards showed one and then the other go down. Each had taken a head shot. Tony appeared over them.

Spencer was in shock, Beers confused. Callista's hand appeared in her view and she sprayed each of them in the face with something she held in it. They both slumped over, passed out.

In the street one of ours, weapon out, crouched at the side of the man on the pavement and took his neck pulse. He swept his finger across his own throat, signaling us.

"What's he saying?" I asked Ryan.

"The guy's dead."

Our man then checked the other four men inside the vehicle and swept his finger across his throat again. They were all dead.

"The General," was all Ryan said.

Our man lifted the dead security man off the pavement and shoved him back into the SUV.

Tony stepped into view in front of the mansion to check Spencer's driver. He was dead.

Four more of our men appeared on the street and began ventilating the four SUVs by starting them up and lowering their automatic windows. That precaution taken, they all got in behind the wheels and drove them off with their cargoes of dead men.

Inside the house Tony and Callista wrapped up the bodies of the two guards and carried them out to the SUV. Another one of our men showed up to drive that away.

Then one of our vans showed up and Tony and Callista brought Spencer and Beers out, both still unconscious, and put them in the back. The van took off and Tony and Callista went back inside, to tidy up, I assumed.

The back door to our van opened and the General stepped in and took a seat behind Ryan and me.

"The plan was altered," Ryan said flatly.

"Just slightly," the General said.

"We've killed twenty-three men," Ryan said.

"Yes," the General said, "and you see," he waved his hand palm up in front of the camera shots on the laptop screen, "all gone. No mess."

"My idea was more elegant," Ryan said.

"Good idea," the General said, "too much margin for error."

Ryan brusquely cleared his throat, but didn't say another word.

45

"That irritated you, didn't it?" I said to Ryan after the General left us.

"Him changing the plan?"

"Not telling you he changed it."

"No. There was a chance of failure, both ways. He made it less likely. What irritated me was that I passed right over his option without giving it a thought."

"You didn't immediately think of killing those men inside their vehicles," I said, "because it violated your principles."

"That's probably right," he said. "On the surface, killing men in that way does violate my principles."

"But below the surface?"

"Below the surface they were the private army of a man who just planned and financed mass murder, which we stopped with this much to spare." Ryan held his thumb and forefinger a hair apart.

"Were they culpable in that?" I said. "I mean, it's unlikely they knew anything about it. They could not have formed guilty minds about it if they didn't know. Under law, they could not have been convicted as accessories to Spencer's conspiracy."

"This wasn't an action taken under civil law," Ryan said. "Spencer is, was, waging war, asymmetrical war, planning it, and advancing his plan to execution. He turned those men into combatants. My plan would have shown them mercy and just left them unconscious and later confused, with headaches. But you heard what I was saying before. I didn't think the plan would work and we'd wind up with a live fire fight. The General eliminated that possibility or, I should say, greatly lowered its probability."

"He did the right thing?" I asked.

"Absolutely the right thing. He was also taking final responsibility for ordering the operation."

"Still," I said, "those were probably good men."

"Probably were," he said. "I probably could have used them on our team. But they got caught working for the wrong insane billionaire at the wrong time."

"And they would have killed our people for trying to get at Spencer," I said.

"Precisely," Ryan said.

"But," I said, "if we had shown up with a warrant for Spencer's arrest, that entire army, all those security men would have stood down."

"O.K.," Ryan said, "but we don't have any legally obtained evidence against Spencer under the terms of civil law. We couldn't present an affidavit to a judge seeking a warrant because we're not law enforcement."

"But we could set up a civil law enforcement agency with sufficient evidence," I said.

"Not on this one, with this time frame. These two things, civil justice and the asymmetrical battlefield, they occupy the same time and space, but they are totally different. Each has its own rules, and trying to pass the events of asymmetrical battle into the realm of civil justice could set off a conflict that would make us more vulnerable by having our own civil values working against us. In fact, that is one of the secondary goals and primary tactics of terrorists. They love getting their target societies caught in that double-bind. Charles Spencer, and Beersy, both put a lot of their cash into groups that press that angle, and lots of people buy into it."

"Am I one of them, you think?" I asked.

"I think you might have been," he said.

"Past tense," I said.

"Past tense," he said.

"But I still ask questions," I said. "I have to. It's my nature."

"We all ask questions, Mara. But doing what we're doing, we can't afford not to have answers. The General made a call tonight that was a battlefield decision. It was about warfare in an unconventional battlespace, with its own rules and its own ethical considerations. Try to put this in a civil justice context and you allow Spencer or any potential terrorist to shape the battlefield his way and lock you in. He makes you guilty of defending yourself."

"But where is the line of authority here, Ryan?"

"'Here' is a shadow world that doesn't exist, Mara. This team doesn't exist. This mission didn't happen. And there is no line of authority to it."

"But you have an identification card, Ryan, that requires local law enforcement to give you a countersign before stepping away."

"Yes, that seems to contradict what I just said."

"Well," I said, "what is that about?"

"That's classified," he said, smiling again.

"How can something that doesn't exist be classified and come with a magic card?" I asked.

"It's like quantum physics," he said.

"Like what?"

"Quantum physics. It's not anything until you look at it, and so you had best not look at it."

"I am lookin' at it, brother, but it ain't turnin' into anything," I said, reaching for some saving irony.

"That's to the better," he said.

"Can I say something to you in confidence, Ryan?"

"Absolutely," he said.

"I think that the General is a lunatic, every bit the lunatic that, say, Franklin Beers is."

"The General has his eccentricities."

"The General," I said, "walked into that building in the jungle and shot the White House deputy chief of staff in the head while she was shackled to a chair. That's more than 'eccentricities'."

"That was a legit battlefield execution, Mara. She was in essence a spy and a very dangerous one. Spies get shot. She had confessed and she had no remorse."

"The General shot her in anger," I said.

"That's true. He wasn't in his clearest mind."

"And you thought she had more value alive," I said.

"But not that she deserved to live, only that she could give us more. The General's reasoning, despite his anger, was that if she got away from us, was rescued, she would be right back inside the White House, more dangerous, much more dangerous."

"But, really," I said, "what were the chances we would have lost control of her?"

"Are you kidding?" Ryan said. "There was a massive, fully mobilized search for her. We had to ditch and burn two of our facilities."

"But we made it O.K. Did we really need to kill Garvin?"

"First of all, that was no small item, having the Pensacola facility blown. Second, even if you could calculate a final decision of 'need,' Garvin was still executed on the basis of her guilt and the danger she continued to pose if we lost her. Yes, the

General pulled the trigger in anger, but he knew what he was doing, and he knew that it was justified."

"Still," I said, "it looked right to me in that moment, but in retrospect it looks wrong."

"Well, use your reason, not your feelings or the look on the General's face to evaluate it. Go back again to the facts. She worked in the White House, a top aide to the President of the United States. She was complicit in a plan to murder tens of thousands of Americans in a terrorist attack. She had no remorse. She confessed. She literally was the enemy. She would have been even more powerful if she had been rescued. She would have destroyed us, and become a national hero, constructing a new web of lies. That, not the General's anger, is why he angrily shot her in the head."

"Now I want to shoot her in the head," I said.

"Got you worked up, did I?"

"I think I'm feeling what the General felt."

"No, you're thinking what he thought and then feeling how those thoughts made him feel, and now you're right there with him, putting that bullet in Allison Garvin's head yourself."

"You did that to me," I said.

"You wanted to understand the General's decision, but you couldn't see it outside the context of his anger. His anger distorted the picture for you. And you must have seen, in your career, a judge hand down a decision or sentence a criminal and be angry even as he gave his reasoning."

"I have seen that," I said.

"And how did you handle it?" Ryan asked.

"I noted the anger and gave my attention to the judge's reasoning."

"Did you ever come to anger from reasoning?"

"You mean my own reasoning?"

"Yes."

"Of course," I said.

"Did you feel that the anger that arose from the reasoning invalidated the reasoning?"

"No," I said.

"Well I'm pretty sure the General has a clear conscience about killing Garvin, despite his anger. And if the General has anything, it's a fully formed conscience."

46

Charles Spencer, hedging against his own abduction, had three microchip implants that signaled his location, each at a different frequency. Those were the first thing our team looked for, and they were disabled while Spencer was still unconscious. I wasn't surprised by the redundancy of microchips, but I was amused. Franklin Beers, the purer and even more murderous revolutionary, had no such implants. In addition to not caring about anyone else's life, he had liberated himself from caring very much about his own.

Part of the General's intent in refining Ryan's plan was to again make use of the ruse, especially with Spencer, that he had been taken prisoner by his own side. He was to be allowed to believe that he had run afoul of a revolutionary faction intent on denouncing and purging him. That ruse was already begun with Beers, who believed Callista to be the most promising revolutionary murderer since Mao.

I was skeptical that Spencer would buy in wholesale the way Beers had, but I also doubted whether the charade could be maintained with Beers. Beers was loopy but he wasn't stupid. But against either of these men I didn't want to underestimate Callista, who was a symphony orchestra of psychological manipulation. Having watched how she unhesitatingly walked right into Beers' life and used his sex addiction to get him to buy into her revolutionary fervor, I wouldn't bet against her. Spencer, though, was paranoid and hyper-vigilant. He suspected everyone. And Beers, for his part, had already been fooled once.

Ryan, Yael, and I arrived by helicopter at a makeshift facility in New Mexico that consisted of a large metal building and two house trailers. Everything about the building and the trailers was beaten-up and ad hoc. Spencer and Beers were both awake and in separate interrogation rooms inside the metal building, which had no air-conditioning and was beastly hot.

We were in an observation room with a large fan and two closed-circuit television monitors, one featuring Spencer and the other Beers. Both were shackled to chairs. Beers looked sleepy, while Spencer managed to look coldly annoyed.

Callista went right in with Spencer after we arrived.

"You know why you are here, Spencer?" she said.

"That's Mr. Spencer and I not only do not know why I'm here, I do not care. You, you filthy little whore, are dead. You'll find that out soon enough. When my security people get hold of you and your gang – are you all listening? – your head is going to explode, literally, and that lovely face of yours will look like one of my Picassos."

Callista let him finish. She maintained such a flat affect that it was making me slightly nauseous.

"Your failure, Spencer, your repeated failures, plural, in New York and elsewhere have set the movement back years, perhaps decades," she said.

"Shut your mouth, you tramp," Spencer shouted. "Don't dare presume to lecture me about the movement. I am the movement. Do you realize that?"

"There is your problem, Spencer, the source of your failure," she said. "You believe that you embody the revolution instead of serving it. That demonstrates a counterrevolutionary error, a fatal flaw, and it explains your failures."

"Listen to me, you filthy, disgusting whore," Spencer said, struggling against his restraints, "when I get out of this, before my men kill you, I'm going to have them do things to you that you cannot even imagine. I'm utterly serious. I'll have them carefully pluck your eyes out of their sockets so that they'll hang down your face, and that will be the start."

"Oh," Callista said to that, "did you think that the microchips we found implanted in your body were still active? There's no one coming for you, Spencer."

That focused his attention.

"Who are you?" he said.

"I work for the new leadership in North America. You've been purged for your failures. I'm here to interrogate you before you are tried. And your security force is dead, by the way. So there's no cavalry left to ride in to save you."

"The new leadership, you say?" Spencer said, "And who might that be?"

"I'm sorry," Callista said, "but that's not something you have any need to know."

"Well here's the deal I have for you, you stupid bitch. Right now there are five, got that, five operations in motion that will address my so-called failures, as if you had any idea about the delicacy and complexity of a serious operation. Each of those five, any one of them, will turn the U.S. domestic situation on its head. Do you hear me? Do you understand me? So you go to this new leadership and you tell it that they are screwing the bloody pooch. All right? I need to manage the aftermath of these operations, and if I don't they will become wasted opportunities. Any of that sinking into that revolutionary brain?"

Callista greeted these proclamations with a smirk.

"So many, many years of failure and suddenly you have perfect plans. The new leadership discussed letting you live in retirement, but I'm inclined now to recommend you be executed. You are making me sick, with your sudden perfect plans. How many years, how many opportunities have you wasted? I should kill you right now, myself."

"No, dammit," Spencer said, "listen to me. You have no idea what you are doing. This is ridiculous. Get me your superior. Get him in here. I have to explain this to someone who can make rational decisions."

Callista let her face fall further into affectless disinterest and it visibly drained Spencer. He was breaking. She turned and left him alone.

Seconds later she walked into the observation room and, as if she were an eager novice, her demeanor transformed and cheery, she asked us how we thought it was going.

I just smiled. Ryan enthusiastically said it was O.K. Yael said, "Great, keep at him."

"He's a little full of himself, don't you think?" Callista said.

"Yeah, just a little," I said, holding back a laugh.

She spun around, happy with our approval, and left. We all looked at one another in mild disbelief. Seconds later she was back in the interrogation room and threw a pad and pen down on the table in front of Spencer. Then she asked him which hand he wrote with. He said his left. She unshackled his left arm but to compensate bent his right arm more tightly around the back of the chair and secured it forcefully.

"Write a full confession and the new leadership will consider your case. If you choose to, you can use the pen to commit suicide. No one will try to stop you. So your options are clear. If you write I advise you to be thorough. I'm already sick of talking to you and having you waste my time. Think of the revolution first, instead of yourself, for a change."

She left the room again and Spencer hungrily went at his task. He appeared convinced that he would save his life, even restore his own power and position.

Callista now went in with Beers, who was withering in the heat. He got lively at the immediate sight of her.

"My darling," he said, "thank goodness you're here. Where is here, by the way, and can you please let me out of these contraptions."

"Beers," she said, rushing to loosen his restraints, "I'm so sorry you've been treated like this. My comrades are fools. They assume that you are like Charles Spencer. I'm talking to them, trying to explain your value, your purity."

"Well first things first, darling. Can I get a glass of water and a quick piece of ass? That will restore my strength."

"Beers," she said, "you mustn't talk like that. Some of my sisters don't understand your ways."

"So send them in here one by one, or all at once, and I'll educate them," Beers said, undaunted by the threat of Callista's puritan sisterhood.

She held her forefinger to her lips to warn him to keep silent and left him alone and unshackled. He rubbed his wrists, trying to take the numbness out of them. She returned with two bottles of water and Beers began to gulp one down.

"Have you killed Charles?" he asked hopefully.

"Not yet," she said, "we're having him write a confession first."

"How wonderful," Beers said. "How perfect. You people do things the old way, the proven way. I hope you had to beat it out of him. Did you? Did you beat the damn confession right out of him?"

"He's telling us now that he has five terror operations in motion, Beersy, to make up for that fiasco in New York." She stood back a bit and let that sink in.

"He says five?" Beers said. "It's not like Charles to say five when all he'd need to do was convince you that there was one plan. If he was lying he'd just say one. He must be telling you the truth. Maybe there's hope for Charles yet."

47

When Charles Spencer finished writing, Callista went in and took the pad and left without saying a word to him.

"Are we going to see that?" I asked Ryan about Spencer's confession.

"I don't know," he said, "but something feels wrong here."

"What?" I said, looking from him to Yael and back again.

"That man looks awfully pleased with himself," Ryan said.

"He does, doesn't he," I agreed.

We silently watched Spencer. A few minutes later Callista stuck her head in the door and called Ryan out. She had only been there for a moment but her appearance struck me.

"Did she seem pale to you?" I asked Yael.

"Yes," Yael said, "there's something wrong."

It was a funny thing to say again, that there was 'something wrong,' in the midst of all this and where we had been. But something was wrong, and it was crackling in the air around us. It had to do with what Spencer had written.

Ryan was gone for a half hour. When he returned he sat down and I could see he was focused on controlling his breathing. His face was tight but without expression.

"Let's have it," Yael said.

"Spencer has got his hands on a nuclear weapon."

"Where is it?" Yael asked.

"It was in Indonesia, in the possession of an Islamic group there, but Spencer purposely took himself and everyone else in his network out of the loop. The team carrying the weapon is on its own. Spencer planned it like that. He doesn't know where they are or who they are."

"Do we have a target?" Yael asked.

"Spencer left it at New York, D.C., or Los Angeles. It's at the discretion of the bomb team. When the weapon is detonated in one of those cities, they get the rest of their money."

"How much?" I asked.

"Seventy-five million," Ryan said.

"That's a lot of motivation," Yael said.

"How soon?" I asked.

"Very. The best Spencer could estimate was within days because the bomb team has a lot of latitude, with the directive to get it done right."

"What else?" Yael said. "Spencer bragged about five distinct plans."

"Well, the others are planned to more or less converge after the nuclear blast. There's a massive cyber attack he's contracted for with a Chinese group. There's an array of attacks on major urban water and sewage treatment facilities, which he thinks will start cholera outbreaks. That dovetails with a mass mailing of anthrax intended, at minimum, to shut down the postal system. The final touch is an attempt to crash the electricity grid in the northeast. The nuclear weapon is the centerpiece. The General believes we can shut down the other attacks, but the way the nuclear attack is set up, it's out of our reach."

"What's our plan?" Yael asked.

"We don't have one yet," he said. "The General is taking a moment to control his rage."

"He's angry?" Yael said.

"He thinks that Spencer needs to be dead."

"Spencer holds the keys to this," I said.

"That's what I told the General," Ryan said.

"How did he respond?" Yael said.

"He said that he knew that and didn't need to be reminded. And I said 'but you'll kill Spencer with that still out there,' and he cooled off a little."

"So is he going to kill Spencer or not?" Yael asked.

"I think he'll wait."

As Ryan spoke we saw on the monitor that the General had gone into the interrogation room that Beers was in."

"And who are you?" Beers said to him.

"I'm the grim reaper," the General said.

"You've come to kill me, have you," Beers said.

"Yes," the General said.

"Well get on with it or bugger off," Beers said, "death will be easier than looking at your boy scout face. You were a boy scout, weren't you?"

"What made you who you are, Beers?" the General said.

"Money," Beers said. "You can't see through the world without money, and I have seen through the world. It's rotten out there and I've always wanted to just blow it up. I'd kill every last thing but the prettiest girls if I could. And if I found things in a bad way one morning, I'd kill myself, without another thought about it. That, my dear boy scout, is the real revolution, the real utopian dream."

The General expressionlessly pulled his nine millimeter out from underneath his suit jacket, pointed it at Beers' knee, and fired. Beers went flying off his chair onto the floor in agony. He was screaming.

"How was that?" the General asked calmly. "Are you in full revolutionary spirit?"

"You mother fucker," Beers screamed at him.

"What? What's that, Beersy? Where did your casual world weary tone go?"

Beers looked much younger, his face more serious in pain. He was using both hands to compress his knee. He looked at the General defiantly.

"What do you want from me?" he asked the General.

"I want you to have never existed, but short of that I'll take this," and he fired another bullet into the same knee through the back of Beers hand.

Beers screamed again and then began to moan rhythmically.

"This is wrong, Ryan," I said. "Stop him now."

"No," Ryan said, "let it play out."

"What's wrong with you," I said and bolted from the room and found the door to the interrogation room.

"General," I shouted as I entered.

He turned, looking over his shoulder at me.

"Are you coming to the rescue?" he said.

"Yes, that's enough," I said.

"Is it?" he said, turning back to Beers. "Is it enough for you, Beers?" he said.

"Yes," Beers said. He was asking for mercy.

"O.K., then," the General said. "I want the one thing you've got on Charles Spencer that made him fear you. What is it? Tell me and I'll bring someone in here with a medical kit who will stop that bleeding and give you morphine."

"He's a pedophile," Beers said, "Charles is a pedophile, he does it with children."

"See," the General said to me as he turned and left the room.

I followed him out.

"You're telling me that you had to do that to get that out of him?" I said.

"No, I'm saying that I needed that right now. The pace is picking up and the time for games is over. Now, I'm going in there," he said, pointing at the door to the other interrogation room, "to have a talk with Mr. Spencer. Would you like to come and supervise, or retire to the observation deck? Your choice."

I took option two and rejoined Ryan and Yael.

"Method, madness," was Ryan's only comment. Yael shrugged. We watched the General on the monitor as he entered the room with Spencer.

"Edward!" Spencer almost shouted when he saw the General. "Good god, man, are you involved in this?"

"Hello, Charles," the General said, "you seem to have gotten yourself in quite a fix. Some here want you dead. Others say no."

"These people, Eddie. They are just thick. But I don't understand. Why are you here? Do you belong to this group?"

"Yes, Charles. I'm part of the new leadership in North America."

"What? That's absurd. How did you ever get involved in the revolution? You were once a military man, weren't you? Why this is just crazy."

"I've been a loyal soldier in the movement since my days at West Point, Charles. I was recruited directly by the KGB. Obviously my cover needed to hold up through my military career and beyond. Not even you knew about it, Charles."

"So you've seen my report," Spencer said. "You understand the brilliance of my plan and the absurdity of charging me with failure. Get me out of this chair, Eddie."

"I can't do that quite yet, Charles."

"Why not?"

"There are questions still. They need answers," the General said.

"Like what? Ask me, I'll tell you."

"We have many assets. Many valuable assets, in the target cities for the nuclear attack. We need to delay the attack and we want you to tell us how to do that."

"It can't be done," Spencer said. "Can't be done. Simple as that."

"You must have kept a key to delay it, Charles. No one is that irresponsible."

"Eddie, I'm sorry, but I had to make it so that nothing could call this attack off. It was my decision. Now we have to prepare for the aftermath. But calling it off, it can't be done."

48

"I don't believe you," the General said to Spencer.

"Believe or not believe as you please," Spencer answered. "It won't change the facts. I relinquished control over the nuclear operation."

"You've never relinquished control over anything, sir," the General said. "You certainly wouldn't let go of something this important."

"Well, look, Edward," Spencer said, "maybe there is a thread that could be pulled, but first just get me out of this chair. My damn fingers are numb."

"You need to give me that thread first, Charles."

"No. I have nothing for you. You want to continue humiliating me, then I'll let you guess about what I know. Stop treating me like a dog and I'll be more forthcoming."

"Here's what I'll do for you, Charles, if you don't tell me how to delay the nuclear attack. I'll let you go, get you all cleaned up, back to your tip-top condition and send you on your way, back to your life, and as you arrive back at whichever estate, the news will break, here in the U.S. and around the world, that you are a pedophile."

Spencer froze. It was as though he turned into polished marble, the transformation was so immediate and complete.

"Yes," the General said, "we know all about your secret life. Did you think that you would be allowed to accumulate all that money and power without us retaining methods of control? We don't care about your habits. But we know how attached you are to your grand reputation in the bourgeois world, and what this revelation would do to you."

Decades of cultivated arrogance drained out of Spencer in a matter of seconds. The General had the thing that was worse than death for him. Spencer hung limply in his restraints.

"There is a way for me to delay the nuclear attack," he said.

"That's all we want, Charles, a delay. Your plans and your work have been brilliant. Your dedication complete. But you failed to consider the entire picture for us. We need time to prepare."

"Honestly," Spencer said, "I believed I was doing the right thing in the right way."

"You were, Charles. We all want to see the U.S. brought to its knees and punished. It stands in the path of everything we believe in. Your miscalculation is minor."

"Who besides you knows my secret, Eddie?" Spencer begged.

"Only a select few, Charles. No one who would judge you by it."

"That's the key," Spencer said, regaining some color, "that no one presume to judge me. I have served the revolution, and that is what should be judged."

"Let's get to how we can delay the nuclear plan," the General said, softening his demeanor, now a trusted counselor, a friend of Charles Spencer, a compassionate minister even.

Spencer gave the General a cell phone number from memory. He said that the person who answered at that number should be told to 'hold.' That message would get to the bomb team.

"Where is the bomb team?" the General asked.

"That I don't know. They could be anywhere, but I would assume that they are already in the U.S., somewhere. They are free to find their way to one of the three targets. These men are not stupid, but they are fanatics. The smart side of them would send them to L.A., because that is the least bottled up location, from a security standpoint. But their fanatic side covets New York as a target. D.C. would be the middle choice."

The General released Spencer from his shackles and told him to be patient. Someone would come by to attend to him. And the General left him alone.

Yael looked at me and nodded, acknowledging the exacting work of the General. I wanted to ask about the General's relationship with Spencer, how they knew one another, and whether the General's first name was really Edward. That sort of question, however, I now understood to be out of bounds and would at best be answered with a shrug.

Ryan left us and I asked Yael if she thought the General was angry about my bursting in after he shot Beers in the knee.

"I don't think he's angry," Yael said. "It's hard to say for sure, and it would be pointless to ask, but I got the impression he was expecting you to do that."

"What makes you think that?" I asked.

"You were in there, so you had a cleaner view than I did watching it on the monitor. When you went into the room and shouted at him, the way he looked toward you, over his shoulder, and his line about you coming to the rescue. Maybe it was his real reaction, but it seemed played right at Beers. It was funny because that let Beers give it up, what he had on Spencer. He chose in that moment not to die, or suffer, to hold onto it, and I think it was because, as the General characterized it in that moment, you were coming to Beers' rescue. It was like a chain reaction of psychological transferences, and the General played it instantaneously. That is what made me think he was expecting you."

"You saw all that?" I said.

"I think I did," Yael said.

"What did Ryan say?"

"He said, 'oh, shit,' his precise words, as you shouted at the General."

"I know that Beers is a sick, evil bastard, but I couldn't watch that. I still have a human reaction to another human being in pain," I said.

"When I was watching that, Mara, I was thinking of all the anguish Beers would be happy, excited to inflict on innocent people."

"But shooting a 78-year-old man in the knee," I said, "aren't there drugs that can be used to get the truth out of him."

"You know, Mara, the clock is running. The General knows the options; I trust his judgment about what the situation called for."

"Still," I said.

"One of my instructors," Yael said, "who taught me all sorts of fighting techniques, when I asked him what his favorite moves were, he said he always liked to give his opponent a good shot to the face before trying any of that fancy stuff."

"Your point being?" I said.

"My point being that dancing is nice when you have the time for it."

"Is Beers not a human being?" I asked.

"That's a good question," she said. "It wasn't until the General put one in his knee that he showed any signs of being human. Moments before that, and everything we saw up to that point, he seemed like a parody of a rich, goofy lothario with such a nihilistic impulse that he had reduced himself, saw himself as no more than an animated bag of water that only resembled something human. And that was the value he placed on his life and the lives of others, essentially nothing. It was only after the General shot him in the knee and you came to his rescue that he seemed to even remember that he was alive. Now, tell me what sort of consideration he's entitled to? Hasn't he by his own volition renounced his humanity?"

"I get it, Yael," I said, "but I'll only go this far. What the General did was justified. It was demanded by the situation. But Beers does not have the power to renounce his own humanity, and we have no power to accept it if he tries. If he commits suicide, he does so as a human being. If we kill him, we kill a human being, whether it amounts to justice or not."

"I'm signed on for that, then," Yael said, "and the justice we're working with here turns on clear right and wrong. Beers and Spencer are murderers, but not past or future murderers. They are in the act, right now, present tense. Their money and power has them abstracted back from the immediate act, but they are still in it. They have information. They are holding information that is the weapon itself. They are at the scene holding and using the weapon, and they have to be treated in that way in precisely that context at precisely that level of culpability."

"O.K.," I said, "I see that. But let's not pretend that killing either Spencer or Beers or Allison Garvin, for that matter, stops their criminal conspiracy. We can administer battlefield justice, but that can't be conflated with stopping the murderous act. It is not acting in either immediate self-defense or the immediate defense of others to kill any one of them."

"Then we settle on this," Yael said, "getting what we need from Beers or Spencer justifies how we get it because they are immediately culpable in transpiring acts of murder. Killing them, however, would not stop those acts, but can only be a matter of justice. In the case of Garvin, the General had a legitimate fear that if she was rescued she would be an even greater danger, while her execution was justified by her complicity in a terrorist plot and her spying on behalf of the plotters."

"If this is a war and we are on the battlefield," I said, "then you have it right."

"This is a war," Yael said, "and we are on the battlefield."

"I agree," I said, "but how do we know when the war is over and we are off the battlefield?"

"I believe," she said, "that we'll know it when we see it."

49

I wondered about that, if we would indeed know it when we saw it. I also worried that we would never get the chance to know it because we would never see it. We would never see the end of this war because the enemy had replicated and spread with the mindless precision of a virus. What I was seeing, and perhaps what the others had already seen but could not explain to me, was why war was a constant. This enemy, being but the latest form of the virus, had worked its way past all the ancient and modern concepts of armies and military defenses.

Ryan returned to the observation room.

"We're moving," he said. "Five minutes."

"Destination?" Yael asked.

"Northern New York State," he said.

"They're coming down or they've already come down through Canada?" she asked.

"It's not clear. They took the call from Spencer's contact right near the border," Ryan said.

"Is there any radiological signature?" Yael asked.

"No. The satellites don't show anything. If they have the weapon, it's shielded," Ryan said.

"They're going to be the most normal looking people up there," I said, offering the single intuition to step forward in my mind. "And they'll be engaging in everyday, utterly mundane travel."

Ryan looked stoically at me and nodded.

"Let's go," he said.

I followed them out of the room and as we were exiting the building the General was standing outside the interrogation room that Spencer was in. As I looked in his direction he smiled and winked at me. That meant I was still O.K. with him, or maybe even more O.K. I smiled and gave him a 'what do you want from me' shrug and left the building.

The copter took us to an airfield about twenty minutes away. We boarded a small jet and were in the air immediately.

"Shouldn't this be out of our hands now?" I said.

"No," Ryan said. "I understand what you're saying. We've got a lot of backup working with us, but we don't want the federal response teams to come stumbling into the middle of this. If this gang thinks they are surrounded they'll detonate the weapon. Our people will do this right."

"Ryan's right," Yael said, "this isn't an occasion for a handoff."

"Did I suggest a lack of confidence in our people?" I asked, seriously.

"No," Ryan said, "you assumed, though, that there's an agency daddy out there who can step in now and do this. But there isn't. We're it for this one."

"How the hell did I ever get mixed up with you people," I said.

That raised smiles and silence settled in. Ryan's cell rang a few times on the flight, but the callers must not have been on point because he let them all go unanswered. We were all unplugging from anything that wasn't immediately in front of us. I could feel it and see it happening. For such a remarkably stripped down crew I wouldn't have thought that there was any baggage left to throw overboard.

We took our landing at a strip near Malone, a town at the north side of the Adirondacks. There was a pick-up truck waiting for us, with the keys in the ignition. Yael drove, Ryan took the front passenger seat, and I had the tight back seat to myself.

Less than a mile from the airstrip we pulled into the lot of a motel. We already had room keys in the truck's glove compartment.

"Let's take fifteen minutes to get cleaned up, then we'll meet in my room," Ryan said.

Our rooms adjoined one another. In mine there were fresh clothes waiting. They were 'local clothes,' neither old nor new, neat, slightly worn, an ensemble of jeans, flannel shirt, and a down vest. The support team that had made the selection got my sizes, if not my tastes, perfectly. A fresh pair of hiking boots were nicely broken in. I was in and out of the shower like a robot. Drying off I looked in the mirror and guessed that I weighed twenty pounds less than I had days earlier. As I dressed I looked at the bed and thought about what an odd thing it was. Do people still use these, I thought, and actually stay in them for hours and hours.

I was at Ryan's door with two minutes to spare on my fifteen minute allotment. Yael was already there. Ryan was cleaned up and on his cell. We all looked as local as local gets.

Ryan finished with his call.

"We haven't got anything more," he said. "When Spencer's contact passed along the 'hold' message the nuclear team went quiet. They ditched the cell they took the call on."

"What's next then?"

"Every bit of data within a hundred mile radius of the tracking point where the call from Spencer's contact was taken is being run to catch anything that looks suspicious. That's every surveillance camera, every credit card purchase, every pay phone call, basically anything that leaves a record or image. We've got observers in place at every gas station and convenience store, some in person as workers and some watching with surveillance cameras."

"The bomb team will be doing what we're doing," I said, "trying to blend in. We're looking for our mirror images. They will be secretive, confident, methodical, and they'll look like they belong in the neighborhood."

"Mara's right," Yael said.

"So they'll be driving a pick-up?" Ryan asked.

"No, I don't think so," I said. "I think it will be an SUV, and it will be one of the most common models people drive around here. They'll have done their research. It will be an SUV because that won't stand out when they get into Manhattan. A pick-up wouldn't blend in as well down there. They're not that common in the city."

"The General," Ryan said, "is telling me that the 'hold' command, according to Spencer, will keep them from carrying out the attack for three days, and then they proceed."

"What about an 'abort' command?"

"The General hasn't gone for that yet. He's still working on Spencer as a comrade, keeping that going. He says that this attack is for Spencer the vindication of his entire life, and the General thinks that Spencer would die before allowing an order to abort it. Even asking him about the order could trigger his suspicions. But the General is working on it."

"The quick way around that barrier," Yael said, "is to convince Spencer that the attack has happened and then milk him while he's rejoicing."

"That could be cobbled together," Ryan said. "I think it works." He started to pull out his cell.

"Make sure," I said, "that the General comes at Spencer with outrage that the 'hold' didn't work and then have him grudgingly acknowledge Spencer's grand accomplishment."

"Got it," Ryan said.

He left the motel room and had his conversation with the General outside.

"We need to get in motion right away," I said to Yael.

"But to where, Mara? Our leads haven't come in."

"I know," I said, "but they are here, now. If we're moving, my gut tells me we'll find them. We'll be able to pick them out. There's going to be something."

"Don't go mystical on me," Yael said. "We succeed when we go with the facts. Our hunches flow out of the facts, they don't create them."

"I understand," I said, "but when Ryan is done with that call we need to get into the truck and drive."

"Mara?" Yael said, cautioning me to stay with reality.

"We should head south," I said. "These are people who will cheat in the direction of the target. They will allow themselves that much. They'll 'hold,' they'll take the order, but they'll satisfy their fanaticism by moving closer, so that they don't feel like they are losing any momentum."

"O.K.," Yael said, "you're saying that we can't take 'hold' too literally."

"Yes," I said, "that's what I'm saying."

"But what about their pace?" she asked.

"They will make it more leisurely. They will move forward, but take their time, cheating forward like kids told to stay away from something but gradually working their way, willfully, back toward it."

Yael was squinting at what I was saying, and starting to buy. When Ryan came back in, before he could speak, she said,

"Mara sees it this way…," and gave it to him with the mystical edges trimmed.

He got her version of it immediately.

"And if we're wrong," he said, "and we get called back in this direction, we turn around. Let's get at it."

We went to the truck and drove south.

50

"Here's what we are looking for," I said. "It's going to be one of the larger SUV models, a big one. If it's parked somewhere, at least one member of the bomb team will be with it, either inside it or leaning against it or right near it. They would not leave it unattended. I say it's going to be a three-man team, like us. They'll be dressed appropriately for upstate, northern New York, but on close inspection, under a hard glance, they won't seem right."

Ryan looked back at me. He was skeptical, as he had to be, but listening carefully.

"What are they?" he asked, "Middle-Eastern? Central Asian?"

"No," I said, "not this crew. They'll be light-complexioned, European, maybe even blonde and blue-eyed. But they won't fit the clothes…no, that's not it. They won't fit the place and the clothes will not hide it."

Ryan's eyes were narrowing on me. He had the picture, but he knew it could all be wrong.

"What is the age range?" he asked.

"Spencer said they were fanatics, but they're still looking at a huge payday. So, young enough to still be insane and reckless but old enough to be methodical, meticulous and disciplined, and old enough to want the full price for the job. Late twenties to mid-thirties. Fanatical cynics, and that contradiction will show on their faces. It will sit right there on their mugs, wrapped transparently in the murderous impulse."

Yael was driving slowly, occasionally pulling over to the side to let traffic behind us get by. We watched every vehicle. We weren't just looking for the target I was describing, but any element of it.

"The weapon won't be heavy," Ryan said, "but the radiological shielding might be, so take note of low suspension over rear wheels."

He paused and held up his hand as if to stop all our thinking in that moment.

"And we can't let them make us while we are making them. They're going to be hypersensitive and paranoid. They'll have it contained. But they are after all driving around with a nuclear weapon. If they get a clear sense that they've been made they could detonate the thing, or set it for detonation while they flee. They could be ready to go either way, go up with the thing or flee, giving themselves enough time to get out of the blast area."

"They would need a second car then," Yael said, "if they wanted to flee."

"Yes," Ryan said, "and it's going to stay right with them."

"They'll be talking to one another," I said. "Can we get a track on cell phone traffic, car to car in this region?"

"That should be possible," Ryan said, reaching for his cell.

Yael pulled over. We were in a heavily forested area, with nothing around. Ryan had a satellite connection. He stepped out and walked away as he talked.

Yael and I sat quietly, watching every car that passed.

"Something isn't right," she said.

"You mean about the profile we've put together or them?"

"No, back there," she said, looking in the rear-view mirror at Ryan.

"What is it?" I said.

"His shoulders. They've slumped down. He doesn't do that."

I swung around and took a look. Ryan's back was to us, but Yael was right, his shoulders were slumped. It didn't look like him. He finished the call, turned around, and walked back in our direction. He had squared his shoulders, but his face was showing that something, as Yael had said, was not right.

"What is it?" Yael said as Ryan threw himself back in the truck.

"Trouble at the facility in New Mexico," he said.

"Go ahead," she said.

"Some kind of private force, trying to fob itself off as a federal agency, has the facility under siege. The General speculates that it's a contingency plan related to Spencer."

"What does Spencer say?" I asked.

"The General is keeping him in the dark about it. He doesn't want to blow the routine."

"Has the force asked for Spencer?"

"No. They're pretending it's a generic drug raid. Tony is there with a sufficient tactical team and enough firepower to take the private force out, but it's going to create a mess and there are complications."

"Complications?" Yael said.

"Yeah, the state police got wind of it and they are racing there with a fleet of vehicles. One of their copters is on the way too. The General is trying to get them called off, but the contact who can do that can't be reached, which is unusual, to say the least. So the General's options are narrowing. That's where we left it."

"Any luck on the cell traffic?" Yael asked.

"That's coming."

"How soon?"

"Minutes. Let's move. Let's focus. What happens in New Mexico isn't going to change what we have to do."

"One more thing," I said. "These guys we are looking for, they'll pass, superficially, for Americans. They will look the part, dress the part, but they won't have the movement or the grit down. Even when Americans go off their grooming, they go off it in an American way. These guys will be off their grooming, but they'll look sloppy in a European way."

Ryan, fully squared up and restored, looked back my way and gave me that amused crooked smile of his. It didn't say he was buying, but neither did it say otherwise.

He took a call and listened.

"They isolated what was clearly car to car cell phone traffic down to a town south of here called Tupper Lake."

"I've been there," I said.

"Then the cell traffic stops there, which might mean they're holding up, for now, in Tupper Lake. It fits your theory, Mara. Let's get there fast."

Yael hit the gas and our leisurely pace was done. She kept it around ninety, passing cars in a way normally understood to be maniacal. At one point we picked up a state police cruiser that came after us, flashing for us to pull over. Yael flicked the truck's light controller on and off several times, beating out a code, and the state police cruiser slowed down, killed its flashers, and let us go.

"Impressive," I said.

"Come on, Mara," Yael said, "you're not that easily impressed."

"Well, it wasn't as impressive as when you two took down and cuffed the cops outside of Beers' mansion."

"They were fake cops," Yael said.

"Former cops, I thought."

"Former cops pretending to be cops are fake cops," she said.

"Once a cop, always a cop," I said.

As we approached Tupper Lake, Yael fell back to our 'just ambling along' pace. It wasn't a big town, but there were plenty of SUVs on the street. I suggested that we cruise past the restaurants. We had a map up on the laptop and we drove slowly around, using the restaurants as checkpoints, but looking at everything.

"Let's be careful," Ryan reminded, "not to stare at any potential suspect, not look too long or too hard. Keep it casual."

We cruised the main drag and the area around it three times without picking up anything. I was about to suggest that we try the nearby shopping plaza and then hit all the motels, when I saw him.

"There," I said, "that guy." I was directing their attention to a thin, handsome, poorly groomed man about thirty years old. He was standing at the back of a large SUV parked in front of a small grocery store. He was staring down at a hand-held computer no larger than a paperback but looking up from it compulsively to check his surroundings. He didn't fit.

Yael continued on past him for a hundred yards and then parked on the street, on the same side as the grocery. Yael would walk back up and go into the store. Ryan would take the opposite side of the street.

"You'll need this," he said to me and handed me a cell phone. I hadn't had one since the townhouse. His and Yael's numbers were in the directory as 'R' and 'Y.' He had had it ready for when I would need it. In this business cell phones were apparently more dangerous than guns.

My role was to trail Yael by half a block and remain inconspicuous.

"Don't let this guy make you," Ryan said to me as he began to cross the street.

51

The man standing at the rear of the SUV stepped onto the sidewalk and looked my way. Rob had told me that one of the ways he made drug dealers when he worked street narcotics units was by the way they walked. He called it 'walking the walk to nowhere,' and he said it had a distinct signature. It was very difficult to look like you were actually going somewhere if you had no real destination. Applying that lesson to myself, I made a determined move into a newspaper and tobacco shop. My eyes did not settle once on the man at the SUV.

If Yael made the man's friends inside the grocery store she would grab some items and get to the check-out line behind them. We hadn't seen his friends, but we believed there would be two of them inside, and that they would stand out as obviously as he had.

To this point I had kept myself numb to the fact that we were after a nuclear weapon. It was too much to internalize. But now that we were right on top of what we thought was the bomb team, it was not possible to ignore the immediacy of the vaporization zone. It produced a buzz inside me that was no easy thing to deal with.

I thumbed magazines near the front window. The target was not visible from there. I could see diagonally across the street to where Ryan was supposed to be, but he wasn't there. He was probably doing what I was doing.

My new cell phone rang. It was Yael.

"I'm waiting on line," she said. "They had what I needed. Are you at the car?"

"Yes," Ryan answered.

I was part of a three-way conversation.

"I'll be there in a minute," I said.

"O.K., hun, bye," Yael said and got off.

"Mara," Ryan said, "as Yael comes out behind them she's going to take them right there on the sidewalk. I'll be on top of the one already on the street. We're going to want their hands up and out, no reaching into pockets, no touching of clothing, up and out, so it's shock and surprise. We want them to react directly to our command. If they don't, they go down. You'll be the trailer here. Ready?"

"Yes," I said.

"Now," he said.

I dropped the magazine and left the store. Five paces up the sidewalk and my hand went unconsciously for the nine millimeter. I could see Ryan in position directly across the street from the target, and then the two other men exited the grocery store. The target on the street turned to greet them, dropping the hand-held to his side. Yael came out right behind them, her gun already drawn and she barked very forcefully at them.

"Get your hands up now."

Ryan had crossed the street and was on top of the original target pushing his gun into the back of his neck, so that he would feel it. And then he had him on the sidewalk, spread-eagle.

Yael had both of the men from the store on their knees, and Ryan had them covered from the front. They were all complying perfectly.

Then the target who had carried the plastic bag full of groceries made a try for the front pocket of his jacket.

Yael shot him in the head. He fell forward from his knees. The sound of his face hitting the sidewalk was dull and final.

Ryan and Yael carefully brought the hands of the two men still alive down behind their backs and secured them with plastic restraints. Pedestrians wanted no part of all this and stayed back. Ryan looked up at me and nodded that it was O.K. to approach. He and Yael found handguns in the waistbands of both men. They were .45 caliber semi-automatics. Neither man said a word. Either they were too shocked to speak or it was part of their training. I couldn't tell for sure.

Ryan went to the dead target and gently rolled him over. With the care of a watchmaker he went into the front pocket of the jacket, and there it was, the detonator. I looked up and around at the people frozen in place on the street and those looking out from inside the grocery store. Nearly everyone was silent. Those who spoke only whispered. None of them knew or would ever know what had just happened and what had just not happened.

One of our vans pulled up in the street, but no one got out. I assumed that they were waiting for Ryan to give them the O.K. Then a state police cruiser, and then another, showed up and one of our men got out of the van and dealt with them. They pulled their cars back and began directing traffic away from the street toward alternative routes.

More state police arrived and they went to work moving the pedestrians out of the area and getting everyone out of the storefronts. Soon enough the street would be empty.

Ryan and Yael carefully went through the pockets and clothing of both of the living targets and the dead one. Another one of our vans arrived and two men got out and put the body of the dead target into the back of it. They just carried it. There was no ceremonial stretcher. The two live targets were lifted roughly to their feet, which were now tied together with plastic restraints, and dragged away to the first van. Both of the vans drove away and we turned our attention to the SUV.

"There's nothing in here," Yael said, looking inside.

"There should be another car," I said. "It will be in that one. It's the reverse of what we thought."

"Ryan had a key set he had taken from one of the targets that didn't belong to the SUV."

"He aimed it around the street pressing the lock button until we heard the beep of the car's lock system responding. It was parked down the street on the other side, in the direction where we had left the truck.

As we approached the car, a Buick Skylark, it was obvious that the rear suspension was low, weighted down by something in the trunk.

"I'm not going to pop that trunk," he said. "Not here. We'll get this vehicle out on a flatbed and get it somewhere the bomb specialists can have at it. I don't want to touch it."

He got on his cell and walked away from us. Before he was done another one of our vans pulled up alongside the target SUV and two men got out who began to examine its interior. After a short time one got back in the van and backed it up while the other man got behind the wheel and drove the SUV away.

Ryan finished the call and went back to speak with the team in the van. We followed him and waited on the sidewalk in front of the grocery store. The street was deserted and I stared down at the pool of blood left from the head wound of the target Yael had just killed.

"It's a good thing you didn't hesitate," I said to her.

"That's one thing bombers depend on," she said, "hesitation. Give them even that much and you're dead."

"There would have been a whole lot of dead with that bomb."

She nodded and looked down at the pool of blood.

"This one," she said, pointing to the blood, but referring to the dead target, "I could tell, standing behind him in line in the store, that he wouldn't go alive."

"What told you that about him?"

"It was in the attitude that had shaped his face," Yael said. "It was like a crust of permanent anger. His eyes were roaming beyond the store. I could feel how distant he was from the immediate circumstances. He must have felt like he had history itself in his pocket along with that detonator."

"He did," I said.

"Hesitation on my part was all it would have taken for him to make that history real," she said.

"Were you tempted," I asked, "to hesitate?"

"Hell, no," she said. "I made it clear to him exactly what he needed to do. He did otherwise. I pulled the trigger. If I hesitate there would be this big bald spot in the Adirondacks where Tupper Lake had been."

"Yael," I said, "I think I might have hesitated."

She looked at me, narrowing her eyes.

"I don't think so," she said. "Not anymore."

52

"Things have not gone well in New Mexico," Ryan said, "but they could be worse."

"Tell us," Yael said as we got back into the truck.

Two members of Tony's team were hit in the exchange. Neither is fatal, but their wounds are bad.

"Did the General manage to keep the state police out of it?" I asked.

"No, but he got them into it with the other side. Don't ask how. I don't know yet. But while that was underway he got everyone out of there in the two copters we had on site. A state police copter started after them, but we were able to signal them and back them off.

"All in all," I started to say.

"All in all it's a huge screw-up. The General's contact to handle the New Mexico cops didn't respond and we don't know for sure who or what that private army was. And it cost us two of our best people."

"We did just thwart a nuclear attack, Ryan," I said, flashing a smile his way.

"That's old news," he said, getting as close to grumpy as he was capable.

I got it. Ryan's thing was to run silent, run deep. Yet here in Tupper Lake we had just shot a man in the head on the sidewalk in full view of dozens of people. They had seen our faces, vividly. They had no idea what had happened, and while they would get some sort of cover story it wasn't going to add up. There might be some stray video out there that would wind up on the internet.

And while the shooting stopped the detonation of a nuclear weapon, Ryan was waiting for aftershocks, both from the public explosion and from whatever network the terrorist crew was hooked into. The situation in New Mexico also troubled him, a lot. For Ryan, the finish of one battle only cued the beginning of the next one.

We were heading to an interrogation facility and Yael was driving fast. She picked up another state police cruiser – it was good to see them doing their job – and she flashed the truck's lights impatiently to signal them off.

We didn't leave the Adirondacks but wound up much farther south at the beautiful and unearthly Blue Mountain Lake in a large thickly built cabin. Ryan warned us that this was mostly an open space, without the usual interrogation rooms. The two bomb team members still alive, he already knew, were not saying anything, not a word. I assumed that for them dying was just the next item, and their last pleasure would be to not discuss it. I had looked at their faces as they were taken into the vans and they were blanks.

We didn't go right into the cabin. It was a beautiful mountain afternoon. The chill air seemed drinkable.

"There are a lot of people who will go on living and a lot of life that will move down the road because we stopped these miserable bastards. We're in a grace period here," Ryan said. "I don't want any reactions in here," he said looking at me, "nothing audible, nothing on the face, that opens even a hint of light for either of them. This is a different kind of questioning of a different kind of human being. We need to keep that in mind."

Ryan led us inside. It was a big empty room with a kitchen at one end, some folding chairs, and the two surviving members of the bomb team in the center of the floor, tied with plastic restraints. The clothes they had been wearing were gone and they now wore white paper coveralls. They didn't look at us. They didn't speak.

One of our guys sat near them on a metal folding chair holding his nine millimeter in front of him. These men were tens on the one to ten scale of dangerous. Given a split second of opportunity they would kill anyone, anything, or themselves. They never expected to be stopped and certainly not to be caught, taken alive.

Ryan went to the countertop in the kitchen area. There was an array of drug vials and disposable syringes and he loaded up two syringes, drawing careful amounts into each from three separate vials.

He went to our two captives and like a hospital nurse who had done it a thousand times before found veins in each of the men and emptied the syringes into them. I looked at Yael as if to ask what he had given them, and she shrugged in response. She didn't know. It wasn't a good time to casually step over to the kitchen and examine the drugs.

It didn't take long for the injected drugs to affect the demeanors of the men. Each became slightly agitated, moving the best they could under their restraints, as if they were trying to stretch and get at itches at the same time. Their faces showed immediate concerns, too immediate, like the agitated faces I had once seen in a psychiatric lock-up.

Ryan watched them carefully and then told our guy to take one of them away and he lifted the one Ryan indicated and half-dragged him to a back room and closed the door from inside.

"I can give you what you want," Ryan said to the one that remained, who now looked at him, very anxiously, for the first time. "I can kill you, if you want that. I can get you whores. I can arrange for you to live on an island paradise. But I can't let you not tell me what you know."

The bomber looked at Ryan feverishly. The drugs were cascading inside him.

"I don't know anything," he said excitedly, but in passable English.

"You know where you came from," Ryan said. "You know what you were doing and where you were going. Now, I just need you to know everything that all that connects to. Every name, every place, every friend, every dollar, everything."

The man began to shake, his face showing simultaneous fear and wonder and stupefied joy about what was happening to him.

"Make this stop," he said to Ryan.

"Talk to me, pal," Ryan said.

"I can't. Make it stop. I'll tell you everything."

Ryan went back to the kitchen counter and loaded another syringe. He returned to the man's side and showed him the needle.

"Give me a little something before I give you a little of this," Ryan said.

"We're all from Bosnia. We trained in Pakistan. They brought us into New York as workers. Our families. We have our families taken care of, no matter what."

He was in his early thirties, sandy-haired, with a face that might have been handsome if there was anything left animating it but the purpose of killing people. He was shaking now and gasping and pleading with his eyes.

"More," Ryan said, still holding the syringe on offer, "I need more right now before I help you."

"We all work for a wealthy businessman. He takes care of us."

"He gives you orders? What's his name?"

"No, he doesn't give us orders. He just gives us a front to set up through. His name is Vernacchia. He owns a building management company. He's paid to help us. Please inject some of that into me."

Ryan gave him a jab with the needle, injecting a small amount from the syringe. Then he walked into the backroom and visited with the other bomber for several minutes. The one in the main room with us calmed down just a bit.

When Ryan returned he was still holding the syringe up. The bomber asked for more. He shook rhythmically, in waves, and then there was the rottenest stench filling the cabin. He had lost his bowels.

"Don't worry about that," Ryan said to him. "It happens."

The bomber glanced over at Yael and me.

"Would you prefer that the women leave?" Ryan asked the bomber.

"Please," he said.

Ryan gave us a nod and we happily stepped outside into the fresh air.

"We were there just so Ryan could give him that bit of dignity back by having us leave," I said.

"Not just for that," Yael said expressionlessly. "Transformations like that are important to see."

"It was drug induced," I said as if I had a point.

"That's not important," she said. "What's important is that Ryan re-opened a section of that guy's brain that had been closed down."

"It seemed more like several sections were opened, all at once. What did Ryan inject him with?" I asked.

"I'm not sure what all the ingredients were," she said, "but it looked like it had a good solid amphetamine base." She smiled ever so slightly.

53

Yael and I stood at the edge of the lake and quietly let the fresh air roll through us. There was a scent of pine from a stand of trees up the shoreline.

A muffled gunshot inside the cabin turned us both around.

"I sensed that was coming," Yael said.

"What?" I blurted.

"You heard Ryan offer to kill him if that's what he wanted," Yael said.

"How could I have missed it?"

"It was a real offer, and I had a feeling the guy would go for it," she said.

"How did you know?"

"Those three were elites," Yael said. "They had heavy training and psychological conditioning. Their mission was meticulously planned and way outside any organizational structure. Spencer was the mastermind and the money, but these guys had independent tactical control. They didn't report to anyone until the completion of the mission. When that was done, if they survived, they became immensely wealthy and pitiless terror masters. It would be, literally, their era. They would own it. An act that would trump 9/11 a thousand fold, but no one would ever catch them."

"But we caught them," I said.

"Exactly. That's why I thought he would take Ryan up on his offer. His life ended on that sidewalk in Tupper Lake. With all their training and preparation and paranoia, to them the mission was a done deal. That bomb was going to go off. They would have parked that car in Manhattan and turned around and left and they would be kings after it went off and they took final payment. Now this guy has his hands and feet tied, he's caught, and Ryan gives him a drug cocktail that opens up all these compartments, these human compartments that he had shut down. And he talks, starts giving it up, and then he goes in his pants. That's quite a different scenario than the one he believed he'd be finishing up with."

"But this execution thing, Yael," I said, "I don't see myself getting used to it."

She laughed. "You're already used to it. You know that this is a battlefield."

"Am I? Do I?" I said.

"Back in front of the grocery store, when I shot the one with the detonator, could you have walked to the other side of that scene and joined the people on the sidewalk who watched it go down?"

"What do you mean?" I asked.

"I mean that you understood the stakes. They didn't. They had no idea there was a nuclear weapon down the block. They'll never know that. That will never be declassified because no record will be made of it. You do understand the stakes. You are on the battlefield. Those citizens back there, so long as that bomb doesn't go off, they are not on the battlefield. You know what position you're in, right?"

"Yes, of course," I said, "but what do you mean no record will ever be made of that attempt? We recovered the weapon.

We can't just drop that off at the local dump. That's got to be turned over to the Defense Department or someone."

"Does it?" Yael said.

"It should be," I said.

"Should it?" she said.

"Yes."

"Why?"

"Because that's who handles something like a stray nuclear weapon. They have the authority, don't they?"

"Well, you know," she said, "Ryan and I both know how complicated all that gets."

"But," I said, now with some exasperation, "isn't what we're doing, ultimately, under the authority of the damn U.S. government."

"Not in any way the U.S. government would acknowledge," Yael said.

"But we use their resources. We have links to NSA. You guys are former military. Ryan has some kind of get out of jail free card that causes cops to fall to one knee when they see it."

"True enough," she said, "but everyone over there..."

"You mean by 'over there' the government?" I said.

"Yes, everyone over there who we deal with thinks that we report to someone else. But we don't report to anyone."

"Not even to the President?" I asked.

That got another smile out of her. "Mara, not only does the President not know about us, we're not even in the category of things he doesn't want to know about, which isn't the same as the category of things he does know about but pretends not to know about."

"So does anyone 'over there' even know about us?"

"Of course," she said, "but no one claims us, has any record of us, pretends to give us orders, or takes credit for anything we do, which they don't want to know about anyway."

"Then what the hell are we?" I asked.

"A mist?" she offered.

"A mist?" I said.

"Yeah," Yael said, "that about sums it up. You know from Rob how gummed up the federal agencies are. Well, that's not us. And we could never fit into any of their containers, but they do have resources and we do have access to them."

"How?" I said.

"The General," she said.

"I knew that was coming."

"And," she said, "we don't know who the General is."

"That's just a let's pretend thing, isn't it? That you and Ryan don't know who the General is? Charles Spencer knew who he was?"

"Did he?"

"Yes, he recognized him the second he saw him. Called him Eddie like they had been friends since childhood."

"But that's only what Spencer believed he knew. He bought in instantly that the General – Eddie – was part of the new leadership of the revolution in North America, something invented by Callista."

"So?" I said.

"So I have no idea who 'Eddie' is and if that's really the General's name or not."

"I believe you," I said, "but the whole thing is convoluted beyond belief."

"No, Mara, you have that exactly backwards. It's not convoluted at all. That big undulating bureaucracy over there," she said, meaning the government, "that's what is convoluted beyond belief. What the General does, that's all right clean in your face straightforward. As straightforward as me killing the terrorist on the street as he reaches for his detonator. We got there because we keep things simple. To put it another way, nobody from over there could have gotten to that sidewalk and those men today."

"Then who and what are we?" I asked.

"We're Americans in a position to help America survive and we're doing what we can and what we have to, but you knew that," she said.

"I did?" I said.

"Who else did you think we were or could be, and what else did you think we were doing?"

"I guess I did know that much, but I thought there was more," I said.

"There isn't anything more. It's that simple," she said.

"Is anything that simple?" I asked.

We were turned around by another muffled gunshot from inside the cabin.

"Guest number two has exercised his option," Yael said. "They don't call that the easy way out for nothing."

"Are you sure that was his choice?" I asked.

"You heard Ryan offer the first guy whatever he wanted, including death. I'm sure he gave the second guy the same deal. And Ryan's a man of his word. If they had asked for life on an island he would have given them that."

"But now," I said, "all three of the nuclear bombers are dead. Shouldn't we have kept at least one of them alive, so that we could have looked into his mind."

"Ryan has looked inside the minds of literally hundreds of terrorists. He knows all the furniture and appliances. He knows it all too well, and so do I, Mara. And you're starting to get a pretty good inventory going yourself."

"I haven't seen that many guys like this," I said.

"No, but you're seeing the minds of the people who send them. Spencer, Beers, Allison Garvin, John Marshall Norton," she said.

"People just like you and me, Yael," I said.

"No, Mara, people who are nothing like you or me."

"Aren't we the same as them in some ways?"

"Not in any way," she said.

"Are you sure?" I asked.

"Yes," she said, "I am absolutely certain."

"But, Yael," I said, "we have been acting so far outside the law that we will never get what we have done back inside it."

"We've acted on the principles of right and wrong that the law is based in and that has to be the law for us."

54

Ryan came out from the cabin in a hurry and waved for us to join him. He got into the truck and started it. When we reached it he got out and switched to the passenger seat so that Yael could drive.

"That wasn't a nuclear weapon," he said.

"One of them told you that?" Yael asked.

"No. Our guys told me. When they got inside the case, they found it was a mock-up, not the real thing. These two here didn't know that. They thought they had the real thing."

"Why would someone send them out with a fake bomb?" I asked.

"These guys never got Spencer's hold command," Ryan said. "We had the right profile, but caught the decoy."

"So there's another team with a real bomb," Yael said.

"Should we assume otherwise?" Ryan asked.

"We can't. Someone up here got a call from Spencer's contact," Yael said.

"This team was right where we guessed the team contacted with the hold command would be," I said. "Is that a coincidence? Or somebody's plan? Did you find out when these two last had contact with their masters?"

"They were in motion, on their own, by previous planning, before the attack on the subways that failed. They've trained for this mission for a year. Last contact was a month ago."

"Ryan," Yael said, "then the nuclear attack and the other four prongs that Spencer described were meant to be follow-ons. Spencer characterized them as back-up plans because that's what they became in his embarrassment at the failure of the subway attack. We missed that turn in his mind, probably because he didn't intend willful deception. He was trying to show that he hadn't failed at all. We didn't see the mischaracterization."

"Well," I said, "where the hell is the other team? Did these two know anything about another team?"

"No," Ryan said, "they thought they were it."

"Whoever planned this," Yael began, "made it so that it would turn into a roll of the dice. It's possible that the team with the real bomb was right there in Tupper Lake, and even watched us take down this team."

"But," I said, "didn't know who we were taking down or why, because they had no idea there was another team with a fake bomb."

"Drive," Ryan said to Yael. "Either way we move south, according to our original plan."

"Ryan," I said, "did you find out if these guys were talking to each other, car to car, as they headed into Tupper Lake? That was the signature we followed in there."

"Stop the truck," Ryan said to Yael. "Go back to the cabin. I never asked them that."

Yael looked at him quizzically.

"They're dead, Ryan," she said.

"No they're not," he said.

"The gunshots. We thought…," she said.

"No, that was to make each think the other was dead. I wanted them both to believe any obligation they might have held to the other was ended, and to believe it was up for them, too."

Yael drove furiously back up the private road to the cabin. This was overload for her. She was pissed at herself for having been taken in by Ryan's ruse, and pissed at him too, even though he hadn't intended to deceive her.

"Hurry up," she barked at him as she slammed the brakes in front of the cabin.

Ryan jumped out and hurried inside. It was the first time I had seen a real spark fly between them.

"You wouldn't mind dying in his arms," I said, attempting a cosmic joke.

"I wouldn't mind him dying in my arms, maybe," she said, looking down her nose at the image. "That was a dumb mistake, not to find out if they had been talking car-to-car."

"At least they're both still alive to tell us," I said, coyly stifling a smile.

She looked back at me, getting the drift of my wisecrack.

"Are you getting smart with me, Mara?"

"Never," I said and we both burst out laughing.

Ryan came flying back out of the cabin, his cell phone at his ear. He jumped into the truck and signaled for Yael to take off. He finished his call urging the person at the other end to move fast.

"These guys were not talking car-to-car heading into Tupper Lake. So we had the right tracking, the right profile, and caught the bloody decoy team."

"Why would they be in Tupper Lake at the same time as the other team?" I asked.

"They don't know. They didn't know there was another team," Ryan said.

"Why did they go there?" Was it part of their plan?" Yael asked.

"No," Ryan answered, "it was a random stop. They intended to leave there and drive straight through into the city."

"So this was all coincidence," I said.

"I don't believe in coincidence," Ryan said. "But we're back looking for car-to-car chatter, now coming out of Tupper Lake the last few hours. We're waiting to hear on that."

"We have a second chance here," I said.

"We'd better have a second chance," he said.

"Suppose we miss them," I said. "Wouldn't it be time to just get everything shut down? Put up roadblocks. Search cars."

"Think that through, Mara," Ryan said. "The team we just stopped tried to detonate what they believed was a nuclear weapon right where and when we caught them. The other team will do the same. So suppose they do get jammed up at a roadblock outside the city and detonate right there. Is that some kind of win for us?"

"I don't know," I said.

"The only win for us is to stop them dead," Ryan continued, "and that's not possible if they see they're being stopped. We have to take them by surprise. They have to believe it is clear sailing for them right up to that moment when we take them down."

"What about the General," Yael said, "has he gotten any further with Spencer? Is there an abort command?"

"The General has just arrived at a new facility. He's going back to work on Spencer as we speak."

"Has that ruse failed?" Yael asked.

"No," Ryan said, "Spencer still believes he is being held by his own movement, and that he is more or less on trial. The General said he needs to iron Spencer's mind out a little after that scene in New Mexico which, by the way, no one at that end has sorted out yet. They still don't know for certain where that private force came from."

Yael was driving the truck like the laws of physics had been suspended. I didn't say anything, but I did look at Ryan, who gave me a reassuring half-wink. I wasn't really reassured.

"Maybe," I said, "if we want to get to the bottom of this, we should have someone looking for Spencer's contact."

"That's a possible avenue, but the probability there," Ryan said, "is that the contact is just a relay man, not anyone involved in operational planning."

"O.K.," I said, "but wait, stop, this was Spencer's plan. There are these teams. We've assumed, correctly I think, that there is an operational control. Spencer contracted with, in his mind, bombers. He elucidated his plan, which in his mind the bombers would carry out. Spencer, however, was only immersed in his details, not theirs."

"Right, exactly," Ryan said, "but the operational control end could be in Tibet for all we know. Most likely it's in Pakistan. But the principal fact on the ground is the nuclear weapon itself, which is somewhere right out in front of us."

"But," I said, "if we can get control of the operational communications, maybe we can get control of the operation."

Ryan was skeptical, not because I was wrong, but because the fact of the weapon itself spoke more immediately than the operational chain. But there was no need to pursue only the weapon.

"Pull over," he said to Yael.

She did exactly that, with a jolt, and Ryan got out to make a call, walking away from the truck. He was not afraid to put another ball in play. We had indeed neglected the operational seam between Spencer and his plan and the bombers and theirs.

That was what I had taken away from the existence of this decoy team, at least.

While Ryan was making his call my cell phone rang. I had forgotten I had finally been trusted with one. What had long been part of my daily routine was now a surprise, and I answered the call with a sense of wonder.

"Miss Rains?" It was the General.

"Yes, sir."

"What did you know for certain after the attacks on 9/11?" he asked.

I hesitated for a moment because I thought I was being tested.

"I knew for certain on 9/11 that we were at war," I said. "What did you know for certain on 9/11, sir?"

"That we had gotten off easy," he said and hung up.

55

"The General?" Yael asked me.

"Yes."

"He does that," she said.

I gave the series of quick quarter-nods that indicate baffled acceptance. I couldn't argue with the General about what he knew on 9/11. It was the call out of nowhere that threw me.

Ryan got back in the truck and Yael punched the accelerator and had it up over 70 mph in an instant.

"Mara," Ryan said, "Spencer's contact did not use that cell phone before we called him after Spencer gave us the number. And his call to the bomb team was the last time he used it. If he communicated with an operational command unit, he didn't use that phone."

"Does that exhaust every angle of that?" I asked.

"Nothing exhausts every angle," Ryan said. "But out in front of us the report is that we do have distinct car-to-car cell phone exchanges that began south of Tupper Lake right after we took down the decoy team."

"Where are they now?" Yael asked.

"They just got on the New York State Thruway at Kingston."

"That's getting down close to the city, about two hours out," I said.

"We're betting they don't go straight into the city," Ryan said.

"And if they do?" I asked.

"If they do, then our bet changes just to them holding off on the detonation for the three-day period," Ryan said.

"What about an abort command?" I asked.

"The General is still trying to get Spencer settled down after the New Mexico episode. He says that he is working toward the abort command, but that Spencer is more complicated than he first took him to be."

"He gave up the 'hold' command pretty damn quick when the General threatened to expose him as a pedophile," I said.

"The General thinks that the 'hold' was the maximum Spencer would exchange for that. Spencer believes his life will be vindicated when these attacks unfold," Ryan explained.

"Was it Beers, you think, who goaded Spencer into such fundamental belief in mass violence?" I asked.

"Maybe," Ryan said, "all those years knowing that Beers scoffed at his methods, that might have pushed Spencer in that direction. But then maybe Spencer is just Beers with his pants on and his collar buttoned."

"How about a cocktail," Yael said, "like the one you gave our friends back at the cabin?"

"The General knows what's available, but his plan, I believe, is to bring Spencer out of the sense of duress. Let him begin to believe that he is being rehabilitated by the new revolutionary leadership. And then reversing the polarity, so to speak, where Spencer acts to abort the attack on the belief that it is in the better interest of the movement to do so."

"If there is any abort mode," I said.

"That's why we move forward as though that will not happen," Ryan said.

He took another cell call, listened, and got off.

"They've gotten off the Thruway at the next exit," he said.

"That's New Paltz," I said.

"Yes."

"It's a college town," I said. "I've spent summers in that area off and on since high school. There's a large campus. The bomb team could have connections with students, mutual friends, something along those lines. It's a busy town now, lots of traffic."

"The one thing we'll have is that one of them will stay with or near the vehicle with the weapon," Yael said.

"With calls back and forth," Ryan said. "They don't seem to put much stock in radio silence. They're blissfully confident."

"Do we know what they're saying to each other?" I asked.

"No, we're staying with tracking the signal traffic," Ryan said. "If we ask for the conversations that will set off a national security cascade and we could find ourselves with the federal agencies pouring onto the scene, and the weapon gets detonated."

"It would help to hear their voices, know what language they're speaking to one another," I said.

"But it's not going to help if that brings the federal club foot around," Ryan said. "If the bomb team is spooked they'll detonate. Yael's bullet was the distance between that happening and not happening in Tupper Lake."

"If the bomb had been real," I said.

"I still don't get that," Yael said.

"The fake bomb?" I said.

"The whole bit. Why a decoy team that thinks it is carrying out the mission. And how the hell does it wind up in Tupper Lake in the same time frame with the real team."

"And we go for the decoy," I said.

"That's the part that unnerves me," Ryan said. "We go for the decoy. The decoy thinks it's the real team. The real team leaves town, and neither the decoy nor the real team knows about the other. They had no way to plan being in the same place at the same time like that. They were on their own."

"It reminds me of quantum mechanics," Yael said.

"No one really understands quantum mechanics," Ryan said.

"That's what I mean," Yael said.

"Even when we stop this attack," I said, "we won't get this finished until we get at the operational control where this was put together."

"I think that you'll find, we will find," Ryan said, "that that is an ever-receding horizon. The plans and planners are many, just like software programs, but the resources to put them in motion, those are much more limited. That's what we have in Charles Spencer."

Yael was racing down toward New Paltz, using off routes instead of heading to the Thruway. I knew that town well and it was its own sort of place, more than a little outside the everyday run of things, with a vocal faction of ex-hippies from the 1960s and 70s who still believed that they were at the forefront of everything. Franklin Beers would feel at home there. That settled generation of ex-hippies might even sit cross-legged in a circle around Beers and nod in understanding as he explained to them why detonating a nuclear weapon in their town was something they should be open to, if the weapon was detonated for a cause they approved of.

"The General told me he called you, Mara," Ryan said.

"He did?" I said. "What did he have to say about it?"

"That he enjoyed the conversation," Ryan said.

"That's it?"

"That was it," he said.

"So he's not angry at me?"

"About what?" Ryan said.

"About yelling at him after he shot Beers," I said.

"Hell, no," Ryan said, "he enjoyed that. He thought you showed spunk, although he said he would have liked it better if you had held your gun on him and ordered him to stop. But he understood your reluctance to go that far for Beers."

"What is it, exactly," I asked, "that the General is looking for in team members?"

"Lots of qualities, but the first thing is a fully formed person, with an unmovable moral center," Ryan said.

"Is that what got me my cell phone privileges back?" I asked.

"The cell phone is a ticking bomb in its own right, Mara. You didn't need one until we took down the bomb team in Tupper Lake."

"I understand," I said. "You understand that I haven't talked to my office or Rob or my daughters through all this?"

"And you understand," Ryan said, "that's one of the reasons you're still with us?"

"Yes, but I would at some point like to resume, ah, I guess it would be called 'my life.' Is the General going to be amenable to that?"

"Absolutely. That is up to you. We're all here because we want to be. The cell phone thing, that's just a matter of immediate security."

"I know," I said, "and I'm with the team until the finish, but on the other side of that mountain, there's this life I was living."

"I had one of those," Yael said.

"What happened to it?" I asked.

She shrugged and said nothing.

We were approaching New Paltz. It was getting dark. That day and night thing seemed to keep happening whether I paid attention to it or not.

When we got into town we took a survey of the main drag, which had a nineteenth century feel in the downtown core. Yael parked across the street from the local Starbucks and I went for the coffee while Ryan made a call.

I had never been uncomfortable in my own skin, so that had made me an outsider during my visits to New Paltz over the years. Being uncomfortable in your own skin had always seemed to me to be essential to the local way of life. Busy street corners in Manhattan had more warmth and a much better gift for relaxation. This town was an odd place.

56

We sat in our truck parked in front of a bank, waiting on the call that would tell us the last cell phone location for the bomb team. I had brought back three coffees, black, heavy on the sugar, hot. I had been drinking less coffee because it only reminded me of how little sleep I had been getting. The stimulant of choice on our team was your own adrenaline.

Ryan took a call and was done with it in seconds.

"It's what we thought," he said. "They've landed on the campus."

Yael took a u-turn right out of our parking space and drove up a hill. We had the same profile in mind. Three men, an SUV, a second car, one of the men staying nearby to watch over the weapon. Last time, in Tupper Lake, we expected to find the weapon in the SUV but it was in the trunk of the car.

"This time it will be in the SUV," I said.

"What if there is no SUV this time," Yael said.

"Then I guess we're looking for a slightly out-of-place European male standing near whatever vehicle," I said.

"And if the person isn't European, out-of-place, male, or standing near a vehicle?" Yael pressed.

"Then I'm fresh out of what we're looking for," I said. "Or we're looking for anyone and anyone is easy to find, because he's everywhere."

"We're likely more out of place here," I said as we rode slowly around the campus roads, "than the people we're looking for."

The students we saw along the way had three traits in common. They appeared to be grim, worried, and suspicious. The women added to that a look of aloof and bossy determination. The men fell out along the lines of either too-thin artist types or the sloppy beer and sports look.

"It shouldn't be that hard to pick out the bombers," I said. "They'll be the ones who look like they have a serious purpose in life."

"We're going to have trouble with the campus police," Ryan said.

"Yes we are," Yael said.

"What did I miss?" I asked.

"They're all over the place with nothing to do," Yael said. "They'll pick up on us driving around and want to stop us."

"Can't we flash our lights or show them that card, Ryan?" I asked.

"This is too tight a situation for that. We don't want them to know we're here. Park it, Yael. We'll get out, split up, and do this on foot."

Yael put the truck in a spot behind the library, which looked like it was originally designed as a mausoleum for distinguished Soviet commissars.

I would cut directly through the campus. Yael and Ryan were going to take the circumference, in opposite directions. We would all meet on the other side and take it from there. The bomb team was here, somewhere, and we would find them. But there was a common sense among the three of us that this would not go down easy. We parted on edge.

My path took me up through the main alleyway between the academic buildings, as grotesque an assembly of architectural catastrophe as I had seen in some time. I was in search of a smallish parking lot tucked in close to a large dormitory. We were all looking for the telltale sign of the person hanging close by a vehicle. On my way I asked a group of students, three women and one guy, if they could direct me there. With polite indifference they sent me down past an art building. Along the way I passed a group of stone benches and made eye contact with a pretty young blonde woman sitting on one.

I nodded at her and said hello.

"Hello," she said, smiling. Her voice had a distinct East European accent, but I couldn't place it. Not Polish, maybe Serb.

I should have kept moving, but I clumsily stopped in front of her and looked at her more carefully. She drew me in perfectly with her smile.

The zap to the back of my neck was sending me right down. My head would have clipped the edge of the stone bench. My arms were limp and helpless to break my fall, but the person behind me who had administered the shock and the pretty blonde woman caught me and supported my dead weight. I had walked into a trap. The bomb team knew we were coming and had made us before we made them.

I never went unconscious but I was indeed stunned and they half-dragged, half-walked me to a side entrance to a nearby dormitory and took me inside to a basement dorm room. On the way there my cell phone rang and the person who had zapped me from behind took it from my pocket, turned it off, and heaved it into a small pond nearby. That person was also a woman.

The third bomb team member was yet another woman, also pretty and blonde. She shot me up with a syringe full of drugs as soon as the other two laid me on the floor of the room. Then came the duct tape around my mouth, gagging tight. I had never wanted to breathe through my mouth more desperately. Then my forearms folded together behind me. Then my ankles and knees.

They had my gun. It was gone, at least. They probably grabbed that as I was going down. They opened a closet and put me in it, right on top of the dead bodies of two young guys. They were, I assumed, the dorm room's late occupants, who had met some pretty women on campus not too long ago who quickly invited themselves back to the room. What simple genius it was to make a bomb team of young pretty women. The world will do their bidding. They ask and receive. Doors open. Guards go down. It's done, like that.

In those first moments in the closet on top of the dead guys I realized that the bomb team must have made us in Tupper Lake while we were taking down the decoy team. The real team used the decoy team by following it, which made perfect sense and explained how they were in the same place at the same time.

The decoy team with three men fit our profile. The all-girl team wouldn't stand out, even if it was standing alone, as anything other than three pretty young women hanging or traveling together. But they knew who we were and had brought us to exactly where they wanted us, onto and into the unreal world of a college campus where they could manipulate the unreality as they pleased.

Two things stood out for me. They hadn't killed me. That was a mystery. And they had chosen to trap us instead of evading us. That's why they re-started and kept up the chatter out of Tupper Lake. Perhaps it was the 'hold' command delaying their mission that made them want to dispose of any trackers. In the end, though, if they felt cornered, they could just detonate the weapon, ending the conversation, so to speak.

They hadn't closed the closet door on me, so it was clear that I was being watched and considered. My instinct was to not look at them, or let them catch me directing any of my attention toward them. I tried to keep the look of my stunned, half-conscious state, my weak notion being that I didn't want or need any more work from them. I had caught a glimpse of a bullet wound in the head of one of the guys I was piled on top of and I expected that I was no great distance from getting one of those.

If the men on the decoy team had seemed cold and vaguely non-human, they were warm and fuzzy in comparison with these ladies. The drug they had injected me with was some sort of hypnotic or relaxant and though I was now drifting on the great oceanic tide of being I could feel them, each of them, in the room. They were whispering ice. The language was a Slavic one. My fear was no longer for myself. I was desperately afraid that they would trap and kill Ryan and Yael. What a horrible tragedy that would be, I thought.

My cell phone had rung back outside, while they were dragging me away. They knew that Ryan and Yael knew that I was in trouble. I tried, desperately, riding the oceanic effect of the drug, to work it out like a math problem. Ryan and Yael were this good. These three women were that good. 'A' had this advantage. 'B' had that advantage. If 'A' did this and 'B' did that, then the result would be, what?

One of them reached out and touched my neck with two fingers. She was taking my pulse. She closed the closet door on me. Then I heard them leave the room and then their voices briefly in the hallway.

They were on the hunt.

57

What my captors did not have was the advantage of being an American girl with older brothers. My two brothers thought it was their duty to protect me when we were kids, but also to find as many safe ways to torture me as they could. One of those ways was to tie me up and leave me in the garage or the tree house or my room.

I got tired of it and became an escape artist, and a good one. Soon it became a game. Tie Mara up and see how long it takes her to get loose. My brothers would bring their friends over and bet them they could not tie me up securely enough so that I could not escape. By that time I was a partner in the enterprise and getting one-third of the winnings. Some of my brothers' friends refused to accept defeat and kept betting, tying me up, and losing. My brothers and I still laugh out loud about it.

The duct tape wasn't going to be a problem on its own, but the drug had left me feeling like a rubber band. I was weak and discoordinated. I think I was supposed to be out as well, but I had become a master at keeping myself awake, following the masterful examples of Ryan and Yael.

Now, while I began to work my arms free, I was also forcing the sloppiness out of my mind and body. Duct tape is strong and they had wrapped it with vigor and certainty, but the mind acting through the twists and turns of the muscles is stronger. It took me just a few minutes to free my arms.

I pushed the closet doors open and threw myself off of the two dead guys onto the floor of the room. My ankles and knees were still bound so I looked for the sharpest thing in the room and saw a set of keys sitting on a desk and dragged myself over to them. I gouged at the tape around my knees, got a good rip in it and tore it off. Then I did the same to the tape around my ankles.

Before removing the tape around my mouth I went looking for my gun. I went right to the desk drawers and there it was in the second one I opened, with the clip still in it. I chambered a round to be ready and then went to work on the tape wrapped around my mouth. Getting that off was the greatest relief because the drug had made me want to vomit, or maybe being left on top of the dead students was what did that. But I knew that if I vomited I would choke to death under the duct tape.

Just as I got rid of the last attachments of the tape to my skin and hair and threw it on the floor I heard a key go into the door. I suppressed an impulse to fire through the door, which was a good thing, because it wasn't one of them. It was a young man who didn't seem to have anything to do with the bomb team. I wasn't taking any chances and held the gun on him. His jaw fell open when he saw me.

"Come on in," I said calmly but with command. "Close the door. Now, who are you? What are you doing here?"

"I'm Jamie," he said. "I live in this room."

I had to think fast and talk even faster. He probably thought I was someone's insane mom, broken out of a mental institution. I had to convince him otherwise, give him clear instructions, and scare him sufficiently to assure he followed those instructions.

"Look," I said, "we've got just seconds to get this right. You need to get out of here, get to the most crowded public place you know of, and stay there. Do not contact the campus police.

You'll just get them killed. I can't explain this to you. But you must do exactly as I say. Now. Do you hear me?"

"Yes," he said.

"Go."

He turned and left the room. I stood in the doorway and told him to take the long way, directing him away from the side exit near the room.

"You'll be O.K. if you do what I told you," I said as he walked quickly away. He believed me, and he was going to sit somewhere frozen in fear long enough so that this could play itself out.

I stepped back into the room and closed the door. The three women on the bomb team were perfect predators, cold as reptiles. They were out looking for Ryan and Yael and they knew what Ryan and Yael looked like. As hard as I had tried, I couldn't calculate how that contest would turn out. For starters I didn't think that either of them would fall prey to the ruse that had trapped me, and I wasn't sure whether they would, either of them, go down from the shock of a stun gun.

But if either one was taken down the women would bring them back here, assuming they were not killed. If I waited in the room, I had the advantage of surprise. They thought they had secured me. I would have enough control over the situation to kill all three of them when they returned, I thought. If I left the room, then the entire campus was in play, and these women had already demonstrated their skill at getting behind me.

Then I would have to factor in what would happen if the young man I had just scared off ran to the campus police instead of following my instructions. I would be arrested, and Ryan wasn't around with his magic card.

If I left the room, and the bomb women came back with Yael or Ryan as captives and found me gone, then they might just execute Yael or Ryan and run. They could move to another location or, if they were convinced a trap was closing on them, detonate the weapon.

My options were reduced to one when I heard the heavy sound of something being dragged toward the door. I grabbed a pillow off of one of the beds. My instincts told me to muffle my gunshots any way I could.

"She's just very drunk," I heard one of the bomb team say in her Slavic accent. She had Yael.

"It's so early," a young woman who must have just come down the hall responded.

"She started at lunch," the woman bomber answered.

She waited until the student had left the hallway, fumbling with the keys in the meantime, before opening the door. I stepped to the side where I couldn't be seen from the doorway. She struggled a bit as she dragged Yael inside. The other two were not with her. They were still out after Ryan. As she pulled Yael inside I fired a round through the pillow into her head. Blood and brains spit out the exit wound and splattered on the wall next to the door as feathers from the pillow snowed down. She slumped over on top of Yael, and I yanked her off and laid her down in the middle of the floor, right about where they had first put me when they brought me back.

I stepped over Yael and looked into the hallway. A clump of brain had found its way out there so I grabbed it and threw it back into the room and wiped my hand on my jeans.

Closing the door I grabbed Yael and sat her up against the wall. Her eyes were open. She had seen the whole thing go down and was nodding her approval.

"Good," she managed to say.

"They zapped you and then used a syringe?"

She nodded.

"Fight the drug," I said. "Throw the effects off. There are two of them still out there after Ryan."

That got her adrenaline pumping. I could see her start to snap out of it. The dead woman had taken Yael's gun and stuffed it in her waistband behind her back. I grabbed it and showed it to Yael.

"That was some close work," she said.

"Too damn close," I said.

"You didn't hesitate," she said and I think I managed two-seconds-worth of a smile.

Then I searched the dead woman, looking for car keys or a detonator, but she had neither. I got a palm-sized .45, her stun gun, and her cell phone.

I couldn't stop myself from thinking about how I would love to use the stun gun on the other two bombers. My anger was surfacing over how they had trapped me and I suppressed it immediately. There was no time for anything but cold precision.

There was some bottled water in the room's mini-refrigerator. I gave it to Yael and she splashed her face with it. She sat up straight and pulled her knees back and began assessing whether she could stand up. We were maintaining silence now. She was ninety percent back and she looked at me and we had a simultaneous rush of fear.

What if the other two women had taken down Ryan?

58

Yael held out her hand, signaling that she was ready to get up. I grabbed it and pulled her to her feet.

"There's a kid," I said, "who walked in and found me here. It's his room." I told her what I had instructed him to do. He was a variable. We had to factor in that he might alert the campus police.

"We have to find Ryan," she said.

I shrugged, indicating that I had no clue how we would do that.

"Either they have him or he's looking for us," she said.

"They're very clever," I said.

"I know," she said.

"They made us in Tupper Lake. They were watching while we took down their decoy team. This was a trap." I gestured to indicate the whole deal with getting us to the college.

She focused on the shards of duct tape I'd thrown on the floor.

"Yours?" she asked.

I pointed to the closet, and the two dead kids inside it.

"They bundled me up and put me on top of them."

She looked at the remnants of tape again, but didn't ask.

"If they have Ryan," I said, "they will bring him back here."

"Not necessarily," she said. "He might be too much for them."

"Then they would kill him and dump him out of sight."

"Yes," she said.

"We have to move, take our best shot at finding him."

Yael crouched over the dead bomber. She was the not-blonde one. In death it was even clearer how perfectly generic the young woman was. I couldn't imagine a place in America where she wouldn't fit in. She was well-groomed, pretty, in-shape, the basic all-purpose pass to mostly anything in the United States. Her training in cold-blooded murder and terrorism showed nowhere on the surface.

We left her right there as we abandoned the room. I gave Yael the cell phone I had taken from the dead woman's jacket.

"Should you call in the cavalry?" I said.

"That's too dangerous," she said.

We went out through the same side door of the dormitory we had both been dragged in through. It was raining, not hard but steadily.

"What's our best bet?" I asked as we hit the nearby walkway.

"To see them before they see us," Yael said.

She took the lead, moving quickly like she knew where she was going. I gave her some room and followed ten yards back. Both of us played to the rain, acting as though we were just trying to get somewhere to get out of it. That worked. None of the few people who were out, most of them with open umbrellas, took any serious notice of us.

We passed through a large cluster of dormitories and then Yael hurried down a bank of concrete stairs. It was as though she had instantly calculated a bundle of factors with her instincts and caught a mental scent of Ryan. I could almost sense what she sensed as the intensity of her purpose radiated back to me.

At the bottom of the stairs the path ahead cut to the right toward another cluster of dormitories. To the immediate right there was another parking lot. Ahead to the left was a lawn leading down to a pond. Yael scanned it all, and she saw them.

She pulled her nine millimeter and pointed in the direction of the pond at about forty-five degrees left from the bottom of the stairs. They were just visible over the top of an incline that fell down to the edge of the pond. Yael didn't hesitate.

They had Ryan down on the grass. Anyone who saw it would have thought 'college girls with drunk guy in rain.' It was that generically unsuspicious. They were crouching on either side of him when one of them saw Yael approaching, gun first. Yael fired once, twice, hitting the one who had seen her in the head, putting her right down, moribund if not dead. The second woman bolted like a deer, and ran like one. Yael fired at her and she stumbled as though hit but kept running, filled with the adrenaline of flight.

Yael slid to her knees over Ryan, who was unconscious. She checked his pulse.

"His heart's stopped," she said and began rhythmically pumping his chest with her joined hands, and then one hand as she used the other to call for back-up.

"Mara, you've got to get the other one. Kill her before she can detonate the weapon."

I was no match as a runner for the third terrorist, but if Yael had hit her she was going to be slowed down. She had run around to the front of a large, square, squat building and into another parking lot. If she had stopped, she was probably lying in wait for me. I didn't see her anywhere in the distance at any point where her pace would have taken her so I circled quickly to the right where I could get an angle on her instead of getting caught in one she was readying for me.

I had made my move before she could pick me up. She was crouching on one knee behind a car, her back half-turned from my position. I continued on for a better angle and then went down behind the next row of cars, moving up behind her. She heard me as I approached and spun in my direction, firing as she turned, but without having a bead on me. It was the pretty blonde who I had first seen on the stone bench, who had lured me into the trap where her comrade hit me with the stun gun.

She wasn't smiley-faced now, just expressionless, as her tactical training guided her, and my first shot hit her in the chest, dead center. She went down. I approached and stood close to her. She still held her gun. A fantastic predator to the end she tried to jerk herself into a position to fire on me. I shot her in the head, without hesitation.

By now Yael's earlier gunshots had been reported and the campus police were responding. I assumed that our back-up had already made it to Yael and Ryan, and I desperately wanted to get back there. But I needed to search the dead woman for a detonator and for her car keys. The nuclear weapon had to be secured.

Now there were campus police on foot headed in my direction as I searched the blonde terrorist. I found her keys, but not the detonator. Something told me to look under the car she had positioned herself behind, and there it was, a small black plastic control with a digital readout and two square buttons. It looked like a garage door remote. She had taken it out and was ready to detonate the weapon if she sensed her odds had dwindled.

I looked at the remote detonator and it took a few seconds for it to sink in. The digital readout at first looked like it merely showed the time, but that was only what I expected it to be, or wanted it to be. But it was a timer, and it was counting down. It was at twenty-eight minutes. She set the weapon to go off and left herself enough time to make a decent run for it. She was not, in the end, committed to suicide. But I knew instantly in my gut that there was no way that this countdown could be aborted or the weapon disarmed before it detonated.

I had to find it and get it out of there but here came the campus police, two of them, guns drawn, giving me orders. I dropped my nine millimeter and threw my hands up, but there was no time for this. I had to get them to stand down immediately.

"Federal anti-terror task force," I shouted at them, trying my best to approximate what we were. "This is a national security emergency. I need your immediate assistance." I sold them on taking a look. They saw the dead woman. Didn't like it.

"She's a terrorist," I said.

They were buying and not buying at the same time. Why hadn't Ryan ever given me the magic words or one of those cards. Maybe because he knew I could do it without them. The two campus cops lowered their weapons, and I lowered my hands but I didn't reach to pick up my gun.

"What do you need?" one asked.

I showed them the car keys. There were two sets linked together, one for each of the bomb team's cars.

"I need to find both of those vehicles. They might be in this lot. There's something in the back of one of them. It's very heavy and the rear suspension will be riding low. I need to get that vehicle out of here right now."

59

The campus cops misunderstood, thinking that I needed them to find the vehicles, and the more forthcoming of the two reached for the keys I had shown them. There was no time for that. I grabbed my gun from the pavement and began searching for the vehicles by pressing the lock system remotes attached to the key rings. I got a response from both vehicles. They were parked five spaces apart on the far side of the lot. If they had been in another lot, then the campus would have been vaporized. It would have taken too long to find them. The ladies bomb team had gravitated back near their weapon. Once they finished with Ryan and were rejoined by Yael's assailant, who would have killed both Yael and me back in the dorm room, they would have been on their way.

The Chevy sedan was sitting too high on its rear suspension to have much weight in the back. The SUV, a Land Rover, was carrying the weapon and I got into it and started the engine.

One of the campus cops held up his hands indicating that this was all happening a little too fast for him.

"O.K., ma'am," he said, "I need an explanation here."

"No you don't," I said, "you need to get out an alert to all local law enforcement that this Land Rover needs a path cleared into Rosendale, and that it's going to be traveling upwards of 100 miles per hour."

"Wait a second," he said.

"There is no second," I said, backing the Land Rover out of the space. "Do exactly what I just told you to do."

A campus police vehicle, lights flashing, pulled into the lot as I barked my orders to the cop. An older pudgy uniformed cop got out. I thought I saw sergeant's stripes, but I didn't really look at him as I hit the accelerator and went for the exit of the parking lot.

The only thing I needed to do right now, besides drive as fast as I could without crashing the SUV, was to talk to Yael. She had the cell phone of the bomber I had killed back in the dorm room. I had the cell I had just taken from the dead woman in the parking lot.

I hit the re-dial for the last number called on her phone.

"It's Mara," I said as soon as Yael answered.

"Don't say anything," I said, "just listen. I have the weapon, and I'm on the road with it. It's set to go off in," I looked at the time readout on the detonator, "twenty-three minutes. You have to call the General right now and get him to do what I'm about to tell you."

"Go," she said.

I told her that there was a huge underground facility in Rosendale, an old limestone mine inside a mountain. It was now a secure document storage facility. The General had to get it evacuated and ready for me to drive the Land Rover inside it, as deep as I could go and still get back out. The massive door then had to be lowered and everyone needed to be out of the area.

She got it. There was no time to ask about Ryan. She needed to get to the General and have him commandeer a private underground facility for what would be essentially forever. I had known about the facility for decades and had even gone there once on the off chance I could talk my way into a tour. If the General did his thing, I would be getting the quick tour now.

I had the SUV's emergency flashers on and was leaning on the horn as I raced through the local traffic. Scared and angry drivers pulled to the side as they saw me coming. It was dark, still raining, and the roads were slick. When I got on the direct route north to Rosendale, I punched the Land Rover up to 110 mph, passing cars in front of me, forcing everyone else off the road. A police vehicle cruising up in front of me, trying to clear the way, gave up and pulled over to let me by.

"Too rich for your blood?" I muttered as I passed him.

Yael called me back.

"The General is on it," she said.

"What are the odds?" I asked.

"That if you get there, it will be ready."

"How's Ryan?" I asked.

"I'm with him in the ambulance. His heart is beating. He's unconscious. We're on our way to the hospital. They almost killed him."

"The third one," I said.

"Yeah?" Yael answered.

"She's dead."

"Good."

"When you get confirmation from the General," I said.

"I'll let you know," she said.

The ride into Rosendale included a near miss with a kid driving a boom box car. I heard the pounding, throbbing beat of rap music as I watched him spin out on the wet pavement. What came flashing into my mind was how much I'd wanted to have a boy. Then I could sense my two girls and how much I wanted to just go shopping with them and take them out to lunch. Such mundane thoughts to have with a nuclear weapon in the back, set to go off now in seventeen minutes. Life could be very simple.

I made it into Rosendale and went the wrong way up a one-way street to avoid the main drag. Coming out at the other side of the commercial district I headed straight for where I thought the underground facility was, but I missed the entrance and had to turn around. A guy driving a pick-up came around a curve in the road and slammed into me while hitting his brakes.

The SUV was badly damaged but still drove and I pulled away without even acknowledging the other driver. I found the gate to the facility and noticed that four or five people who appeared to have been working inside had come out.

A guard was waiting for me.

"Get them out of here," I said. "How far into the mountain can I get?"

He didn't get it. He wanted to mull it over and answer me after he finished assessing the situation.

"Look," I said, "there's no time for you to think. Answer my question."

"About a quarter mile. That's about how far you can get inside," he said.

"Who's going to operate the door?"

"That's me," he said.

"O.K.," I said, "once I get in there you lower it down to about three feet from the ground so that I can slide back out. When I come back through, close it all the way and get as far away from it and here as you can."

"Lady," he said, "what the hell is going to happen here?"

"Hell," I said, "is what's about to happen here," and I punched the gas and drove through the oversized entryway into the cavernous inside of the mountain.

My thought on seeing the inside of the facility was that it looked like the refinished basement of a medieval king. My second thought was that it was a big enough and strong enough box to contain a nuclear blast, but then that was the wildest guess I'd ever made. I believed that the best I could hope for was a substantial mitigation of the blast and to get back outside and far enough away to survive it myself.

The driveway inside the mountain forked off, with one fork heading down further underground. That was the one I wanted.

I checked the detonator. I had eight minutes left. It was time to think about letting this baby go. I stopped the Land Rover in the middle of the drive, pointed the wheels straight ahead toward the next bend, put it in neutral, got out and gave it an extra shove from behind as it rolled off. I turned and headed for the exit, never looking back. It was going to land where it was going to land.

There were seven minutes left and I was about a hundred yards inside the mountain. That I was running only occurred to me well after I started. Nothing had ever seemed so far away as the way out of the facility. When it came up in front of me, with the huge metal door left exactly as I had asked the guard to leave it, I thanked God for the remnants of sanity and precision left to us.

Rolling under the door and outside I picked up the guard immediately and motioned to him to lower the door the rest of the way. He was in a booth, a glass booth like the ones the team had so often found itself in, and I reached it and him as I heard the massive door close behind me.

"Come on," I said, telling him to follow me. I looked at the detonator. We had two minutes. I never knew a two minute span with more life in it. I led the guard as far away from the door and around the side of the mountain as we could go. I checked above us to see what could be thrown loose by a blast and chose a spot where we were protected by some boulders.

Then we just sat down.

"What's your name?" I asked the guard.

"Chris," he said.

"Mara," I said, shaking his hand.

"What is this?" he asked.

The ground throbbed beneath us, heaving like the body of someone having convulsions. The air seemed to go flat and my ears began ringing. There was a sound like a freight train or a gigantic wind. I looked at Chris.

"That is what," I said.

"Oh," he said.

60

When the earth stopped heaving and the peculiar buzz in the air faded, I wanted to confirm that the massive door had held. I was sure that if it had not held, anything that could burn that was anywhere near it would be on fire. There was no sign that anything was burning, no smell of smoke, no glowing embers drifting in the dark.

Chris followed me as I headed down to a position where we would be well away from the entrance but would have an angle on it. When we had a line of sight to it we could feel it radiating heat, but it had held. The blast probably threw many tons of rock up behind the door, shielding it from inside. But no one was ever going inside there again to find out.

This place would be a problem for the rest of history, but it had served to stop Charles Spencer and his plan to remake history.

The first people on the scene were local cops and firemen, who stayed back, looking confused and uncertain about what needed to be done.

The cop who looked like he was in charge ambled over in my direction.

"You the woman who drove that thing in there?" he asked me.

"What thing?" I said.

"The thing that just exploded inside the mountain," he shot back.

"What explosion?"

"O.K.," he said, "I get it."

"Are your cell phones working?" I said, reaching for the one in my pocket. He went for his own.

"The signal looks fine," he said.

I smiled at him. "I think you're all too close here. Maybe you should just get everyone back a quarter mile, just to be safe. People will show up who will take charge of this."

"People?" he said.

"Yeah, people," I said. "You saw Men in Black, right, with Will Smith and Tommy Lee Jones. People."

He appreciated that and laughed.

"O.K., ma'am," he said, "nothing happened here. You're not here yourself. And people will show up to confirm all that. I'll pass it along."

"And don't forget to shoot any reporters on sight," I said.

"That's our standing policy," he said, smiling like a coyote.

I hit the redial on the cell phone.

"That was a geophysical event," Yael said.

"You felt it?" I said.

"Sure did."

"Ryan?" I asked.

"He's looking better right now. I'm at the hospital. The General is sending in a surgeon who is experienced in gunshot trauma."

"Gunshot?"

"Yeah, they shot Ryan in the gut. His heart stopped again in the ambulance. The EMTs got it started. Meanwhile, our people are all over this place. It's in a virtual lockdown."

"Why's that?"

"The General thinks that we're being hunted now."

"By who?" I asked.

"He wasn't clear about that, and I've been too busy standing around the trauma unit looking like I'll kill everyone here if Ryan doesn't make it to ask the General for details."

"Keep that up," I said, having been through enough hospital emergencies to know that patients need someone around with a big neon sign flashing 'malpractice' on their foreheads to ward off slack attitudes and relaxed treatment decisions.

We finished the call. I needed to get hold of a vehicle. Chris was still following me, so I thanked him profusely for his perfect work and recommended that he stay as uninvolved with the people who were going to show up as he could.

"Don't volunteer any information. Don't offer help. Don't remember me. And don't tell them your name," I told him.

"You sure?" he said.

"Surer than sure," I said. "That thing there," I said, pointing up toward the facility, "is over. The only thing you did here tonight was evacuate like everyone else, as you were instructed to do. Don't do anything to stand out in the crowd. If they corner you, tell them the truth but as little of it as you can."

"I need to protect you, is what you're telling me," he said.

"Hell no, Chris," I said, "I'm telling you to protect yourself. Don't worry about me."

I thanked him again and left him as what looked like one of our vans rolled up on the stretch of highway that ran past the facility.

The General himself got out, impeccably dressed as always.

"Ah," I said to him, "the men in black have arrived."

"Could you have disarmed that bomb?" were his first words to me. It was a good question.

"I don't know, sir. It was my first nuclear weapon."

"Indeed," he said. "You did the best you could."

"Well, it didn't go off in Manhattan or on the college campus. Those are good things, right?"

He smiled. "It did wipe out a century's worth of records, not to mention two hundred million dollars worth of art masterpieces, as I have been vigorously told."

"Yet," I said, "not even the security guard was killed or hurt, so we're even on that score."

"Good work," he said as he stepped forward and gave me a little hug.

"Aren't you the sentimental old fool," I said. "Yael just told me you're concerned that we are being hunted?"

"The bomb team you eliminated," he said, "they weren't alone. They had a shadow team that was ready to move in to help them when the gunfire brought the university police on the scene."

"How did you find out about that?"

"Our back-up team picked up their movement but then Ryan became the priority. Everyone followed the ambulance to the hospital."

"What am I," I said, "chopped liver?"

He liked that. "No, you had every available cop in the area looking out for you. They closed the roads off behind you so that no one could follow you."

"You saw to that?" I said.

"I did," he answered.

"So this team shadowing the bomb team, you think they won't just go home. They're after us now?"

"Think, Miss Rains," he said. "If some of ours are taken down, do we run and hide?"

"Are these people like us?" I asked. "Those women that we killed…"

"Were better trained than anything we've ever seen," he said, finishing my sentence his way.

"So you're saying this shadow team wants revenge. Why wouldn't they just regroup and make another terror play?" I asked.

"We took their big play away from them," the General reminded me. "Charles Spencer and his money and network aren't there to boot up another operation. This shadow team and the bombers are and were jihadists. You think they maybe want to get to the people who not only stopped them but killed their best assets, the pretty American-looking blonde girls who could do anything?"

While we were debating the question the federal agency people began to arrive. One very important looking man approached us and told the General that he wanted to speak to him. The General didn't say a word to him or even look at him. But it was as if he glared at the man with the back of his head. The man walked away without another word.

I squinted at the General, as if to say 'what the hell was that.'

"You learn how to do that at the Pentagon," he explained, "if you don't want to spend your life talking to people like that. Don't respond to them and they usually go away."

"We do the same thing in Manhattan, to street lunatics," I said.

"It's the same principle," he said, smiling.

"Suppose you need a favor from someone like that, down the road. Won't he remember that you dissed him?" I asked.

"Yes, of course he'll remember, and he'll fall all over himself to deliver the favor."

I got it. The General was right. "Why is that?" I asked.

"He wants to be treated better in the future," he said.

"So what's the plan for dealing with this shadow team?" I asked as we got into the van.

"We'll have to kill them," the General said matter-of-factly.

"Before they kill us," I said.

"Exactly," he said.

"Anything more specific to the plan than that?" I asked.

"Yes, we don't know where they are at the moment. They have us at a disadvantage. We need to find them by letting them find us."

61

It was Tony at the wheel of the General's van and he acknowledged me with a friendly nod. He drove about 30 mph above the speed limit, but compared to my trip in the Land Rover it was slow going.

Ryan was in surgery at a hospital across the Hudson in Poughkeepsie. The General had already been told that the place was a tactical nightmare, but it would be at least twenty-four hours before Ryan could be moved. Between now and then we had to control the hospital, all comings and goings, without provoking internal revolt. The General believed that the terrorist shadow team would have their best shot at us while we were there and that they wouldn't care at all about it being a hospital. That would make it an even more attractive target for them.

As we crossed the river at the Mid-Hudson Bridge my gut spoke to me.

"This bridge needs to be watched," I told the General.

"Already done," he said.

"What did you do with Charles Spencer, if I may ask?"

"You may," the General said. "Charles and Franklin Beers, who is recovering from his gunshot wounds by the way, are both at a temporary foreign facility."

"Still alive," I offered in redundancy.

"Their fates are up in the air," he said.

"You weren't so hesitant with Allison Garvin," I said.

"That was a special case," he said. "She had infiltrated the Executive Office of the President of the United States. She needed killin'."

"I see your point," I said. "Whereas Charles Spencer only planned and financed a nuclear attack on New York. So his fate is up in the air."

"Well, Miss Rains," the General said, "we have our priorities. We first have to kill all the lawyers before we get to Charles Spencer."

I laughed out loud. "Very funny, sir."

"Was I joking?" he said.

"Is your name really Edward?" I asked, while the mood was light, about the name Spencer had called him.

"Yes and no," he said.

"Is that your final answer?"

"For now," he said.

We pulled up at the emergency entrance to the hospital. I recognized some of our people outside doing a good job of looking inconspicuous. Inside it was clear, to me at least, that things were tightly bottled up. It was our people in the security guard uniforms and Callista was there playing doctor. As I looked around I saw that most of the hospital personnel in the receiving area had been replaced with our people. Even some of the people sitting in the waiting area were ours.

This was not the sort of place where you wanted to face down murderous attackers, however.

The General led me into an elevator and we went up to the floor where Ryan was in surgery and found Yael in the waiting room.

"Nice work, Mara," she said.

"Any word?" I said.

"He's been in almost an hour. Nothing yet," she said.

The General looked displeased.

"Do we have anyone in the operating room?" he asked Yael.

"No sir," she said.

"I need more information," he said and left us.

"Ryan's his boy," Yael said. "Where the one ends the other begins."

That was a way of saying it. If the General put a little effort into being mysterious, Ryan was effortless about it. The two of them led the team in its major competition, the race to zero fear. I could tell from watching Ryan that he had contempt for death. He hadn't been cheating it all those years in Iraq. He had been smacking it aside and stepping over it.

"It was the pretty blonde I killed in the parking lot who shot Ryan?" I asked Yael.

"I believe so," she said, "the other one, her weapon hadn't been fired."

"She wanted to mess him up more than she wanted to kill him," I said, "so she shot him in the gut instead of the head."

"That's right," Yael said.

"I wonder how much was raw meanness and how much was a tactic to burn our resources," I said.

"We'll never know," Yael said, "but that crew was as cold as it gets and I've seen cold."

"Did they bring her body here?"

"They did. All three of them are here in the morgue, along with the two guys they killed in the dormitory room."

"I want to take a look at the one who shot Ryan," I said. "Come down with me?"

"Sure," Yael said, without questioning me. She asked a nurse to tell the General that we would be back in a quarter hour or so, and we took the elevator down to the morgue in the basement of the hospital.

There was nothing more daunting than the medical examiner's morgue in Manhattan. I'd been there more than once. The one in this hospital was no competition, but no morgue was a place I would ever get used to, and this one had the same awful smell and ghastly atmosphere as the big one in the city.

She was on a gurney under a sheet. I had put her there and was glad to have done it. In death she didn't look that much more blank than she had when I saw her alive. She was wiry and fit. I remembered her last move, already shot in the chest, to try to bring her gun to bear on me. It seemed that at that point she might have thought about giving up, but she didn't. She had used the detonator to arm the nuclear weapon, and she gave her last breath gambling on getting off one more shot. What a strange life she had led, I thought.

Surely the thing, the group, the terror organization that had trained her had taken away her soul. I recalled how Chelsea Fall, when she finally dropped her mask of sanity, declared herself already dead. If Chelsea Fall truly was already dead inside, then this woman had been through death and been brought back as a form of zombie, a taut bag of flesh programmed for mass murder. Not anything like the hot-blooded terrorists so often portrayed in the media.

Before we left the morgue I looked at the bodies of the two boys who I'd been thrown on top of in the closet. Now, at a distance from that and no longer in the midst of my own struggle to survive, the perfect rottenness of those women killing these boys and throwing me on top of them struck me like a wind out of hell.

"Let's go," I said to Yael.

When we got back upstairs we found the General arguing quietly with one of the doctors from the surgical team.

"Don't tell me that again," I heard him say to the doctor and I had the feeling that things were going wrong.

The doctor walked back inside and the General turned to us.

"They want to let him go," he said as he broke down. "I told that son of a bitch to get back in there and save him. I told him that letting him die was not an option."

Yael took the General aside and tried to calm him. None of us were prepared for this. Death out there, in the action, was one thing, but we had gotten Ryan to the hospital, to the doctors, as far as the operating room, and the General was right, the sons of bitches ought to be able to take it from there.

Then the three of us sat together, waiting, praying, saying nothing. Each minute that passed without the grim reappearance of a surgeon was a victory. Soon we had fifteen one-minute victories, then thirty. All three of us were imploring God to keep Ryan alive. We got to an hour along a path of time that seemed both endless and instantaneous.

In that long moment my mind penetrated the hard shell Ryan kept in place around him. I remembered Allison Garvin taunting him, calling him 'soldier boy,' and how I could almost hear him thinking, 'you got that part right, lady.' Ryan wasn't in this for the action or simply because he was the consummate professional. He was in it because of what he loved, and what he loved was right over wrong. That was at the very core of all that he was.

The surgeon appeared in the hallway at a distance. His body language expressed exhaustion. He walked straight toward us, his face tired and neutral.

"He's going to have a very long recovery," he said, "but he will make it."

"Thank you," the General said, "thank you for saving him."

"You should thank God," the surgeon said. "It's a rare thing that anyone that far gone makes it back."

62

Ryan was moved to a post-op unit and the three of us stepped in there to see him. It was the usual mess of tubes and monitors. Inside it all Ryan looked pretty good. He wasn't awake yet, so that test hadn't been passed, but we were pleased just to have him still with us and to have a look at him.

Yael stayed with him. The General and I took the waiting area just outside. We were well into the middle of the night. My body was screaming at me to let it crash, but my mind wouldn't listen. The General looked as crisp and punctual as a businessman waiting on a late lunch meeting. He was on his cell taking inventory with our people positioned around the building.

"We're ready for them," he said to me when he got off.

"What are the chances they'll take a run at us?" I asked.

"About one hundred percent," he said.

"That certain? It's possible that they don't even know where we are, isn't it?"

"Not only do they know where we are, they know who we are, and they know we're waiting for them. In every sense, they've got us surrounded and they'll come at us with everything they have from the best angle they can find."

"You're making it sound dire," I said.

"It is," the General said. "We're vulnerable. For us, the way we play the game, this is right out in the open. We never let that happen, but here we are."

He had that right. We usually moved around like ghosts, leaving one location for another if the wind so much as shifted.

"Is this shadow team going to be men? More women?" I asked.

"They're going to be hornets, Miss Rains, and they're going to be mad. It's only in that certainty that they hand an advantage back to us. We are being treated as unfinished business, when the smart move for them would be to move on. Again, this is about revenge."

"There are a lot of things I don't know and understand about how we operate, sir," I said.

"It's all need to know," he said.

"But for instance," I said, "we, or you, seem to have a lot of power, a lot of resources, and a hell of a lot of intel at your disposal."

"And your question is?"

"My question is who the hell are you, sir?"

"That's classified," he said with a twisted grin.

"Allison Garvin knew you," I said.

"She thought she did, yes," the General admitted.

"Well, here I am, sitting with you, talking to you. We both know what's been going down. What's the big freakin' mystery?"

"There will always be plenty left of that, Mara," he said, his face changing for me as he called me by my first name.

"Plenty left of what?"

"Mystery," he said, "and more of that than even your penetrating curiosity can handle."

"You're saying it gets deeper than lunatic rich ideologues paying for nuclear terror?"

"Yes, is the short answer," he said.

"O.K., then lay it on me, I'm ready. We could wind up dead here tonight. I'd like to know the whole story."

He began to chuckle, so thoroughly amused by me.

"You're laughing at me," I said. "What's the big mystery? Is it something like the President is an alien from outer space?"

"No, not that I know of," he said. "At least the President never struck me as that interesting."

"So, is that an admission that you know the President?"

"Well," he said, "I don't really know the President. Not to drop by and play cards anyway."

"How about this," I said, "does the President know who you are?"

"No," the General said.

"But you've been to the White House to meet with him?"

"More often to Camp David," he said.

"But he doesn't know who you are?"

"That's the arrangement, yes. I am deniable. You see, unlike you, the President has a restrained sense of curiosity. It helped get him where he is."

"The team, through you, has access to the highest levels of U.S. intelligence," I said.

"It does?" he asked.

"That's the question I'm asking," I said.

"Oh, that was a question. Well, I'll let you in on a secret that no more than a few thousand people know," he said. "U.S. intelligence, levels high and low, has become virtually an open source utility for those with the means to access it."

"What does that mean?" I asked.

"It means that the vast secret U.S. intelligence industry, even when it's not leaking like a sieve, is being accessed day and night by everyone who has the capacity to do it, friend and foe, and that's a whole lot of folks."

"Al Qaeda?" I asked pointedly.

"No, not directly, but they can buy some at the day-old bread counter."

"What?" I said.

"You heard me," he said.

"So everything is for sale?" I said.

"There's that. But those who pay retail these days are mostly buying from those who steal it first. Which is not to say that the intelligence bureaucracies are not riddled with spies and traitors. They certainly are. Look where Allison Garvin was sitting. Do you think she was an anomaly?"

"I was hoping she was, yes," I said.

"Think of America, not just the U.S. intelligence industry, but the whole society, as just this huge superstore doing a brisk business. First, then, let the principle sink in that where there is a buyer there is a seller. Then think about how even in that environment there will be shoplifters, thieves, some of whom are undaunted even by the stuff that is kept locked in the glass cases."

"You are one cynical bastard, sir," I said.

"Me? Cynical? Not at all," he said. "I'm well informed. Cynical is when you toss away your values and beliefs in the face of it. What I do is the opposite of that, I hope."

"I apologize," I said. "I was reacting to your characterization of America as a store where everything is for sale."

"But I didn't say that *everyone* was for sale," the General corrected me. "I said that where there is a buyer there is a seller. There will always be a whore available, but that doesn't mean that everyone is a whore."

"But there is a little whore in everyone," I said.

"Now who's being cynical?" he said.

"Am I right?" I said.

"I don't see your inner whore, not from this angle. Do you see mine? Most people, I find, try to do the right thing, most of the time, with the notable exceptions of criminals, academics, and politicians."

The General took a call and slowly stood up, straightening his suit jacket with his free hand. He held up his index finger signaling me to wait and he stepped back into the recovery area. He was going to speak to Yael.

There was a buzzing sensation in the air. I was reading it as the approach of the shadow team, come to wipe out the lot of us. The General had said they knew we would be waiting for them, so I knew this was going to be a fast ride.

When the General returned he had already drawn his nine millimeter and was holding it at his side. He nodded at me to get mine in hand as well.

"There are just three of them, all women," he said. "That gang likes threesomes. They had themselves delivered to the morgue as corpses. How sentimental of them."

"Where are they now?" I asked.

"They've split up, but one of them is headed our way up that stairwell," he said, pointing to an exit at the opposite end of the elevator area.

"So what are we doing?"

"We're getting ready to kill her when he or she arrives," he said.

"That's the plan?" I complained.

He was moving to get his best angle on the stairwell door. I looked for mine. We fell naturally into a triangle with the target area.

"She knows we're waiting?" I asked.

"Not precisely," the General said, "we haven't let on that we know they're inside. She expects to surprise us. But, you see, we're going to surprise her."

63

It was but a split second's worth of too much presumption on her part, to think she would surprise us, and it was fatal. Her body armor did her no good. The General shot her in the head in the very instant she turned through the door. He did not hesitate. He was completely relaxed.

She was a beautiful kid, in the abstract, but even in death it was clear that her face had gone pretty well unused as a vehicle for human expression. It was hard in sleep.

"She should have considered that their plan was working too smoothly," the General said as he looked down, squinting at her delicate, cold features. "Did she really think we were taken in by the morgue ruse?"

The General got on his cell and checked in. He walked away, listened, and spoke too softly for me to hear. When he was finished with the call he came over and grabbed hold of the body armor at the back of her neck and dragged her out of the doorway over to the side of the elevators.

"The other two?"

"Callista – she's just something, don't you think – administered the last rights to one. The other one made it back outside the hospital when she realized the plan was blown, tried to take a hostage, but Tony killed her."

It didn't feel right to me.

"If they knew we were expecting them," I said, "then why were they so easily stopped?"

"It wasn't that easy. I had to shoot this one in the head," he said, gesturing toward the body.

"Be serious, sir," I said.

"We made a big show outside. It wasn't a show an ordinary person would notice. It was for the benefit of these women. They would see it. There was no direct way for them to get by it. We were checking everyone coming in, and had enough firepower to repel an assault."

"So you expected them to evade that and get in anyway?" I said.

"We hoped for that," he said.

"Hoped for it?"

"Sure. It was inside the hospital where we had everything under control. All the surveillance. We knew the building plan," he gestured toward the stairwell.

"They got in through the morgue, by having themselves delivered as corpses?" I said.

"Yes," he said.

"Why did we let them get that far?"

"They had us fooled that far. We only picked them up on surveillance when they let themselves out of the body bags inside the morgue."

"Didn't we check the body bags as they arrived?" I asked.

"Ah," the General said, "the fine point of the matter. Yes, we did check. They got by us."

"How?" I said.

By making for good corpses, I assume. From the appearance of this one, the performance wasn't a stretch. But at bottom we expected them to get through."

"I don't get it," I said.

"Here's what you need to understand," the General said. "Plans are not anything until they happen. So you layer in contingencies, and you stay awake, stay relaxed. These women played it the same way. But their mistake was having no purpose higher than revenge. What were they coming here for? Once they were inside their plan dissolved into 'go kill them,' but there was no 'them' to kill except for, maybe, this one going after Ryan, to finish him."

As the General spoke his voice seemed to be echoing in the distance. I felt that same buzzing sensation in the air that I felt as we waited for the corpse in armor to arrive from the stairwell.

Back toward the waiting room I saw a doctor in surgical scrubs reading a medical chart. The buzz came at me in a wave. The doctor looked up at me and our eyes locked. He bolted behind the empty nurse's station and back into the recovery room.

I don't remember having ever shouted as loudly or with more purpose and intent than I shouted Yael's name. Then came four gunshots, the first two from separate guns in a rapid exchange. Then two more from one gun.

The General and I moved into position outside the recovery area. Whatever was done in there was done already.

I called for Yael and she walked out, her gun hanging at her side. The General was on his cell.

"Are you hit?" I asked.

"No, are there more?" she said.

"I don't know. We thought they were all down and then that one showed up from nowhere," I said.

"He's not a problem now," she said.

"He fired his weapon," I said.

"Into the wall. I hit him in the center of the chest. His armor stopped it but his shot went wild and I got him in the face."

"Ryan?" I asked.

"Sleeping like a baby."

The General finished his call.

"We missed that one," he said.

"Where did he come from?" I asked.

"Damned if I know," he said. "We'll have to run through the surveillance tapes to find out."

The General stepped into the recovery area to take a look at the body, then came back out.

"Good work, Yael," he said.

She nodded. "Are there more?" she wanted to know.

"When aren't there?" he said wearily. "But right here right now we don't know. If I had to guess, he has two teammates unaccounted for. These people seem to run in packs of three. But who knows. We're sweeping the building, re-checking everywhere and everyone."

"We got sloppy," I said.

"Did we?" the General said.

"This one got by us," I said.

"Did he? He doesn't look like he got by us," he said.

"I mean," I said, "that he got inside the hospital undetected."

"We'll see," he said. "There's another possibility."

"What's that?" I asked.

"That he's a real doctor who either worked here or had access to, and legitimate credentials for, the hospital."

"How is that possible?" I said.

"He could have been a sleeper who our lady friends activated," the General said.

The very prospect of that threw a chill into me. I didn't like doctors to begin with.

An elevator arrived with a team of our people. They come to remove the bodies and to re-check the pared down medical staff, who had been keeping to a station at the back of the recovery area. The General asked one of our guys to get a digital image of the dead doctor and show it to the staff.

I began to feel the buzz again. Looking one way, then another, I felt the hairs on my neck standing up. Yael and the General were watching me.

"It's nothing," I said. "You damned people have turned me into a paranoid."

Then their weapons came up as they looked past me to the elevators. Another one had just arrived and a maintenance cart was rolling off it, pushed by a man who didn't fit with it. He panicked as he saw the guns and tried to reach under the cart. They waited. This time they hesitated. I could hear my heart beating. The man pushing the cart only wanted to show he belonged there. He had a schedule in his hands.

"I might not have hesitated," I said.

Yael smiled. She understood that I was talking about the thin line between yes and no.

The General went over and checked the maintenance worker himself. Then he had him stay right there while he went back into the recovery area to retrieve the digital image of the dead doctor. He returned and showed it to the maintenance worker, speaking softly to him, and the man shook his head. He didn't recognize the doctor.

I sensed now that this was it. We weren't going to face or find any more attackers in the hospital. When Yael stepped back into the recovery area and the General and I were alone again I challenged him.

"I still think we got sloppy," I said.

"You mean we let our guard down?" he said.

"And took a satisfied attitude," I said.

"But your instincts were completely alert. You saw right through the doctor," he said. "You picked him up after he'd made it through the net."

"O.K.," I said, "but after we put down the three women on the shadow team we were assuming it was over."

"Oh," the General said, "that was just a way of pausing. It's never over. You must know that by now. This isn't ever going to be over."

"You're switching contexts on me, sir," I protested. "I'm talking about our immediate situation not the long war."

"One is the other," he said. "I expect that someone will try to kill me every minute, and I'm ready for it. You're almost there yourself."

64

Twenty-three years living with a cop gave me a lot of practice being ready for a killing close-by. I worried about Rob, his partners, his squad mates. I knew the wives and the kids. I knew the fear.

The General, however, wasn't talking about the risk level inside law enforcement. He wasn't even referring to the level in military combat. He meant an unrelenting threat that he would face straight through to the end of his life. There would be no freedom from it, not even on the back porch in his dotage. The General had reached into the darkness and he expected that something would reach back out of it for him. His answer was to not fear it.

Things stayed quiet at the hospital into the next day. Ryan woke up. He was in ghastly pain. I could see it in his face before the doctors relieved it with morphine. Most important was that he did fine on the neurological tests.

The General wanted Ryan moved to Bethesda Naval Hospital and overruled the local doctors when they raised objections. It wasn't going to do Ryan any good if another team of assassins came for him and all of us. At Bethesda the security could be ramped up to where we needed it.

Yael and I went with Ryan on the copter down to Maryland. He was in and out of consciousness on the trip, unable to speak, but starting to get the light back in his eyes when he looked at us.

This was not going to be a long recovery process for him. The surgeon was wrong about that. It would happen quickly. That's what I knew.

The General had disappeared, as he always seemed to, into the mist. By the end of the day Yael too was there one minute and gone the next. She didn't say goodbye. She went out to get coffee and never returned. Ryan was sleeping when I left the hospital so I left him a note: "See you later. Mara."

I decided to take the train back to New York and first rode the Metro into Washington. From there it was a trip I had done many times – Amtrak from D.C. into Penn Station in Manhattan – when I was working on a huge case involving my then-firm's Washington office.

Here I was again on the evening commute. I looked more like a combination mountain climber and horse farmer now than I did a lawyer. I tried sleeping but it didn't work. Conversations and quiet, papers rustling, pages turning, human smells, I was fascinated to be back in the taken-for-granted world, where one minute followed safe and sound on another. I would be rejoining that world, but would never be fully a part of it again.

As the train rolled up through northern Jersey, and Manhattan appeared on the horizon, the thought occurred that, yes, it was still there, open for business. Those big old boxy towers that were once down at the south end were gone. I used to really enjoy seeing them full of lights as night fell.

Over the next week I grabbed my life back by armfuls. My associates had covered for me, but a couple of clients were barking about my unavailability. I had dinner with Rob.

"You've changed," he said.

"What a detective," I said back, being a smartass.

We talked about our girls and stayed away from the rest. It saturated us. There was no need to discuss it. Maybe we would in six months.

The strangest thing was the idea of the night's sleep. I couldn't do it. I didn't get this thing about lying in the same place for an hour, let alone eight of them. Maybe I would get the hang of it again, but it wasn't that appealing to me. It felt dangerous, something like a vacation used to feel when I was a young associate.

After a week of pulling things back together at work I took some of the staff out for drinks at Rembrandt's. It was only a gesture expressing my thanks for keeping the watch in my absence.

Jenn Marcus was there, having coffee at the bar.

"Mara," she said, looking me up and down, "you've been to a spa."

"No," I said, "but you're close."

"Did you see the news?" she said. "They've found a woman's foot washed up on the gulf coast in Florida. Preliminary DNA tests say it belongs to the missing White House chief of staff, Allison Garvin."

"Deputy chief of staff," I said. "She was deputy White House chief of staff."

"Right, sorry," Jenn said. "I knew her."

"Yes, in fact you once introduced me to her."

"Did I? Right, yes, I remember that. You were with Rob. She was so smart. So talented. And now this."

"They found just her foot?" I asked.

"Yes, only a foot. It's an incredible mystery. She left the White House and never returned. She vanished," Jenn said.

"May God forgive whoever did this to her," I said.

"She was the one person in the White House," Jenn said, "who I thought really understood this whole phony war on terrorism business."

"You think the war on terrorism is phony, Jenn?" I asked blandly.

"Come on, Mara, when was the last time we were attacked. They knocked a couple of tall buildings down here, years ago, and the national security types have dined out on it since. Allison Garvin saw right through that."

I nodded, pursing my lips.

"Yes," I said, "and maybe she knew too much and it got her killed."

"Don't get carried away, Mara. I think she just stepped into the wrong neighborhood at the wrong time. And then when whoever abducted or killed her found out who she was they drove down south and ditched her body in the gulf."

"Sounds plausible," I said.

"I never attribute things like this to politics," Jenn said. "People in that field are timid about almost everything, with the possible exception of taking payoffs."

"You liked and admired Garvin, though?" I asked.

"Oh, dear God, yes. She was fantastically smart and right at the top of her game."

"At the top of her game?"

"Absolutely. This is a real loss to the nation," Jenn said.

I didn't say anything to dispute a word of it.

My week back turned into a month. A month became two. Ryan, Yael, the General, they didn't write, they didn't call.

I found myself gravitating more often to the gun range. On the other hand, I couldn't stand going to the gym and did workouts at home.

It was a Friday afternoon. I was in my office with the door closed, catching a ten-minute nap on the leather couch. My cell phone woke me out of it.

"Miss Rains," said the voice on the other end. It was the General.

"Yes sir," I said.

"We need your help."

"Yes."

"Downstairs. Ten minutes," he said.